BATTLE OF THE BLUE HOUR

BATTLE OF THE BLUE HOUR.

Copyright © 2020 by Greg Rosshirt.

Printed in the United States of America.

Library of Congress Control Number:2019916983

ISBN 978-0-578-52994-3 (paperback)

Cover design by Sergii Golotovskiy

First Paperback Edition: January 2020

10 9 8 7 6 5 4 3 2 1

Believe without bending, for the good in the world perseveres

1

"Good people of Zanoma," Chancellor Daiton Tibs greeted to begin a live video broadcast through all of the public and private monitors within the City of Zanoma, while slumping over his bocote wood desk with his charcoal hair slicked back from the furrows across his ivory tinted forehead. "Today marks ten years since the Battle of Treton—a day devastated by unspeakable warfare. Nonetheless, we must not forget that day, but rather, remember what we have learned through humanity's greatest tragedies.

In order to restore our world to what it once was, we must be united. We must pick up our neighbors when they kneel before their fears of the future. We must sacrifice ourselves for a greater purpose—to ensure the survival of our species. No longer are we inspired by the actions of Zanoma's enemies; we are fighting forces much greater than any military can defeat, forces that threaten our very existence. We must operate as one great, big machine, with all parts functioning as they're meant to, together, with one common goal—prosperity. The Republic of Zanoma remains commited to nurturing our people as we apply our unique skills and passions to our roles for the new age. Together, as healthcare providers, engineers, agronomists, energy specialists, architects, political leaders, environmental scientists, guards, parents, and much more, we will restore this world. We are a community of intelligent and persistent people. Together, we will be ultimately indestructible.

As many of the last remaining survivors of the Black War, it is our duty to make certain that the treacherous acts of violence that once plagued our planet do not define our future. We will preserve our identity through fire and rain. We will carry the legacies of Medrik Malva and others that have been lost to the evils of the world, and we will create a better world in their honor. Thank you all for listening."

Transmission was terminated, and Chancellor Tibs stood from the seat of his desk, which was surrounded by an office with dark walnut floors, a rug of beige and ruby patterns, standing lamps in the two corners near the desk, a ceiling fan with a light, beige walls, and, on the opposite side of the room, a wall of wooded shelves, a perched camera that sat on a tripod, and a member of Communications Sector, an older woman with brown hair, operating the camera. Tibs paced slowly, bowing his head in reflection, toward the expansive windows at the edge of the common area of his suite, which had polished concrete floors, beige walls, ceiling lights, and tables, couches, and chairs scattered around. He lived comfortably without family to accompany him, only memories of past lovers or an occasional doxy when he felt lonely. Tibs' suite was within the upper levels of the Zanoma Tower, which loomed over the City of Zanoma. The lands that he governed laid below, ranging from the Zanoma Tower to the city walls, through the Industrial District that surrounded the superstructure, and through the city's major boroughs. Wrexon's End was to the east and Milbon Hill to the west, each housing those who worked within the government sectors in upmarket tower blocks and smaller apartment buildings. South Village, south of the Zanoma Tower, was a far more expansive, and far inferior, borough of tower blocks. The people of Zanoma informally called this borough the South Village Slums, an area where residents who were not granted a working role within the Republic were restricted to limited rations of food from the Sustenance Sector after government employees elsewhere were taken care of, leaving many malnourished and susceptible to illness.

Ductways wrapped with metal floors, metal ceilings, and polyethylene glass walls connected the second stories of the Zanoma Tower to each borough's hub, joining at the Central Node, a disk-shaped enclosure standing just south of the Zanoma Tower. On top of the Central Node was the city's largest television receiver, which connected to a ring of monitors within the node, to monitors throughout the public areas of the city, to monitors inside of the homes of viewers, and to hand-held tablets. Additional private ductways for authorized government employees connected the upper levels of Industrial District buildings, though still well below Chancellor Tibs' suite.

Zanoma's Military Commander, Evarand Nap, entered the suite from a private elevator after being granted access by Tibs' personal assistant, Morin Malva, the slender, blonde-haired son of Medrik Malva. Matching Chancellor Tibs, Morin was in his typical attire—black pants of flexible fabric and illusionary seams, a plain long-sleeved grey shirt with four black buttons down the chest and a Z over his heart, a synthetic leather black belt and low-top black shoes. Commander Evarand Nap was an imposing blonde figure—tall and bulky, with a square jaw and swollen knuckles. Like the guards under his control, he wore black boots, black khaki pants, and a long-sleeved black shirt covered by a black protective vest. His vest, unlike those of his men, had a Z on the chest just like Morin's and Tibs' shirts.

He stepped next to Tibs, peering down at the Central Node, where some restless residents were shuffling about, seemingly chanting in unison while facing the Zanoma Tower Ductway, the shortest of the ductways. It connected the Central Node to the Zanoma

Tower, though it was only accessible for authorized government employees commuting to work, including top officials who were granted suites to live in the tower itself. The residents in the Central Node could not pass through.

"There's a crowd of angry protestors at the gate again," Nap said, causing Tibs to focus his sights on the gate that blocked the Zanoma Tower Ductway from the Central Node. "They're growing."

"Make it known that we won't tolerate agitators," Tibs said with a sneer. "Have your men clear the area and do so carefully."

"Yes, sir."

"And keep a close eye on your men. You remember what happened during the riots in Milbon Hill. I don't pay you to create anarchists."

Commander Nap nodded, left the suite and descended to the second floor of the Zanoma Tower. Attached to the second floor, on the south side of the Zanoma Tower, was the Zanoma Tower Ductway. Several guards stood along the ductway, black helmets on their heads, awaiting Commander Nap's guidance. As Nap approached, the guards stiffened their stance, holding their arms still to their sides.

"You know what to do," Nap said as he stepped toward them. "Clear the area."

"Sir," one guard retorted, straightening his back as he spoke. "The protests are getting larger."

"Yes, there is certainly more hostility in the air," Nap said, addressing all of the guards. "Your jobs are difficult, and necessary, which is why you've all been granted comfortable homes, where your families can eat their plentiful rations while staying protected from the cruelty of the slums. It would certainly be difficult to live there with all of the sickness and the hunger, or even to find a new home for your families when such little space remains in those congested tower blocks. You have one job and one job only—protect the Republic at all costs. Take care of this situation, and I expect you all to report back to me when the area has been cleared."

The guards scanned one another before turning their backs to Commander Nap and stepping forward along the ductway. The Zanoma Tower stood tall behind them. Tibs returned to his office, trusting that his guards would douse the flames flaring in the eyes of the jaundiced residents.

. .

Eleven years prior, Medrik Malva, Chancellor of the Republic of Zanoma, stood in front of a jet on an airstrip north of the Zanoma Tower, preparing to take off to Ainkia, the other military pillar of the world. He was wrinkled, his head covered with fluorescent white hair, his eyes drooping in fatigue over the ongoing tension between the governments. After a deep breath, he turned around to face an early teenage Morin and his partner, Morin's mother, Nena, whose curly blonde hair was beginning to fade to grey.

Medrik kissed Nena, smiled, and said, "I love you, Nena."

"I love you, Medrik," Nena said with a smile back. "Promise me you'll be safe."

"Peace will bring safety," Medrik said with a slight nod before leaning down to Morin and placing a hand on his son's shoulder. "I love you, Morin. I'll be back as soon as possible."

"I love you too, Dad," Morin said.

With a smile still on his face, Medrik stood upright as Morin looked up at his father in admiration. Chancellor Malva walked away from his family alongside Commander Nap and several guards. After ascending up a staircase to the jet, he waved to Morin and Nena, who smiled and waved back to him.

Chancellor Malva boarded the jet with Nap and the guards. The jet took off into the skies on the cloudless morning. Medrik gazed out of his window at the land below, patched with lush landscapes, clear blue waters, and sprawling city structures between Zanoma and Ainkia. There were heavily travelled roads through farmlands and meadows, lesser known roads weaving through valleys and around mountains, and curling roadways around the cities.

"We're so fortunate to live in such a beautiful world, despite these tribulations," Medrik said, still staring out of his window, sitting across from Commander Nap. "Wouldn't you agree, Evarand?"

"Yes, Chancellor," Nap responded, looking at Medrik. "Very beautiful. To me, the most beautiful place in the world is the Ornaian shoreline—the soft sand, the cliffs creeping over the crashing waves. Someday, I hope to move my family there."

"As much as I'd like to say a province of Zanoma like Ornaia," Medrik began. "Nothing takes my breath away like Storo Peaks—those magnificent snow-capped mountains, and those beautiful women catching the sun down in the valley."

"You always veered toward adventure," Nap said with a smirk, causing Medrik to smirk as well.

"It's a shame we as humans can't seem to figure it all out," Medrik said, his smirk fading. "There's so much room for life, yet so many clawing for scraps."

"It is a shame, sir."

"I feel good about this trip, though, Evarand," Medrik said, prompting Commander Nap to nod in apparent agreement. "Ainkia has taken advantage of us for quite some time, but I think there's hope for a new arrangement."

"You're the first Chancellor in fifty years to visit Ainkia. That should make an impression on their people, maybe enough to sway public opinion."

"Peace will never be established with Ainkia and their allies unless I put my presence behind it, unless we put our presence behind it."

The jet eventually began its descent into Ainkia and landed at the nearest airstrip to Zanoma's embassy, a four-story steel building with thick glass windows, west

of the City of Ainkia. Two Zanoma guards were
stationed outside of the main entrance of the building.
Chancellor Malva was swiftly guided in by his men.

*   *   *

An adolescent boy with tawny trimmed hair,
wearing black pants of flexible fabric and illusionary
seams, a plain white shirt with sleeves tracing the
bottoms of his shoulders, a synthetic leather black belt
and low-top black shoes, stood closely behind his
mother, who wore clothing of the same colors, though
pressed to the skin, with minimal cosmetics, some silver
on her fingers, neck, and ears, and her tawny hair tied
up. In front of them was their partner and father, a
black-haired man with broad shoulders, who matched
his son besides the grey shirt.

They were joining fellow residents of the City of
Zanoma in the Industrial District. The people of
Zanoma gathered below the ductways, facing the
Forum, a room that spanned the first floor of the
Zanoma Tower. It was the only floor of the Zanoma
Tower to be accessible for the public. Between the
people and the Forum was a platform, where Daiton
Tibs, Vice Chancellor of the Republic of Zanoma at the
time, was prepared to give an unbidden briefing.

"Excuse me—only authorized individuals
beyond this point," a guard said to the father,

referencing the smaller semi-circle of approved
correspondents and government employees within only
a few degrees of the government's true foremen.

"I am Riklin Amaranth," the father said,
revealing identification cards for he, his partner, and his
son. "I am the Director of Wrexon's End Distribution
Center. She is my partner, Tera, and he is my son,
Elsan."

The guard nodded, and turned to allow the
Amaranth family in. Riklin, Tera, and Elsan weaved
through the outer layer of correspondents before
stopping with a view of the Forum doors sliding to the
sides, allowing Vice Chancellor Tibs to walk out of the
Zanoma Tower and onto the platform alongside several
armed guards, with Nena Malva and Morin Malva
following from behind, weeping and embracing each
other as they stepped forward. Elsan looked behind him,
sensing the perplexity in the eyes of a female
coorespondent, who held a tablet with both hands.

"Good people of Zanoma," Tibs began, quieting
the chatter within his audience. "As you all know, we
have a hostile enemy far to the southeast. Ainkia has
taken advantage of Zanoma for decades, and has
continued to threaten us when we defend our economic
position. Tensions have escalated as of late, through
trade wars and attempts to control our precious
minerals, manufacturing materials—now even our
sources of food and water. Economic gain is and has
always been their goal, even at the expense of our right

to life. We must never give them the opportunity to destroy our home.

I organized this briefing to report an unparalleled act of war. While travelling to Ainkia with the intention of reaching a peaceful agreement, Medrik Malva, our Chancellor, was murdered by Ainkia's guards, who infiltrated our embassy. Medrik Malva would do anything to protect Zanoma, so now we must do as he would have, in his honor."

Residents stood aghast with their mouths and eyes wide open, glancing left and right at their neighbors as Tibs continued the report. Tera covered her mouth with her hand, stared down at Elsan in concern, and turned to Riklin, whose eyes remained fixated on the Vice Chancellor. Vice Chancellor Tibs finished his speech and turned to wrap his arms around Nena and Morin, who saw their beloved Medrik for the last time that morning.

Within days of the announcment, Daiton Tibs, the newly appointed Chancellor of the Republic of Zanoma, ordered his military pilots and crew to drop nuclear warheads over the City of Ainkia and its closest provinces. Firestorms miles in diameter deteriorated the enemy territory, believed to have killed every human and animal within tens of miles of the strikes with radiation, flames, and even debris. Ainkia's allies were left to fight for themselves, besides a small number of survivors from Ainkia's territory, who fled their homes for ally territories while those who remained were overcome with over twenty forms of cancer, commonly bone cancer and leukemia. Newborn children had birth defects, many dying before their first birthday. Lacking the resources to rebuild their side of the world, the desparate leaders of Ainkia's allies used their ballistic nuclear missiles provided by Ainkia's government to attack Zanoma, though the missiles were intercepted while traveling above Tocano, a province just east of Zanoma's walls, and Cronen, an ally far south of the City of Zanoma. The missiles detonated after dropping from the air, decimating Tocano and Cronen. Of few survivors, many fled to Zanoma, leaving behind their neighbors in sickness and despair.

As contamination spread, essentially eliminating most allies on both sides of the war, Ainkia's allies made one more attempt to isolate Zanoma by territorial gain. Ainkia's allies invaded Treton, a province west of Zanoma, with all of its remaining military forces, including one nuclear warhead and a plan to poison Treton's water supply in the process. Many Treton residents who survived the nuclear attack began blistering, vomiting, and tragically falling to their deaths. Tibs determined that there was no choice but to indelibly defeat Ainkia's allies, beginning the Battle of Treton. Zanoma's military mowed over their enemies, making Zanoma the only true military pillar and government in the world.

Zanoma homeowners hid inside while survivors from Treton and survivors still trekking from other provinces and territories of the world fought to gain entry past Zanoma's city walls. With the gates open, guards who were assessing right of entry at the city's limits were unable to stop the desperate people from finding a way in. Swarms of people clawed their way past the walls and the guards, crying frantically as many were shot down.

Chaos struck Zanoma and the only people allowed to stay were the fortunate residents of the City of Zanoma, though many outsiders were kept in hiding or blended into the South Village Slums. Chancellor Tibs solidified the city's borders in a state of emergency. Those that legally belonged in Zanoma were blocked off, and many who did not belong in Zanoma managed to force their way in, causing the permanent closing of the entrances. The entrances were not opened again. Those that were left outside of Zanoma's walls and even many within the city borders suffered from the dissipating radiation in the air currents and the contamination of their food and water.

The war would forever be known as the Black War, for after all of its devastation, fifteen million tons of soot rose into the upper atmosphere, absorbing incoming sunlight and drastically lowering the planet's temperatures, contributing to crop failures, which were also a result of contaminated groundwater and soil, as well as a decrease in precipitation. The ozone layer depleted, and it was not expected to fully recover for fifteen years. Water bodies contained byproducts of nuclear, biological and chemical weapons. Sea floors, especially by the shores, accumulated radioactive particles—even fish became radioactive.

It was estimated that it would take ten to twenty years for the air to be healthy again, though no one knew for sure. Temperatures were expected to rise again, though only gradually, as soot would eventually drop from the upper atmosphere into water bodies and soils. Soils were not expected to be healthy again for at least ten years. Yet, Zanoma residents were fortunate for their geographic location. Wind currents generally traveled south of Zanoma, around the semi-circle of mountains bordering the city. Winds from the northern shore were the only to strike Zanoma, and enough of the forests survived to provide oxygen to the city.

Still, as residents of enemy territories were, Zanoma residents were overcome with over twenty forms of cancer and genetic disorders. Food, air, nor water could be trusted. Outside of Zanoma's walls, generally only insects and fish lived on besides a few survivors of most species of land animals and birds.

After the Black War was won, the battle for resources came to the doorsteps of Zanoma's residents. To some, the only solution for surviving the spread of radiation seemed to be cooperative production, and to some, a fight that only the fittest of the survivors could win. What no one knew was whether or not their efforts would allow them to experience a breath of fresh air once again.

During the decade after the Black War, there were countless thefts of the food surplus by residents of the slums and by foreigners not authorized to eat. There were countless attacks on the Zanoma Tower. Violent outbreaks between the guards and the people were frequent, as the people aggressively protested what they believed to be war crimes commited by Chancellor Tibs, and crimes against his own people. Anger, mistrust, and desperation molded the minds especially of those in South Village, who looked for answers for their constant struggles in any of the many rumors that spread throughout the city. Violent outbreaks between residents of the South Village Slums and the neighboring boroughs, Wrexon's End and Milbon Hill, became frequent as well. South Village residents commited many thefts against the neighboring boroughs, and impassioned residents of those boroughs often stepped between South Village protestors and the Republic to protect the government that kept them safe, while Chancellors Tibs, Commander Nap, Morin Malva, and other officials watched the violence perpetuate from a distance.

Residents of Zanoma, especially those in South Village who lacked priority in healthcare, lost their lives to starvation, illness, food and water poisoning, and cancer, though Tibs and a majority of Zanoma's residents continued to defend his actions taken before, during, and after the Black War. The population continued to reduce, the burial grounds nearby Zanoma's core filling more and more. Yet, the heartbeat of humanity persevered.

Whatever path we set foot upon is ultimately a route back home, Tera would say.

Elsan, alongside his parents within their home, halfway up a tower block in Wrexon's End, often spent time watching from the windows and on their television projector as residents, both authorized and unauthorized, revolted within the Industrial District, the ductways, and the Central Node. One day, when Elsan neared his late teenage years, there were riots near Elsan's home. It was started by South Village residents who raided the homes of several of Elsan's neighbors, inciting guards to protect Wrexon's End residents. Violent outbursts ensued between South Village residents and the guards, causing further loss of life within the South Village population.

Until Elsan became an adult, Tera and Riklin refused to allow him to step out of their home without one of them to accompany him. Elsan often dreamed of a day when he would be free again, when he could escape Zanoma's walls and explore the forests once again, but the dream was always short-lived. Many Zanoma residents found purpose within the Forum, praying to the heavens within aisles of benches lined in front of a cast stone statue of Medrik Malva. As all people do after they die, Medrik became a symbol—a symbol of peace, sacrifice, and prosperity, shining upon the faces of those who fought blindly for the future.

2

Elsan, a young adult, and Riklin bustled through Wrexon's End Ductway, passing concrete nodes that connected the ductway to various buildings, as well as elevators and staircases leading to outdoor streets and corridors generally travelled by foot, often by light armored military vehicles, and infrequently by tanks and electric cars cruising low to the ground. Sunbeams curled through the polyethylene glass walls. Wrexon's End Distribution Center, where they had spent myriad days, months, years to alight upon such a day, was at their backs as they ventured toward the Zanoma Tower. On the edges of the ductway were transporters, aisles of moving floors that accelerated one's movement, though Elsan and Riklin chose not to rush their first commute for work within the Zanoma Tower.

They were on their way to the Energy Sector for their first day in new roles, having been granted access to the Zanoma Tower for the first time. Trust tended to be given to government employees until lost to disobedience. Riklin was promoted to Assistant Head of the Energy Sector, while Elsan was beginning his first role as an energy data analyst.

As the father and son trudged forward, Elsan held his black tablet in his hands. For the first time since his mother's birthday, his hair was slicked back, his eager brown eyes digesting the journey that would become his daily routine. Riklin wore nearly identical attire to Elsan's, which consisted of similar clothes to those that Elsan wore as an adolescent, besides the size. The only difference was the royal blue of Elsan's shirt, and the deep red of Riklin's.

Riklin watched ahead of Elsan, worried his son would walk into a rush of rigid laborers as he took a moment to stare down at his tablet. Weaving around them were women in typical attire, shirts and pants pressed to the skin, minimal cosmetics, gold and silver wrapped around their fingers and necks, or through their ears, and men with different suit colors, hats, and footwear. There were men wearing synthetic leather jackets with magnetic zippers and synthetic leather gloves to repel the cold of the outdoors, where few spent an extended period of time after the Black War. After walking by two of these men, Elsan picked up his chin and turned his attention to Riklin.

"Good news from the Environmental Sector," Elsan said, projecting his voice over the crowds of people before putting his head back down to continue navigating the tablet. "They're saying that we'll pass below predicted exposure levels of plutonium waste by the end of the year at this rate."

"That may be," Riklin replied, seemingly uninspired by the news.

"Well, doesn't that excite you? We might finally breathe some truly fresh air again. There's hope for the near future. It's been a decade, Dad."

"Yes, we're getting close."

"Don't you ever want to leave this place, even just for a short while? It's been more than a decade since we hiked the Tocano Mountains."

"Of course, I do, but we need to be careful trusting estimates like that and focus on our work," Riklin said, only to receive a blank stare from Elsan. "This is a big day for you—for both of us. We can't get complacent now."

Elsan took a deep breath and said, "I won't. I just hope we all make it out of this soon."

"It's been a long ten years," Riklin said, nodding in agreement.

Riklin led his son through the commotion of the Central Node, which was filled with the chatter of countless residents, as well as the echoes of monitors broadcasting a correspondent's report on the state of the environment. They approached the private Zanoma Tower Ductway. It was a new experience for the father and son, as Riklin worked only at downstream energy distribution centers for the Energy Sector and Elsan completed training at Wrexon's End Distribution Center just one week prior. They were not previously authorized to enter the Zanoma Tower Ductway, nor the Zanoma Tower besides the Forum. Other levels of the Zanoma Tower were accessible only to specific government officials and employees, and only felicitous personnel could access them all.

"You can do the honors," Riklin said, pointing at an identification pad adjacent to the gateway to the Zanoma Tower Ductway. "Go ahead and place your finger here."

Elsan lifted his finger and placed it upon the identification pad. Two guards stood on either side of the translucent doors. A green flash of light bordered the gateway and the doors slid sideways into the walls of the Central Node. Riklin and Elsan stepped through the gateway and scanned the premises of the city's core as the doors sealed shut behind them.

"It's unfortunate that we'll need to pass the burial grounds every day into work," Elsan said, pausing to stare out of the ductway to the expansive area northeast of the Zanoma Tower.

Riklin sighed and replied, "We lost a lot of people. We'll think about them every day, which might hurt, but we thought about them all anyway."

"Right, and we'll make the world better in their honor."

"Yes, it is motivating in some twisted way. After the Black War, I felt that I was the most unfortunate man in the world. I survived such a travesty only to lose many that I loved and be left with the remains, but I eventually came to realize that we're lucky. We're lucky because I'm one of very few who have the opportunity to rebuild the world the right way."

"Well, it seems like we'll have a say in the matter if that's where we're working," Elsan said pointing toward the Zanoma Tower.

"Don't get distracted by the prestige of it all, Elsan," Riklin retorted. "Just do your job well and do some good for Zanoma. Focus on that."

"I will, Dad," Elsan said, though he couldn't help but to be captivated by the superstructure.

Awe-inspired, Elsan eventually tilted his head back down, looking back at the crowds of Zanoma's workers, who scattered to their respective buildings within the Industrial District. Riklin and Elsan arrived at the entrance of the second story of the Zanoma Tower. After Riklin placed his finger upon another identification pad, a green flash of light bordered the doorway and the doors opened, sliding into the walls of the Zanoma Tower. As Riklin and Elsan stepped inside, Morin Malva walked toward them with a cheerful smile, his black shirt with the Z on the chest lacking a single wrinkle.

"You must be Riklin and Elsan Amaranth, is that right?" he asked, raising his eyebrows.

"Yes," Riklin said, holding out his hand. "It's an honor to meet you, Morin."

"Fantastic to meet you, Riklin," Morin said, shaking Riklin's hand as he spoke. "My name is Morin Malva, son of Medrik Malva and personal assistant to Chancellor Tibs."

"We know," Riklin replied with a cordial smirk. "You're greatly appreciated by the people of Zanoma, and by us specifically."

"Thank you, Riklin," Morin said, holding his hand out to Elsan.

"It's an honor to meet you," Elsan said as he shook Morin's hand.

"It's nice to meet you as well, Elsan," Morin replied before taking a step back to address both the father and son. "I understand this is your first day and you both are eager to get settled, but you should be acquainted with your new workspace. How about a brief tour to start?"

"That would be great," Riklin said, beginning to study his surroundings. "Thank you."

Morin led Riklin and Elsan to an elevator at the end of a curling hallway with saffron lighting and lacquered metal walls that curled ever so slightly as their eyes traveled up. The three entered after the elevator doors opened and Morin pressed a black button with the letter "F". He sighed, closed his eyes, and tilted his head down for a moment while Riklin and Elsan stared at the floor.

"I'm sure you two saw the view of the burial grounds on the way in, is that correct?" Morin asked, picking his head back up.

"Yes," Riklin answered. "It's difficult to digest, but it's humbling."

"It's a terrible thing to think about all of the lives we've lost, but it reminds us all what we're fighting for," Morin said, staring at Riklin and Elsan with a soft smile. "As does the first floor of this building, especially for me, as you might imagine."

"Yes," Elsan said. "W-We're very sorry for your loss, Morin."

"Your father was an admirable man, a true proponent of peace," Riklin added. "You must be very proud to be his son."

"Yes," Morin said. "Thank you both for your kind words."

The elevator came to a stop and the doors opened. After passing through two more doorways, including one secured with an identification pad, the three were in the Forum, a giant room with gold tinted lighting. Much of the Forum was an immense empty space, meant for assemblies, while a small section of statues and adjacent benches aligned along the far end. Stock-still beneath an encompassing golden light was a cast stone statue of Medrik Malva, as he was remembered during his reign, before being revered as a great sacrifice after death. In the early hours of each day, residents of Zanoma were admitted into the Forum to pay their respects to Medrik Malva's legacy, as well as the cast stone statues and legacies of the ancient luminaries, Woryn Wrexon and Brint Milbon. Elsan did so frequently, his parents sometimes as well, though not as frequently as when they would accompany an early teenage Elsan in the years after the Black War.

"My presence in this section of the building may exceed others' by a great margin, but as you already know, the Forum is frequently visited by residents of all boroughs and all socio-economic statuses," Morin began. "Of course, all lives lost during the Black War and the years after were of equal value to my father's, but he represented our final pursuit of peace and he gave his life for it. Our guards protect the Forum against those who seek to vandalize my father's legacy, literally or figuratively."

"I see," Riklin said, waving to a guard who stood in the far corner of the room, wearing black boots, a black helmet, and black protective armor over his black khakis and black long-sleeve shirt. "Well, Elsan and I certainly embrace the vision Chancellor Malva had for Zanoma. Elsan looked up to him as he grew up."

"Great," Morin said as the guard waved back. "That is particularly important in such a high speed and high stakes workplace, where there can never be too much motivation."

"Your father was a brave man," Elsan said as Riklin stood silently nodding. "He would have done anything for Zanoma."

Morin smiled, placed his hand on Elsan's shoulder, and said, "As should we all."

Morin pointed his hand away from the statue and continued back toward the elevator to return to the second floor. Riklin and Elsan followed, Elsan's arms at his sides and Riklin's folded. The elevator doors opened and Morin led the father and son through the lounging area, near the center of the second floor.

"This is where you eat," he said, pointing inside a room with pristine black tables and sparkling silver tiled floors. "And this is the lounge, where you can relax and talk to your friends and, well, in your case, family members."

The lounge was extravagant, with red silk couches, televisions playing old entertainment, and stations for mindless games. Elsan's eyes expanded at the sight while Riklin impassively scoped the room, knowing that there would ultimately be little time to spend so freely. Replenishing the world required steadfast commitment, and Riklin was well aware that there was no time for games.

Within the lounge, the Republic's personnel pecked at their rations for breakfast, generally in silence, besides a few with bare plates. Simply staring into this vibrant, warming sanctuary gave the eyes a break from the rapid movement elsewhere. As soon as Morin led Riklin and Elsan away from the lounge, suits of all colors darted in all directions, dizzying those without blinders beside their eyes.

"A lot of newcomers have become overwhelmed on their first day," Morin said, pausing Riklin and Elsan at an intersection of hallways. "And who can blame them? There are bright lights, vibrant people, and polished walls and machinery reflecting it all again. Just try to keep pace, and you'll be alright."

Morin turned and started to walk toward the center of the tower as Elsan and Riklin were cut off by a group of young engineers all paying their attention to a single tablet. Riklin followed closely to Morin as Elsan was impeded by some more of the scattering workforce. Elsan attempted to more aggressively push through the crowd before being shoved by a pair of architects. Neither of the two said a word, so Elsan continued, narrow-eyed, tracking Riklin and Morin as he weaved through rigid joints and stares.

As Elsan caught up, Morin said, "Learning to work in an environment like this is not just necessary; it can be gratifying, too. It's easy to find inspiration in fellow employees of the Republic."

Morin paused and pointed up at a colossal metal structure planted separately from the rest of the tower in the northern end, through floors and ceilings of many of the tower's levels. It was circular, with a radius shrinking with altitude. Eye-level to the three men was the foundation, which consisted of translucent walls, exposing the herds of energy specialists walking about. Above this were only steel walls, besides some emergency windows and ventilation.

"Beautiful, isn't it?" Morin asked.

"Yes, it is," Elsan replied as Riklin stared intently at the facility in which he spent years trying to gain access to. "Breathtaking, really."

"This is where you'll both be working," Morin said. "The Energy Sector. It's where nearly all of your duties will be carried out. You two will spend most of your time on separate floors, but you may overlap on occasion."

"The section at the top—is that where the transmission controls are?" Riklin asked.

"Yes. From there, we control the transmission of electricity to the city's distribution centers here in the Industrial District, in Wrexon's End, in Milbon Hill, and in South Village, where, as you already know, the electricity is distributed to Zanoma's border security, through every home, and to every facility."

"I see," Riklin said, nodding his head. "Where is the battery storage infrastructure located?"

Morin snickered and replied, "Unfortunately, Riklin, there are still anarchists in our world and in our own city; the battery storage section holds some of the most essential assets within the city, if not the most important. It powers our homes, our food factories, our media networks, our air purifying systems, our water and soil purifying systems, our hospitals… everything. For that reason, few people know where that infrastructure is and even fewer can access it. Only the Head of the Energy Sector and some key officials have the authority to monitor the batteries. It is not quite the same level of authority that applies to the transmission controls."

"I mean no disrespect, of course, but how are they held accountable?" Riklin probed.

Morin smirked, stepped closer to Elsan and Riklin, and replied with a sterner tone, "You make a very good point, Riklin, but we have no choice. Unfortunately, few can be trusted with such information. Until the smoke clears, some matters are just not meant for public knowledge. We must all accept our roles, and not deviate from them."

"I understand," Riklin said with a nod.

"Great," Morin said, peering over at Elsan, causing Elsan to nod as well. "Now, shall we go inside of the Energy Sector?"

The father and son nodded and followed Morin toward the base floor of the Energy Sector. Morin used his pointer finger to open the automatic doors and the three entered. Fortunately for Riklin and Elsan, the traffic inside was much less intimidating.

"Gentlemen," Morin said, raising his hand at a tall, thin, middle-aged man with brown skin, black hair, and brown eyes. "I would like you to meet the Head of the Energy Sector, Lealan Wiske."

"It's a pleasure to meet you both," Lealan said, shaking both Riklin's and Elsan's hands.

"Nice to meet you," Riklin and Elsan each said as they shook Lealan's hand.

"What do you think so far?" Lealan asked.

Without hesitation, Elsan answered, "Incredible. The energy in the tower is engulfing."

Lealan smiled and said, "That's great to hear. It's challenging, but it's a very rewarding place to work."

"I'll leave these two with you," Morin said.

"Thank you, Morin," Lealan said.

Riklin and Elsan each shook Morin's hand once more, with a nod of appreciation. Morin quickly turned and paced out of the Energy Sector. Lealan clasped his hands together and opened his mouth to speak once Riklin and Elsan looked back at him.

"Well, let's not waste any time here," Lealan said, lifting his arm to rest his finger on an identification pad to his side. "This is where you will check in and check out. You can do so now."

Riklin and Elsan took turns placing their fingers upon the detection surface to check in for the day. For both, the machine flashed green. As with the identification pads of the Zanoma Tower Ductway and the Zanoma Tower, this signaled success.

"Eight hours and twelve minutes," an automated voice sounded from the device each time Riklin and Elsan used the identification pad.

"Twelve minutes late, but we can forgive that today," Lealan said with a smirk. "Now, let's take a brief tour of the Energy Sector."

Riklin and Elsan followed Lealan as they did Morin, but Lealan was much less vocal of a tour guide. He simply pointed to various sections of the structure that made up the Energy Sector as the three walked by and uttered a few words. The father and son were exposed to monitoring rooms, transmission control rooms, and a range of other rooms that they expected to work with entirely at some point. Even with all the two were exposed to, they did not ascend past the fifth floor, though Riklin would eventually.

"Elsan," Lealan said. "It's my understanding that you have a friend and old classmate working within the Energy Sector; is that correct?"

Elsan's eyes lit with excitement as he smiled and said, "Ermin Muttin? Yes!"

"How would you like to work with him to start and make yourself comfortable?"

"That would be great!"

"Great, just don't slack off," Lealan said with a grin. "We expect a lot out of both of you."

"I won't," Elsan replied.

"Ermin is in room one hundred thirty-four, just down the hallway. He will know how to get you started. Riklin, why don't you and I walk and talk some more. We can make our way to our offices."

"Sure," Riklin said, before turning his attention to Elsan with a smile. "I'll see you later. Remember, don't slack off."

"I won't," Elsan said.

He turned to find room one hundred thirty-four. Swiftly, he raced through a curling hallway with an exterior border of honeysuckles making up the decor. Although Elsan saw Ermin Muttin outside of work, he waited a year to reunite with him in a formal setting ever since Ermin graduated from his training program the prior spring.

Approaching room one hundred thirty-four, Elsan's heart pounded through his chest, strangely, seeing as his visits with Ermin were relatively frequent outside of the Zanoma Tower. The two were neighbors and best friends long before the Black War, crawling together through the parks in Wrexon's End soon after birth, spending much of their time together as cheerful and curious children in the rich outdoors. After the Black War, they met indoors, whether at their homes or in a public space when their youth required some distance from their parents, distance they would have gotten consistently if not for the condition of the world. Nonetheless, they grew into young men together. Yet, within Elsan arised some anxiety as he approached room one hundred thirty-four.

He entered the room, staring in all directions in search of Ermin, though he was distracted by the multitude of monitoring equipment mounted within the walls. Some specialists stared intently at the screens in front of them, while others caromed from one station to the next. Eventually, Elsan spotted Ermin hunching over a desk in the far corner of the room, with his brown hair pushed back, his tan forehead and bushy eyebrows exposed, and his brown eyes bound to the computer screen.

"Ermin!" Elsan yelled, but there was no reaction so he stepped closer. "Ermin!"

Ermin abruptly spun around and yelled, "Elsan! I was waiting for you! How has your first day started? Hard at work yet?"

"Well, I've only taken a tour so far."

"That's good. They run a tight ship around here, so I hope you cherished it while you could."

"I did. This place is unbelievable."

"It's staggering," Ermin agreed. "Well, I should probably teach you a thing or two about monitoring."

Ermin and Elsan huddled in front of the screen as Ermin clicked away. It was time spent far differently from all of the time they had spent together in the past, but it brought greater purpose. Throughout his first day, Elsan had the untiring support of his closest friend within the tumultuous lower levels of the Energy Sector.

．．

In the evening, Elsan stood in line to check out of the Energy Sector, alongside Ermin and Riklin. Their eyes were bloodshot from a long day of staring at computer monitors. After several minutes, the three placed their fingers on the identification pad one at a time—Ermin, Riklin, and lastly, Elsan.

"Eighteen hours and twenty-one minutes," the automated voice sounded for Elsan. "Ten hours and nine minutes elapsed."

Elsan followed Riklin and Ermin out of the Zanoma Tower to walk back toward Wrexon's End. Riklin placed his hand over Ermin's shoulder, reminding Elsan of a time, many years prior to the Black War, when he and Ermin were young boys and Riklin would watch over them as they played in the park nearby their homes. Elsan chuckled under his breath as he recalled a day when Ermin tripped over some sticks and cried all the way home, with Riklin's hand on his shoulder to comfort him.

After passing through the Central Node, the three men turned toward Wrexon's End Ductway. For their commute home, they chose to use the transporters, as most typically did when there were longer distances to travel. The three men reached Wrexon's End Distribution Center and descended to ground-level, where they walked along cracked asphalt with an occasional weed creeping through, between refurbished buildings, toward their tower blocks, a glimpse of the city walls standing some distance beyond. Before the golden hour of the evening could pass, they arrived home. The Muttin family's home was situated two tower blocks down a primarily abandoned street from the Amaranth's.

Tera began preparing dinner at the Amaranth's home, having already completed her shift within Wrexon's End Sustenance Center, where rations were packed for the many residents of Wrexon's End. The borough's Sustenance Center, as well as all Sustenance Centers in Zanoma, received large quantities of raw food from the Sustenance Sector building in the Industrial District, west of the Zanoma Tower. Production facilities were located in that building, occupying much of the first few floors. Some had polyethylene glass wrapped around the upper walls and ceiling in order to allow sunlight to pass through to the rows of food, and others had no sunlight, instead using heat lamps. There were bean plants wrapped in twine, lettuce and tomatoes grown in hydroponics, and potted dwarf banana trees. Barley grass did not grow to the same height indoors, but it was a lucky time of year for Zanoma's residents, including the Amaranths, who had a pot of barley cooking.

Riklin and Elsan changed clothes in their respective bedrooms. All walls of the home were cream-colored. Grey carpets covered the floors of the bedrooms and the common room, and beige tiles covered the kitchen floor. The common room had a projector screen to watch television and a charcoal grey couch to rest upon. Most homes within the tower blocks of Wrexon's End and Milbon Hill appeared similar to the Amaranth's.

Elsan, Riklin, and Tera all salivated at the smell of cabbage simmering by induction on the stovetop, lentils boiling with rosemary, and barley. They had developed a taste for such cuisine, as it was typical Zanoma food given the capabilities of the indoor production facilities. Tera occupied the kitchen as Riklin and Elsan continued to change clothes. Their meal was almost done cooking.

"Dinner is ready!" Tera yelled from the kitchen as she stirred the lentils a last time.

Riklin and Elsan entered the room and situated themselves at the sleek, black kitchen table, their feet planted along the tile floor. Eyes drooping and dry, Elsan and Riklin sat jaded and hungry. It was, howbeit, the only time of day that the family was able to transition to a night of contented company.

"So, are you two ready to tell me about your first day on the job?" Tera asked.

"Go ahead, Elsan," Riklin replied.

"Well, the beginning of the day was amazing," Elsan said, his eyes perking a bit. "We toured the Zanoma Tower and the Energy Sector. Then, they had me work with Ermin at a monitoring station for most of the rest of the day."

"You did see Ermin after all," Tera said, her voice higher-pitched. "That's great!"

"Yeah, for quite a lot of the day actually," Elsan said. "But to end the day, they put me with some older woman to learn about transmission. She was a bit slower, exhausting to watch."

"Respect your elders, Elsan," Tera said, holding a large bowl in one hand while giving Elsan's shoulder a playful slap with the other and pointing to each of herself and Riklin. "And your first day, Riklin?"

"My day went well," Riklin said with his head down. "Nothing electrifying."

"We can always count on you for a stupid joke," Tera said while placing the expansive tray of cabbage, barley, and lentils on the table.

"Dad, you must have something to tell us, don't you?" Elsan asked.

"Well," Riklin began as he reached for the bowl of cabbage. "I learned all about how to tell people like you what to do."

"You can't tell me what to do," Elsan said with a grin. "I'm a grown man, now."

Riklin smirked and said, "Unfortunately, the Black War made it so you're stuck in this home with us, which means you still need to do what I say."

"We'll see," Elsan said, still grinning.

"So, you think you're a man," Riklin began, pausing from filling his plate for an extended moment as he looked Elsan in his eyes. "You have quite a bit to see, my dear son."

.
. .

Hours after dinner, Elsan laid his head on one of his pillows. As it did every night, his mind strayed through his pre-adolescent years as soon as his eyes were shut. It was a time when he could travel by air to his cousin's home a quarter of the world away, or by car to Tocano to see his uncle. It was a time when oceans were swimmable, the air was pure, and birds chirped during the blue hour of the morning. Elsan drifted into sleep, with the spirits of those he loved beckoning him to embody their will.

3

Elsan's hands cramped as he typed and typed and typed and typed energy output data into the monitoring database. The end of his second day on the job was nearing, and this day was spent entirely within room one hundred thirty-four, besides a lull in the lounge at mid-day. It was almost time for Elsan to check out of the Energy Sector and walk home with Riklin and Ermin, who were also finishing their work.

Riklin finished first and stood by the exit of the second floor with a pair of sweat droplets trickling over his temple, not so patiently awaiting Elsan and Ermin. He was leaving his job on time, as he would on any day, but his son needed to finish his daily monitoring report. With his tablet tucked into his front pocket, Riklin decided to place his finger on the security pad, check

out, and wait outside. Elsan and Ermin followed
minutes after and checked out.

"How was your day, Ermin?" Riklin asked as his
voice trailed off with a shortening of breath, before
wrapping his arm around Elsan and turning toward the
Zanoma Tower Ductway with him.

"Are you alright?" Elsan asked before Ermin
could speak, staring at Riklin's glistening forehead and
briskly bobbing chest.

"I'm fine, just did some heavy lifting at the end
of the day is all. You two got out late."

"Yeah," Ermin said. "I just need to get Elsan up
to speed on putting these reports together and we'll start
getting out on time."

"Sorry to hold you up," Elsan said as his father
chuckled.

"It's alright. It'll be worth it as long as we can get
past those walls someday," Ermin said.

"Well, let me fill you two in on a little secret,"
Riklin said, his voice again trailing off, before being
distracted by an older couple in the cemetary east and
below the ductway, kneeling before a small memorial
with their hands holding one another's.

Elsan and Ermin stared at Riklin, waiting for him
to continue, until Elsan said, "Well, what is it?"

Riklin tilted his chin up as the three men entered
the Central Node. He stood still for a moment, causing
Elsan and Ermin to stop as well. Riklin inched closer to
the space between the two young men.

"One night about three years ago, I decided to play a little game," he said.

"A game?" Elsan repeated.

"Yes, a game. You were staying at Ermin's that night. Anyway, I decided to play a game," Riklin began, speaking softer with each word. "We heard some rumors. We heard that some residents of Wrexon's End accessed the hyperloop passageways somehow and escaped out the other end. They carved out the old exits to the surface of some provinces nearby."

Elsan and Ermin stood speechless. Riklin smirked, raised his eyebrows, and turned toward Wrexon's End Ductway to continue the commute home. After staring at each other for a moment, Elsan and Ermin chased after Riklin.

"Where did you hear this?" Elsan asked.

"They must have become ill," Ermin said.

"They were lucky. They had no signs of sickness. None at all," Riklin replied. "The land still couldn't support crops, but it isn't a suicide mission to escape the city, as many might think."

"So, what was the game?" Elsan asked as the three men stepped on the transporter just past the entrance of Wrexon's End Ductway.

"I decided to see how far I could go, but no one operated the hyperloop, of course. All I could do was get far enough past the city walls to climb up and out of the hyperloop pathway without being seen by border guards before I needed to turn back. I wanted to hike the Tocano Mountains and visit the swimming hole, but it was too far away to make it back in time. I didn't sleep that night. I made sure to get back before sunrise, though, so I could come out from the underground while it was still dark. I did get to see the stars without soot or light pollution for first time since before the Black War. I could even smell the living forests to the southeast. Others may have gone farther but they couldn't have come back the same night."

Elsan stared at Riklin, narrowed his eyebrows, and said, "You're bluffing; I know you are. You always do this."

"I might be," Riklin said, as another group of tired residents began trailing closely behind them. "But it's good to wonder, don't you think?"

Ermin smiled and shook his head from side to side as Elsan looked over at him, and they continued to walk beside Riklin on their route home. The farther the three men walked from the Zanoma Tower, the clearer the ductway became. Riklin and Elsan finished the trip swiftly and undeterred, splitting ways from Ermin before reaching home and greeting Tera. Elsan stopped with the door shutting behind him as Riklin walked through the kitchen toward his bedroom, kissing his partner along the way.

"Dad is telling lies again," Elsan said, staring at Riklin as he walked past Tera.

"What now?" Tera asked.

"Dad told me he left the city through the hyperloop passageways."

Tera's eyes lit up before she turned with narrowed eyes to Riklin, who stopped abruptly before the doorway to his bedroom. Riklin turned around, smirked as he looked Tera in her eyes, unbuttoned his black shirt collar, and sat at the kitchen table.

"I just like messing with these young ones," he said as Elsan sat across from his father at the kitchen table, hands folded and resting atop. "They won't do anything stupid, right son?"

"Right," Elsan answered.

Tera glared at Riklin and said, "W-Well, Elsan, don't get any ideas from your halfwit of a father. It's very dangerous out there. In plus, anyone who tries to escape would get into a lot of trouble with the authorities, and there is still contamination—a lot of contamination."

"How do you know for sure?" Elsan asked. "Or have you escaped the city too?"

"Neither of us have," Tera retorted.

"See, now he's thinking," Riklin said with a smile, tapping Elsan on the shoulder as Tera again glared at him.

"I'm going to get out of these clothes," Elsan said, tugging on his collar as he stood to his feet and walked to his bedroom.

He stripped off his daily attire and slipped on a baggy white cloth shirt and black shorts. Scratching his head, he stood dead still. After an internal lapse, he smiled, turned and walked back into the kitchen, where Riklin and Tera looked at each other in silence.

"Remember when," Elsan began but he stopped after seeing, through the doorway of Riklin and Tera's bedroom, his parents' tablets lying on top of one another on a dresser. "Why are you syncing those right now?"

"Dad's tablet is getting old," Tera said. "He wants to back up his data from work."

"Yeah," Riklin said. "It's getting slow. What were you going to say?"

"Remember when we found that swimming hole?" Elsan asked.

"Of course," Tera replied.

"Do you think it's still there?"

"It could be, but I imagine it's discolored, dried a bit, covered by algae."

Elsan sat at the kitchen table, surfacing the memory of a time when he and Ermin tied a rope to a tree by the swimming hole. After climbing to the highest branch to tie one end, and after creating a set of wooden stairs along the steep bank, they swung into the deep pool of fresh water all day long. Daydreaming of the sanctuary left Elsan sitting motionless in his seat with his elbows resting on the kitchen table and his chin resting on his folded hands.

"Are you alright?" Tera asked as she walked to her bedroom.

"Yeah, I'm alright," Elsan responded with a nod. "It's just sad to think that the rope Ermin and I tied up is probably gone—the tree too, for that matter."

"That could be," Riklin said, before nudging Elsan's forearm with his hand. "Let's get cooking."

The Amaranth family would again eat cabbage, lentils, and barley, so as not to waste the leftovers from the night before. Tera heated the food in the same pots and pans, just enough that they did not cook through any further. Riklin prepared the cabbage while Elsan remained seated with a wandering mind.

The tablets in the parents' bedroom beeped three times, signaling the completion of the sync. It took ten minutes, much longer than a typical sync. Recognizing the abnormality, Elsan began to wonder.

"What kind of data do you have on there, Dad?" Elsan asked. "You've only been working one day."

"My job requires a lot of data collection," Riklin replied. "Especially as I get familiar with all of the Energy Sector's databases and networks."

"I see," Elsan said.

He started to help prepare dinner. It was an eerie night, one that chilled the spine and left the heart unsteady. The arching amber rays of the setting sun dimmed as they seeped into a rare layer of fog that floated in the placid air along the edges of every node, ductway, and building.

The Amaranth family paid no mind to the outside at the time. The heat from the cabbage cleared their congested heads while the scent of the rosemary soothed their restive hearts. Steam filled the room, entering their nostrils like georgic to the ear. Riklin pulled his aging gin from the cabinet above the refrigerator and mixed it in a large pitcher with some carbonated water. Elsan set the table while Tera turned the stove and oven off. It seemed to be another savored dinner, and with a kick of alcohol to settle the tension that the new roles in the Zanoma Tower brought.

"Let's eat," Tera said, placing a tray of food upon the table.

"Let's eat," Riklin repeated as he filled each cup with the gin mixture.

"Aren't you worried about your head tomorrow?" Elsan asked. "I don't think I'll be able to work after a night of drinking gin."

"Enjoy it for now, hydrate before bed, and you'll wake up brand new in the morning," Riklin answered. "We haven't celebrated yet."

"Whatever you say, Dad."

After a sip of her drink, Tera said, "Do you remember the nights we used to spend by the shore, just the three of us?"

"Of course," Riklin replied. "That was like our second home. You remember, Elsan, don't you?"

"How could I forget?" Elsan said. "We used to trace constellations for hours past my bed time. It was one of the biggest thrills I got as a child."

"That's right," Tera said with a smile. "I think you discovered some new ones too. You were always the creative one."

"Someday," Elsan began. "Someday we'll get back there and we'll do it all over again."

"I hope so," Riklin said.

There was a knock at the front door of the Amaranth home. Riklin peered through the peephole, then turned his head toward Tera with a perturbed expression. He stood up straight and raised his eyebrows suggestively at Tera.

Tera grabbed Elsan by the arm and scurried with him into the parents' bedroom, leaving their steaming dinner at the kitchen table and Riklin to open the front door. Tera shut the bedroom door behind her son, grabbed the tablets, and moved Elsan toward the closet. Riklin distanced from the front door. There was another knock.

"Mom, what's going on?" Elsan whispered, startled and disconcerted.

Tera was silent, holding her ear toward the bedroom door. Riklin inched toward the front door, intensifying his last two footsepts in an attempt to disguise his delay in answering the knock. Elsan continued to stare at his mother's flushed face.

Riklin opened the door to three guards with folded arms and clenched jaws and greeted, "Good evening, gentlemen. What can I help you with?"

"Riklin Amaranth?" the guard in the center asked with a scowl.

"That's me."

"We've been sent here to search your home. It's an order from the top. Do you have any idea what we might be looking for, Riklin?"

Appearing confused, Riklin replied, "I must say, I can't fathom what that might be. We've lived here forever and this has never happened."

"Well, Riklin," the guard began. "We ask that you kindly allow us inside."

"Of course. Please, come in."

The front door creaked as Riklin slowly pulled it open. The three guards stepped inside, examining the kitchen on their way. The last one to enter gently closed the door behind him.

Elsan's and Tera's hands tightened to fists. Suddenly, the rap of Riklin's face onto the kitchen table sent a jolt through their bones. Plates shattered on the kitchen's tile floor, further terrorizing their already throbbing hearts. They snuck swiftly into the closet.

"Elsan," Tera whispered frenetically, with a tremble in her hands as she reached for Elsan's. "Listen to me. Listen closely."

"You know exactly what we're looking for, scum!" a guard yelled at Riklin in the other room. "Tell us where it is!"

"You need to take this," Tera said, handing Elsan her tablet. "Take this and run."

"Mom, I-I, I ca-" Elsan began before being interrupted by his mother.

"Go to the most southeastern tower block in Wrexon's End and look north. There's an abandoned hyperloop ventilation shaft with a loose grate on the side. Run there, and don't look back. Everything else you need is in here."

"Where are you and Dad going to go?" Elsan asked with fear fuming from his eyes. "I don't understand what's hap-"

"Leave out this way," Tera said, directing Elsan to a chute inside an opening in the back corner of the closet. "Go!"

The bedroom door swung open, cracking the far wall on impact. All was suddenly silent besides the clack of a few footsteps and Riklin wheezing in the kitchen. With the top half of his face pressed firmly against the kitchen table, Riklin stopped panting for a moment, gathered saliva in a pocket under his tongue, and spit at the guard's feet. The guard pulled a black club from his belt and struck Riklin's face, throwing Riklin's weakened body to the floor, where he squirmed in anguish.

"You stupid, worthless rat," the guard said with gritted teeth, glaring down at Riklin's grimacing face.

Tera was forced against the cracked bedroom wall while Elsan slid down the chute without a clue of where it would lead. The chute slanted back and forth down floor after floor, but eventually leveled. Elsan found himself in the tower block's maintenance room. There was a door in front of him. With his bloodstream accelerating in anger and impulse, he tore the door open and sprinted through the corridor outside. The most southeastern tower block in Wrexon's End was within sight, though Elsan's paranoia made it appear farther.

"You can't run forever, Elsan!" a guard yelled just as the Amaranth home became out of sight.

Elsan reached the most southeastern tower block and looked north. There was an above-ground, cement structure with a locked door and grates around the sides. In a frenzy, Elsan stared in all directions, sprinted to the structure, and began tugging on different grates. He found the one his mother spoke of, removed it, ducked inside the structure, repositioned the grate, and stepped onto a ladder leading below the ground, which was attached to the walls of a vertical shaft.

Elsan climbed down the ladders and planted his feet on the steel floor of the hyperloop passageway, the air inside much mustier than he remembered it being as a boy. He extended his arms to feel around in the darkness until he found a switch on the cement wall. He pressed it, illuminating white bulbs every twenty feet to the east. After a glance back up the vertical conduit, the desultory young man darted toward the vanishing point.

4

Huffing, Elsan slowed in relief at the sight of another vertical shaft above a junction of hyperloop routes from Tocano and Ornaia. Without hesitation, he hoisted himself up and out of the hyperloop. He thought he knew where it would lead, but he had not yet gotten to know his new world.

As soon as he arose from the conduit, curiosity overcame his fearful instinct to run. He stared in all directions at the barren lands and abandoned roads under the moonlit sky, suppressing the shock of what appeared foreign to him. Before wasting more time, he tucked his hand back at his side, grasped his mother's tablet to confirm that it was still there, and made his first stride beyond the city walls in a decade. His first breath of air was as he dreamed it would be—inconspicuous and void of bitterness.

As the air coursed by Elsan's face, he began to smile slightly, in levity, but quickly grimaced again and sped up after a tickle to the back of the neck, triggered by the ideation of authorities trailing him. The smack of Riklin's face onto the kitchen table rang in his ears. There was no shield from above by trees or buildings within sight, only the shroud of darkness.

Elsan had not seen the land so dry and lifeless. Sporadic sprouts and petrified tree stumps amplified the unease in his eyes. There were no crops, fields, nor forests at least within several miles of the City of Zanoma. The land was frozen in time, with roots just beginning to crack the surface once again.

Elsan paused for a moment and pulled Tera's tablet from his side. It was charged with nearly five days worth of battery life, though its back cover was a solar charger. Its transmitter was turned off, so as not to allow the authorities to trace him. He opened the file inventory and found a map to the swimming hole in the forests southeast of the city. With renewed urgency, he took off toward what he used to know as Tocano, eager to find the forests that bordered Tocano's residential neighborhoods and the Tocano Mountains. By the time he reached, it was nearly the turning of a new day.

Remnants of once sturdy and occupied tower blocks, as well as commercial and industrial buildings, were scattered across the sienna debris. Eyes gaping, Elsan stared in all directions, horrified by the molten metal, crooked infrastructure, and blasted asphalt. It was one of countless provinces across the planet whose residents were victims of their territory's agenda. They were not well-protected by Zanoma, nor were they prepared for the radiation. Yet, they were a target of Zanoma's enemies.

Elsan resurfaced the unpleasant memories of Tocano residents punching, kicking, and screaming at the border gates of the City of Zanoma after their province was destroyed by Ainkia's allies. It was of no matter, though, in Elsan's trudge up the inclined edges of the decimated enclave, besides the delusion of his suitably eccentric uncle, Loni, resting his feet upon the rail of his balcony. Elsan overlooked the suburb, as Loni would have, roughly halfway up the slope of the steep neighborhoods he and his family passed on their way to the hiking trails. After the humbling sight of the lifeless landscape, he refocused, fleeing up and over the arid crest of the Tocano Mountains in less than an hour with his sights set on the forests.

Elsan opened the map and determined his location. His path became clear as he lifted his chin and spotted a small concentration of vegetation to the southeast. The hum of a military drone froze his feet to the crusted soil for an instant, but it sparked him to sprint toward the swimming hole.

After navigating his way down, Elsan skipped and skidded to the bottom of the mountain, withstanding a struggle for breath and a brume of foreign dust particles to his eyes. At the bottom, the land mass muted the drone's flight, but the hum magnified with each stride over the flat ground. Elsan sensed it would soon hover over the Tocano border with a direct view of him, so he scavenged his soul for an extra boost.

The resonant drone passed over the Tocano border as Elsan dove behind a patch of bushes and under the wilting branches of some trees still clinging to life. The air quieted enough to catch the leaves that persisted swaying in the gentle breeze. Again in relief, Elsan perspired profusely, releasing some of his tension. His chin began to quiver and his eyes pooled tears. He placed his fist against his nose and wept, over and over again, until his tears washed away all of the dust from his eyes. After wiping his face with his shirt, Elsan's eyes were again as dry as the surrounding land. A gulp scratched his dry throat.

Peering through the leaves, Elsan watched as the drone flew over some sable stained forests to the north, in the direction of Ornaia. He pulled out Tera's tablet to look through the files Riklin transferred. There were energy output monitoring program codes and reports written by Lealan Wiske. Much to Elsan's surprise, there was a map of the internal layout of the Energy Sector, including the location of the battery storage section, on the tenth story, along a private staircase only accessible through certain leaders' suites on the upper levels. Elsan scrolled across a decrypted digitalized message, dated the year prior. In a craze of confusion, he narrowed his eyes and read:

Hello old friend,

It is my pleasure to notify you of our recent accomplishments. The milestones thus far this year have all been completed.

Our workforce has exceeded our expectations, giving us the manpower to manage all of the resources we need to power the final stages of development of our new home in Ornaia. Food production has become prolific enough to feed the current population of Wrexon's End and Milbon Hill, while dividing the rest between South Village and the provinces as planned with the increased birth rates, at least for the time being. Our workforce remains continuously motivated by the fight for prosperity, and they continue to fall to their knees for Medrik.

I cannot stress enough the importance of constant surveillance of lands outside of Zanoma, especially the coastline. More and more Zanoma citizens have gone missing this year, and if alive, their intentions cannot be predicted. Survivors from the provinces might someday try to travel this way. We are not yet ready for the civil unrest that will come. A rebellion must occur on our terms.

Thank you. As always, your presence is felt in Zanoma. We trust that you will send a signal upon receipt of this message.

Regards,

Daiton Tibs

There was another set of data in the files. It contained food weights distributed to each of the City of

Zanoma's boroughs, as well as provinces across the world. Elsan knew that survivors across the planet that did not flee to Zanoma were having their societies structured after the Republic, with the support of the Republic, as their old regimes were eliminated during the Black War, but he was previously under the belief that they were self-sustainable, not reliant on the weak support of the Republic of Zanoma, not receiving rations, insufficient rations, like the South Village Slums. He did not know fully what these files on Tera's tablet meant, but he knew that they were not good.

Elsan's face smoldered, but a sudden brush of leaves stole his attention. With the blindness of night settling in, he shined the light of the tablet on a blacktail deer that gnawed at creeping junipers and bunchberry bushes a short distance away. Strange, it seemed to him, not only for the coastal creature to be alive, but also for it to be feeding from the inland forests, where the vegetation was a bit different. Elsan wondered if the shore's shallon may have turned to poison or even ash.

When the gormandizing deer raised its head from the greenery, Elsan was unnerved by a dark bulge below one of its ears. The bulge bubbled down to its neck, leading to a hairless patch on its loin. Its legs were frail and its rump veered to the side. Its black eyes, which connected with Elsan's, contained pools of white clouds.

"Hello," Elsan uttered, though he knew to maintain a safe distance from the deer.

The blacktail deer stopped chewing, seemingly at the sound of Elsan's welcoming voice.

"You don't look well, my friend," Elsan continued as the deer continued to stare back at him. "What are you doing here?"

Elsan stood to his feet and tucked the tablet back into his pants pocket. As he did so, the deer bolted away from its food and between the carmine trunks of some surrounding evergreens. It had forsaken the patch of forested land and darted in the direction of some other partially vegetated areas by the Ornaian shores.

Whatever path we set foot upon is ultimately a route back home, Elsan thought.

Utterly alone, Elsan dropped to his knees and lowered his chin to his chest. He touched his right hand to his forehead, whimpering, though his eyes could no longer form tears. Folding his hands together, he thought about praying to the heavens, as many practiced after the Black War, though he was never sure that the heavens existed. Before the Black War was a world where the heavens were more often considered a fanciful ruse for the adrift people, and the Black War left the sullen searching for hope in the heavens once again. Elsan's family just worshipped the dead, including Medrik Malva after the war. Trapped in a contaminated world without his parents, Elsan no longer felt that he had a way to control the chaos. All that remained was hope that his life and the lives of his mother and father would be among the righteous survivors.

The light from the stars started to dim as some thin clouds passed through the sky. The air became crisp, as it had been every night after the Black War, though Elsan was still warm from the exercise he had just endured. The trees began to breathe. It was time for Elsan to find the swimming hole so he could make himself some sort of bed in a place that he felt more comfortable.

The buzz of flying insects rang between the trees as he crept cautiously into the forest's darkening center. His heartbeat slowed, but with each step came a thud beneath his ribs. A horse fly landed on the side of his neck and quickly bit into his skin.

"Ah!" he yelled with a wince, smacking his hand on top of the fly.

It was the last time for the flies to feed before hiding away for the night. With fewer resources available, the flies stayed out later. The surroundings became completely dark besides the light from the moon and stars above. Elsan used Tera's tablet to illuminate the cryptic land, and he continued under some drooping, yet blooming, branches. He stepped around a small boulder and over a line of short bushes. Hanging from a distant tree was a collection of prop roots appearing as a thick net.

Elsan held the light steady so as not to lose sight of the strange object. It seemed to be natural material, but it was unclear whether or not its shape was a mere illusion. He tiptoed forward, tightly holding the tablet and keeping the tips of his feet prepared for the foreign lands that laid ahead.

"Hello?" he said as he neared the net, but there was no answer. "Is anyone there?"

Still, no answer, but it quickly became clear to Elsan that the prop roots were tied intricately, purposely, into a net. It was attached on either side to a pair of tree branches, which extended from two of the seemingly sturdiest trees he had seen. Up the sides of the trees were holes carved to fit the balls of a foot.

Elsan tilted the tablet down so he could continue under the net. Just steps after the net, he stopped in awe of a reflection of dimmed moonlight on the ground surface. It was the swimming hole. Unlike the millions of swimming holes that were dried or even filled by the debris of nuclear blasts, this one had survived along with the surrounding forest.

With Elsan's thirst came a yawn and a wave of fatigue. The yawn watered Elsan's eyes, so he wiped them dry along with his perspiring hairline. His unsteady knees, which he knew he would need the next day, shook with each step toward the prop root net.

Planting the tips of his feet into the carved steps, Elsan climbed toward the top of one of the net's supporting trees. He turned his back to the net and scanned his surroundings one last time, though he could only see the faint moonlight glowing between the leaves. Falling backwards, Elsan spread his body from one tree to the other along the net, drooping an arm over the edge.

Elsan, he imagined in Tera's voice. *You should go to sleep. It's your first day tomorrow.*

"Yes, Mom," Elsan whispered, his delirious mind hoping to dream.

Elsan, Riklin's voice rang. *Be ready when you wake up tomorrow.*

"Yes, Dad."

Elsan's eyelids flickered as they slipped down, causing his vision to go black. His heart skipped a beat. With the woven bed beneath his back and his weary head rested, he drifted into sleep.

5

At dawn, Elsan awoke, nearly flipping over the side of his new bed at the sight of the dancing leaves above him. Between the leaves was a mellow orange hue, a warming glow after a dark, cool night alone. Elsan's stomach growled, overdue for some of Zanoma's almond and barley rations. Aware that his food supply would be even less plentiful than the scarce supply in Zanoma, he was determined, like the blacktail deer, to settle his stomach.

He climbed down from the net, stepping on some intermediate branches along the way, and planted his restored, energized legs on the ground. The cool, shaded soil softened his landing. As he let out a sigh, the morning sun soothed the back of his neck, but the forefront of his head throbbed.

Elsan stood stock-still, wondering whether any food grown in the forest could be trusted. Fruits and nuts could have grown with radioactive material. Meat, if there were any to hunt for, could have been sickening. No matter what Elsan found, the health effects were unknown. Regardless, he walked around the swimming hole and deeper into the forest. There were no berries, nuts, or other natural foods in sight.

After a step over a fallen hornbeam, a purple tint appeared within a faraway plant. Elsan started to run toward it, hoping to find juneberries hidden in the distant tree. His eyes widened and his mouth salivated at the thought of the sweet, tangy taste, and the burst of refreshing juices.

He skipped across and above ground roots and open mounds of soil, between black spruces and under their overshadowing branches. The berries became closer and closer, but there was a sudden brush of leaves nearby. Elsan stopped to listen.

It was a blacktail deer approaching the juneberry bush. Astonished, Elsan recognized the deer's bubbling neck, but his disbelief of the coincidence quickly turned into a dispirited slouch as the deer chomped at the plant's rich branches. He knew the deformed deer had come in contact with contamination somehow, and any plant could have played a role.

He stepped back over the roots, the soil mounds, and the fallen hornbeam, which had a trunk tinted with the umber of the remnants of war. Elsan lifted his chin to look deeper into the surrounding trees and bushes.

The red oaks had trunks with black spots all over. The trunks of the basswoods had mahogany-colored crust over its partially decayed foundation. Honeysuckles and holly bushes were not quite as vibrant as he remembered them to be.

Elsan closed his eyes, breathed deeply to slow his heart, opened his eyes again, and continued on his path back toward the swimming hole. Looping behind a white oak, he peered through some more trees, but there was no more food in sight. Suddenly, he felt a section of land beneath his feet too solid and flat to be natural, so he abruptly stepped back.

After a layer of soil was kicked to the side, a silver square appeared. It had a handle on one side and small hinges on the other. Elsan lifted the handle and shuffled to the opposite end of the unforeseen enigma to put his shadow behind him. He was overcome with relief at the sight of a heap of grains and nuts piled within the metal cube. Without hesitation, he dug his hand into the unexpected gift from an unknown aide and gorged as much as he could chew. Handful after handful, Elsan devoured the grains and nuts and settled his hunger. He wondered if his parents had gathered the food.

He shut the compartment cover, and looked up to sharpened sunrays. Rejuvenated, he felt an enhanced warmth from the sun, calming his mind. Suddenly, Elsan had nothing more to do—not a single obligation or even an objective direction. He had freedom, though without comfort.

Elsan scrolled through Tera's tablet some more and came across some new files—not from the Energy Sector like Riklin said of the documents, but from the Sustenance Sector. They were filed under the name of Zanoma's Head of the Sustenance Sector, Shylo Cob, and his brother, Fydel Cob, who was Head of the Health Sector.

Along with some more datasets was a transcript from one of Chancellor Tibs' many speeches to the public in the years after the Black War, part of it reading, *It is strange to think about managing our food so strictly and producing our food in ways so rarely done before. One might assume that no artificially grown food will be as nourishing as a crop grown with healthy, natural soils. Although this may be true, and although our pre-war surplus is now gone, our food production facilities have improved operations enough to match the amount necessary for our city's population. Thanks to our innovative agronomists, we expect to make further progress so we can all survive until our world's soils are enriched again. So long as we protect the Sustenance Sector from thieves and keep our food healthy, we will not go hungry. As much as our time, and as much as our energy, we must continue to sacrifice our cravings and temptations. We must resist the gluttonous ways we lived by prior to the Black War. That means being satisfied with the rations that we are able to distribute and, at worst case, being willing to make sacrifices for each other to move us all forward, together. We will rebuild this world together, and together we must remain.*

Elsan scrolled further down the list of files to one labeled "Ornaia Map". It included the northern shore. Northeast of Zanoma and north of Elsan's current location was a star symbol along the coastline with the label, "Ornaian Shores". Elsan decided that he would follow the map to the Ornaian Shores to see what was there, to see why the map would highlight it. There was nothing more for him to do in such a lonely and lost state than to explore, or rather, investigate.

Without further hesitancy, Elsan ran toward the northern edge of the forested area. He dodged trees, leapt over plants, and stopped behind the last tree in his way. He stared across the vast sky in fear of drones and military aircrafts, but he saw none, so he sprinted out of the forest toward the vegetated borders of the northern shore, which was barely in sight.

Vulnerably alone on the impoverished land, Elsan ran faster than ever before. His mind ran rampant as well, with illusions of drones and military aircrafts flying behind his back. With each stride, Elsan neared closer to the forests of the northern shore, the vegetated border quickly appearing taller, the forest appearing denser. Shelter from the defenseless open land was within reach, and Elsan was eager to escape the indefensible air.

He slid behind a towering tamarack at the border of the northern forest, catching his breath under its shield of layered leaves. Sweat formed along his hairline and in his armpits. The forest was in a similar state as the other, with wilting trees and dry, lingering leaves. Elsan slowly stepped deeper and deeper into the plagued, yet prospering, forest. The leaves brightened as he walked closer to the ocean. Plant stems and branches stood more upright, and tree trunks had a more natural shade of brown. Soils started to appear moist and more fertile. Life was plentiful and fortunate.

His mind immersed in a green glow as he recalled the adventures he took as a child, with his family, friends, and the flocks of Zanoma residents from Tocano, Ornaia, and Treton. It was a time when the air was fresh, water was swimmable, flowers emitted scents strong enough to raise the hair follicles on his arms, and fruits were detoxifying rather than toxic. His world was not artificial, but truly alive. He climbed trees, tossed a ball with his friends, built swings out of prop roots so he and his friends could launch themselves into swimming holes, and played in the sand of the beaches. All of his friends were alive and well, excited to take on each and every day. Even Tera and Riklin would join him if his friends were not available, crashing with the waves like they were children once again.

Waking from his daydream, Elsan found himself motionless in between a few red oaks and a patch of moss. He became so distracted by his thoughts that he lost his sense of the northern direction, but his unready ears were overcome with the hum of a military aircraft flying above. He quickly jumped beside a tree trunk so he was no longer in their line of sight.

After skipping over a few fallen maples and a couple of buttonbushes, he lost sight of the aircraft. Elsan continued to make his way through the densely vegetated forest, passing berry shrubs with his initial strides. He manipulated the maze of green and brown, jumping and weaving, staring down each obstacle the moment they came into sight. Wrapping his arm around an evergreen, Elsan forced himself to a halt. The forest seemed to end not far ahead. As he neared the last row of trees, he started to see a mix of sand and soil, until it became purely marigold sand. The salty tang of an ocean breeze and the hiss of plunging waves healed Elsan's anxious heart, if only for a moment.

In stealth, he sunk his body low to the ground and knelt behind a red cedar and a patch of goldenrods. The aircraft was parked on an airstrip that stretched along a coastal cliff that protruded further into the sea than any of the surrounding land. The beach in between Elsan and the cliff edge extended until the cliff became too steep to settle sand.

Elsan could not see faces, but four people were walking inland, away from the resting aircraft. They approached a large building enclosed and concealed by a strangely symmetric array of green ash trees. Having lost sight of the unidentified people, Elsan decided to use the tablet to zoom in on the building they were about to enter.

After focusing the tablet's lens on the peculiar building, Elsan tapped the screen to zoom in. It was a large building, suggesting that it had some special function, though it appeared as a royal mansion. Chancellor Tibs was entering the building alongside Lealan Wiske, Shylo Cob, Fydel Cob, Commander Evarand Nap, and the Head of the Environmental Sector, Powman Pent.

Shylo and Fydel walked side by side behind Lealan and Tibs. Shylo and Fydel, with their tan skin and dark hair, looked identical from Elsan's distance. Nap and Powman followed closely behind, with far more apparent differences. Nap was last to enter the house, with the blonde hair on his head grazing the top of the doorway as he reached out one of his bulky, veiny hands. Alongside him was the blonde, petite Powman, who seemed to be almost half the height and half the width of Nap.

Elsan retreated ten feet and shuffled along the forest's border. The view of the building was at a different angle, one in which the building's backyard balcony was visible. Elsan refocused the tablet's lens at the new angle.

Five guards paced toward the trimmed grass over a tile patio jutting from the building's back wall. There was a set of doors on the back wall, which slid open as another guard stepped outside to join the others on patrol. The guards spoke among themselves, casually, as if they had never been threatened in Ornaia.

Above them was the balcony. The green ash trees obstructed Elsan's vision, so he stepped a few feet further to the right. On one side of the balcony were four men in white suits apparently bellowing in laughter with wine glasses in their hands.

Shocked, Elsan fell behind a patch of goldenrods at the sight of a guard, dressed just like those in the City of Zanoma. The guard held the same long-distance firearm as those on the upper levels of the Zanoma

Tower and along the city border, and it was aimed seemingly in the direction of Elsan.

His chest throbbing and his eyes expanded in alert, Elsan crawled deeper into the forest. With the cover of dozens of tree trunks, he launched himself upright and sprinted with the fear of being chased pushing his fleet escape. His strides stretched farther with each passing thought. He panted in both panic and physical exertion. The forest seemed to have no end.

Elsan dashed through the dense forest, jumping over bushes and fallen trees, eluding the congested branches and thorns. The end of the forest was finally in sight, with a backdrop of desolate land. Elsan's foot hooked into the branch of a fallen tree, which held his leg back as his torso continued forward, sending him flat to the ground.

A bunch of sticks and broken branch ends stabbed and scraped Elsan's face, neck, arms, legs, and abdomen. Blood surfaced where skin was lost, including a trickle down the side of his eye. His head pounded from inside with an animalistic impulse to flee, as he was from the dangers behind him. He was certain that he was being chased.

Shaking the branch off of his foot, Elsan accelerated toward the forest's edge, keeping his eyes on the vegetated ground. Finally, he had reached the last tree in his way, an oak with a ghostly grey hue in its bark. Elsan imagined the tone of the military aircraft's aerodynamic thrusts, though he had not heard nor seen the aircraft in the skies.

Rather than sticking within his skittish mind, he took off again over the open land, which transitioned to a bleaker beige. Even more fearful than before, Elsan rushed across the naked land scared of the open space at his back and above his head. The sunlight sizzled the back of his neck and sweat began seeping from his pores. His heart raced, as tree cover appeared distant.

He continued his rapid retreat from the mysterious coastline, the forests to the south growing nearer. The proximate trees grew taller with each stride. Elsan's legs and heartbeat decelerated as he approached. He had finally reached the forest that he called his home for one night. Most comforting of all was that he had not heard any signals of the military aircraft.

He began to feel safer. He was protected, above and in all lateral directions, from the vision of guards. The shade of the tree leaves gave Elsan a calming moment to temper his torrid skin. The summer sun was imposing its ferocity on the young man, enough to make Elsan's forearms a bit red in such little time.

He began walking slowly into the forest in the direction of the swimming hole, the silent air alleviating the angst from his invigorated brain. The thought of his hand holding a mound of grains and nuts added strength to his shaking knees. He began salivating, though his thirst quickly dried his mouth again.

Elsan stepped over a fallen tupelo, confident that he had reached safety and evaded the grasp of the guards at the curious coastal building. With each step, he grew hungrier and his throat grew drier. He licked his chapped lips and continued onto some open soil between four evergreen trees.

Suddenly, his leg was again pulled out from under him. Unlike the branch he had fallen over, the force caused his torso to fall backwards. The back of his head struck a rock peaking out from the soil. Elsan's vision faded to black as cordage constricted his ankle and raised him into the air.

6

Eleven years prior, a dark-skinned, dark-haired, muscular guard of the City of Ainkia sat in front of an array of monitors with his mouth gaping and his eyes bouncing from side to side. It displayed live surveillance of Zanoma's embassy, receiving signals from camera taps at many corners of the embassy's interior. The man synced his tablet on a sleek, circular black surface on the side of one of the monitors, extracting twenty seconds of footage before stashing the tablet in a pants pocket and rushing out of the room.

He ascended several floors in Ainkia's security facility, his eyes instinctively wide. He planned to find Ainkia's Military Commander, who picked his head up as the guard enterred his office. The guard shut the office door hastily behind him.

The Military Commander noticed the distress in the guard's eyes and said, "Macrum, are you alright?"

"We need men at Zanoma's embassy immediately," Macrum said.

Soon after, a fleet of Ainkia guards surrounded Zanoma's embassy, weapons drawn, but it was too late. Travelling diplomats and guards from Zanoma had already left the embassy in armored vehicles to return to their military aircrafts to fly back to their home territory. Ainkia guards who followed the armored vehicles could not get close enough to stop Zanoma's men before taking off.

Macrum took the footage to media outlets throughout the City of Ainkia, not only to spread throughout his home territory, but through to Zanoma's networks, through Zanoma's allies' networks, through Ainkia's allies' networks, and through other networks around the world. Speculation emerged in the minds of Ainkia's residents, and in their voices as residents looked to their government for answers. As invididuals in Zanoma accessed the footage, pulling from Ainkia's networks, widespread confusion led to protests and riots. Residents of Zanoma's ally territories protested their governments for relations with Zanoma. Yet, before the footage was seen by too many, before the backlash became too strong, the Republic of Zanoma commited to blocking all traces of the footage from its networks and to blocking all network traffic into and out of the City of Zanoma, while Zanoma's media outlets claimed that the footage was staged and doctored.

Undercover operatives of the Republic tracked down and erased all traces of the footage from its allies' networks while promoting the same story.

It was a time when no information could be trusted, no matter how clear it seemed to be. Newly appointed Chancellor Tibs declined to comment on the footage, stating that he would not entertain fabrications. Before long, the footage was forgotten, and the support of Zanoma's military was restored within the City of Zanoma, Zanoma's provinces, and ally territories. In Ainkia's ally territories, in Ainkia's provinces, and in the City of Ainkia, some residents held onto a history of corrupt dealings by the Republic of Ainkia and were too suspicious of the government to defend them, though many more rallied for Ainkia to take action.

In the north side of the City of Ainkia, Macrum visited his mother, who lived alone in a tower block close to the center of the city since Macrum's father had passed away. She sat at her dining table, staring at her son's eyes skeptically. Macrum stared back at her, eyes focused with genuine intention.

"I'm leaving the city," Macrum said. "And I'm not leaving without you."

"Macrum," his mother said. "Don't you think you might be overreacting?"

"Why do you think they would do something like this?" Macrum said, continuing to stare at his mother with piercing eyes. "It's a false flag. It has to be. There's no other explanation."

"My son, I've lived in Ainkia my whole life, and I plan to die here, whenever that may be. I'm not prepared to leave, nor would I want to, no matter the risk. This is my home."

"Mom, you could die here now," Macrum pleaded. "This is bad, Mom. This is very bad."

"I love you, Macrum," the mother said. "I believe you, but I'm getting old. There's no place for me outside of here. I'll let our military protect us like they're meant to. I trust they will."

Macrum tried some more, but he could not convince his mother to join him in fleeing the city. He took off alone, making his way to a neighboring province sprawled atop a plateau that allowed for a view of the City of Ainkia at certain angles. Having found a boarding house, he sat idle in his bed, hoping that the heavens were real, hoping that they would protect his mother from the horrors that he feared would come down upon his lifelong home.

Beside other guests of the boarding house, Macrum overlooked the City of Ainkia, keeping a keen eye on the center of the city. He watched as Zanoma's bombs dropped, incinerating the city and sending dark grey mounds of soot into the atmosphere. Buildings collapsed, others left in flames, and Macrum's distant heart grew cold. In that moment, with tears trickling from his eyes and his breaths erratic, he knew his mother was gone.

Ainkia's allies started to prepare to defend themselves and retaliate. A lone warrior, Macrum fled again, understanding that Ainkia's allies would not survive an attack, nor escape the radiation from nearby acts of war. Zanoma was his destination, though sickening, for it may have been the only place where Macrum could influence the future of humanity.

As he travelled by hyperloop routes across the planet's lands, stopping at boarding houses along the way, Zanoma and its allies continued to trade threats and attacks with Ainkia's allies. As more radioactive particles, biological weapons, and chemicals coated the world's territories, so did the distrust between them. Before Macrum could travel to the City of Zanoma, Chancellor Tibs ordered the removal of the City of Zanoma as a hyperloop destination and ceased travel by any route through the city.

Displaced people from territories across the world were forced to approach Zanoma's walls by foot, hauling the remainder of their belongings on their backs. Some had small children at their sides. The City of Zanoma was the only city in the world with such impenetrable borders, with walls several stories high, leaving the refugees begging the guards for empathy from outside of the gates. Foreigners were not the only ones to approach the gates, though.

Zanoma residents who had been out of the city also sought entry so they could return home. They were granted entry as foreigners were watched over by armed guards. At the gate that Macrum stood by, a sudden rush of scared refugees trampled a row of guards, breaking open the border. Macrum sprinted forward into the city, terrified that, at any moment, a bullet could end his life, but it seemed to happen to everyone around him while he survived unscathed. The crying and wailing of the others sent a sharp pain through his heart, but he continued sprinting forward.

Eventually, after evading the border guards, he found himself on the streets of South Village, hoping to blend in despite the sweat dripping down his face, carrying dirt from his cheeks down with it. Despite the escalation of war, of devastation, throughout the world, South Village's radiant culture persevered. Having visited Zanoma in years prior, Macrum noticed a bit more of a presence of guards at street corners and the borough was always the poorest, but the residents still appeared happy and healthy, waving to one another as vehicles passed by, bargaining at street-side shops.

The crowds began to dissipate. Macrum veered from the hectic section of South Village and stopped in a small park surrounded by tower blocks. Taking a moment to simply breathe seemingly for the first time since watching the live surveillance in Ainkia, he began crying, releasing tears for his mother, for all of the lives that the planet had lost to that day.

"Are you alright?" a tall man with dark skin, black hair, and brown eyes asked, approaching Macrum in the quiet park.

"Yes," Macrum said, starting to wipe the tears from his face. "Yes. I'm alright. Thank you."

"There's an inflection in your voice," the man said. "Where are you from?"

"A-Ainkia," Macrum answered, turning to the man with scared eyes. "P-Please don't turn me in. I'm just trying to survive, like we're all trying to do."

"Don't worry," the man said, reaching out to shake Macrum's hand as Macrum's eyes remained wide, though with calming surprise instead of fear. "My name is Myer Storm. What's your name?"

"Macrum."

"It's very nice to meet you, Macrum," Myer said before signaling Macrum to follow him to a nearby tower block. "Come with me."

Myer led Macrum toward the tower block. Macrum continued to stare in all directions along the way, hoping to blend into the people of South Village, though he was visually anxious. The two men ascended the tower block and entered the Storm family's home. At a kitchen table, a woman and two children looked up, initially appearing confounded, though the strange looks in their faces subsided.

"Macrum," Myer began. "This is my partner, Sola, and our children, Sairin and Mora. Family, this is Macrum. He travelled all the way from Ainkia, and he was a bit lost. I thought he could use a place to rest his head for the time being."

Sola gave Myer a probing look, and he gave a confirmatory nod back while the adolescent son and the adolescent daughter gave Macrum a gentle smile. Sola had tan skin, blonde hair, and big hazel eyes. Sairin and Mora looked much alike, with their mother's striking hazel eyes, their father's black hair, and fallow skin. The three of them stared in curiosity of their visitor, the children with the innocent excitement of meeting their father's new friend.

It quickly became clear that the Storm family intended to house Macrum for as long as he needed. Macrum did not go far from their home out of fear of being confronted by the growing number of guards in South Village, but he did not need to venture. The Storm family fed him and provided him clothing that was typical in Zanoma. Myer and Sola even made Sairin and Mora move into the same room so Macrum could have a private place to sleep in whatever peace he could find in the Storm family's home. Much to Macrum's surprise, the Storm family looked at him warmly, seemingly with blind trust.

Nuclear, chemical, and biological attacks were commited by Ainkia's allies against Zanoma's allies, and over the provinces of Tocano and Treton. Ballistic missiles targeting Zanoma were shot down as well, torching areas surrounding Zanoma in all directions. Soot filled the skies, and radioactive flakes even fell within Zanoma's walls, onto the streets, and in the parks, sprinkling the grass and tainting the air that the residents breathed every second. The people of Zanoma began leaning on their military once again, passionately advocating for retaliation, and Chancellor Tibs seemed to be prepared.

One day, Macrum sat at the kitchen table with the Storm family, and he decided to finally ask, "Why do you all trust me? I've been here for a little while now, but you trusted me from the start. Tragedy after tragedy, all centered around your territory's poor relationship with mine—well, what used to be mine."

"People like us have more in common with each other than we do with our leaders," Sola said before turning her head to Myer.

"Not long ago," Myer interjected. "I saw some things that shocked me a bit."

"What was it?" Macrum asked.

"I work at Zanoma's central receiver," Myer said. "I was one of the first to be notified about a suspicious video that was circulated a bit throughout the city. The source was Ainkia. You might have seen it. The children wouldn't understand, but it was gruesome. We were forced to block any trace of the video from our networks. Our leaders said it was fake and a hazard to the city, but something told me that it was real, and very important because it was real. I can't quite remember what it looked like, but I remember feeling deeply troubled, and that feeling hasn't gone away. Anyway… I feel that the people of Ainkia and elsewhere, the people who have lost their lives, the people who are sick, who are fighting to survive, deserve redemption. You may be just one person, Macrum, but you represent countless people who have seen the world crumble around them. I look at you in your eyes and I see a good man. You aren't an enemy. Not to me."

"Thank you," Macrum said, narrowing his eyes in curiosity before smiling and looking around at the rest of the family. "All of you. Thank you."

"Well," Sola said with a smile. "We could all use some sleep."

The family, including Macrum, went to their bedrooms to get ready to sleep for the night. After a few minutes, Macrum noticed Myer, who was back in the kitchen to pour a cup of water, wearing some ragged clothes. He entered the kitchen, placing his tablet on the kitchen table as Mora peaked over from her's and Sairin's bedroom doorway. The young girl watched as her father and her new friend whispered to each other and looked at Macrum's tablet together. Their faces became steely, and the two men split apart to go to their bedrooms and fall asleep.

Days later, Myer and Sola left for work in the morning, Myer a bit earlier than usual. Macrum stayed home with Sairin and Mora until it was time for them to leave for their classes. It was a normal morning in Zanoma for Macrum, watching the television projected onto a screen in the common area of the Storm's home, waiting for more news regarding the war. There was a sudden glitch in the television reception, and a fuzzy image appeared on the screen.

A low-resolution video began, showing a still room with a walkway, rails on both sides, piping and equipment supporting ventilation and heat recovery systems outside of the rails. Suddenly, a man with white hair wearing a black suit with a Z on the chest ran from around a corner of the walkway, and a big, blonde man followed in a guard's uniform that also had a Z on the chest. The man in the guard's uniform shot the man in the black suit in his back, causing him to flail to the ground. The man in the guard's uniform stepped over the fallen man and shot him again in the back of the head, the video ending after a few seconds of blood spreading along the floor.

"Commander Nap," Sairin said with wide eyes, approaching from behind Macrum. "It's a bit blurry, but it looks like him. It was Commander Nap who killed him, not Ainkia's men."

"That's right," Macrum said solemnly before the screen suddenly glitched again and reverted back to the Zanoma News and the head reporter, Amon Sarato, whose large white eyes and large shiny teeth contrasted his tan skin and dark hair.

"We sincerely apologize for that graphic imagery," Amon Sarato said to the camera. "That appeared to be the supposed footage from the Zanoma embassy in Ainkia that was deemed by independent video engineers to be doctored long ago. We will investigate what just happened and who is behind this. Those who have hacked our television networks will be dealt with."

Macrum's leg began bouncing up and down as he glanced back at Sairin. Mora walked into the room, causing Macrum's hands to shake more, sweat surfacing from the pores of his face. He scratched the back of his head and turned to the children.

"I need to leave," Macrum said. "Will you two be alright if I go take a walk?"

The children nodded, so Macrum gathered his tablet and a few other belongings before leaving the Storm family's home. He swiftly walked through South Village, as he would on any day, so as to act casual while residents politely gestured. The Industrial District was his direction as he used the Zanoma Tower to guide him. As he got closer, angry and confused residents were already starting to gather in the streets, in the ductways, and in the Central Node. Some residents were protesting, demanding answers for the surveillance footage, while others defended the Republic from the protestors. It was a clash that the city had seen before, having had the footage released to Zanoma's networks for some people to view on their tablets in the recent past, but more people saw the footage this time. People gathered in stronger forces, and Macrum took advantage of that as he made his way to the primary hyperloop entrance in the Industrial District.

The hyperloop was shut down. There were three guards at the entrance, who waved their hands, so as to tell Macrum that he could not access it. Macrum paused for a moment before launching forward and over the metal gateways to the hyperloop.

"Hey!" one guard yelled, pulling his gun out, along with the other two guards.

The three guards fired bullets in Macrum's direction, but none struck him before he was able to scurry around a curling hyperloop pathway. The guards shrugged and placed their guns back at their sides, so as to suggest that Macrum had no where to go. It was not clear to Macrum where he would go either.

Sola Storm arrived home to Sairin and Mora, who sat in front of the television screen, still astonished by what they had seen earlier that day. After briefly looking around for Macrum or Myer, Sola's eyes widened, clearly concerned about them. She walked over to her children, sat between them, and wrapped her arms over their shoulders, pulling them closer to her. There was a knock at the door. A few guards stood there, awaiting Sola as she opened the door.

Sola quickly broke down crying at the news that Myer had been shot down by a guard near the central receiver as he attempted to escape. Her eyes filled with rage as she stared in the faces of the guards who defended the Republic, but subdued with the weakness she felt in her heart. Sairin and Mora walked over, catching on to what was happening as they watched their mother fall to her knees. They began sobbing as well, hugging Sola tightly as they leaned into her shoulders on either side. Their father and their new friend were gone, far too abruptly and mysteriously for the young children to understand.

The air in Zanoma was cold, stemming from the soot in the upper atmosphere and a universal feeling of loss through all of Zanoma's residents. The Republic of Zanoma won what was then being called the Black War, but every territory outside of Zanoma was destroyed, ultimately uninhabitable after tons and tons of radiation and contamination and a loss of resources. It was believed that most people who did not make it to Zanoma for shelter were dead as well, and if they were not, they would be in short time. What was certain was that no other organized territory existed, and those that had no government were not counted through the eyes of Chancellor Tibs. They were not counted unless he could govern them himself.

One morning, exactly a year after her father's death, Mora sat with her brother and her mother at the kitchen table, eating the rations that they received from the South Village Sustenance Center, and asked, "Why did this happen? What's the point of winning a war if the whole world is destroyed, if all of those people aren't around anymore to live in it?"

Mora appeared angry, not toward her mother, but toward what remained of humanity. Sairin looked at Mora profoundly, fearful for his sister's well-being. Sola sat in silence for a moment, but looked up at Mora.

"We all have our own eyes with a unique perspective on the world around us," she began, her cheeks narrower than they were a year prior. "There are some people in this world, and in our world's history, that we will never understand. We reached a point in time when we didn't understand our own leaders, in Zanoma, in Ainkia, even ally territories. We reached a point in time when the world's leaders were all mad. Those psychopaths, sociopaths—they had no concern for people like us, and the biggest maniac of all was our Vice Chancellor. He is why this started. He and the other hollow leaders are how this ended."

"Chancellor Tibs?" Mora asked.

"Yes. Chancellor Tibs," Sola said. "Him and the ones in his circle who were as crazy as he is, who knew what he was doing and joined him for wealth, for satisfying their hatred, and most of all, for control."

"Has it truly ended?" Sairin asked.

"It appears that they've won," Sola said.

Suddenly, Sola's vision faded a bit, as she was getting more and more fatigued each day that passed by. She pressed her hand firmly against her lower ribs, below her heart, wincing as if there was a deep ache. As she moved the tips of her fingers back and forth over the area, her eyes widened a bit, her vision clearing up for the moment. There was a lump.

"Are you alright?" Sairin asked his mother as he and Mora watched her closely.

"I-I think I need to go to the Health Center," Sola said.

Sola had felt weaker and weaker, sorer and sorer by the day, though she was never consciously aware of what that meant until that afternoon. Her knees were shaking with each step as Sairin and Mora helped her through the kitchen. Sairin wrapped a jacket around his mother and guided her through the doorway of their home along with his sister.

The Health Sector had become overburdened with sick residents in need of urgent care, particularly in the South Village Health Center, where there was a dense population and less efficient care. Sola was added far down on a list of residents waiting to be assessed and treated for similarly severe conditions. Every day, Health Centers were swamped with residents who had lumps that felt like tumors, fractures that indicated that their bones were weakening, extreme fatigue, nausea, vomiting, and even some unexplainable symptoms. There were children who were ill, some born with smaller heads due to microcephaly resulting from their mothers' exposure to radiation while pregnant. Other children from infants to adolescents had different forms of cancer and disease, the smaller ones clutching to their mothers with their pale hands, the older ones flushed and coughing with their mothers rubbing their backs. Parents argued for their children to be prioritized, but their neighbors were dealing with the same drive to protect their children as well. Arguments escalated between health professionals and residents, and among residents, though some saw themselves in each other. With no other choices available, slow and delayed care was ultimately accepted. Even in Wrexon's End and Milbon Hill, where the Republic of Zanoma began providing more resources, the Health Centers were an ugly scene.

By the time Sola was seen, cancer cells from the tumor on her rib had spread to other ribs, to her lung, and to her lymph nodes. She became frailer and frailer, paler and paler, though her mind somehow became stronger. It was too late physically, and Sola passed away in her home after months of insufficient treatment, poor nutrition, and a lack of hope for a recovery. Sairin and Mora would not forget those final days, nor the look in their mother's eyes when she had accepted her fate. Yet, Sola did say something that Sairin and Mora appeared to attach themselves to as she began drifting out of their world on her bed in South Village.

"I was wrong," she had said, glancing at both Sairin and Mora. "It isn't over, and they can't win. We can't let them win."

After Sola passed away, Sairin and Mora were taken in by the Republic, though ultimately left with one of the Storm family's neighbors to be cared for throughout their teenage years while living in what was becoming known as the South Village Slums, which became riddled with sickness more and more during the several years following the Black War. The lively culture that existed in South Village had dulled. Street-side shops closed, cars were kept off of the roads, and a wave of grief, fatigue, depression, and unemployment made the morose South Village residents mosey around aimlessly under the murky skies. Sairin and Mora had no choice but to eat smaller and smaller rations each day, and they dreamed of a day when their stomachs would be satisfied again.

. .

"He's even more handsome than I imagined he would be," a woman, whose hazel eyes glistened beneath her black bangs, said with a smile, looking down at Elsan as he became conscious again.

"Hu-wh," he mumbled as he blinked his eyes to lucidity.

"It's very nice to finally meet you, Elsan Amaranth. We've heard so much about you."

"Who are you?" Elsan asked.

"Mora. Mora Storm."

Through the haze, Elsan saw her hair draping to the sides of his eyes. Mora continued to smile down at Elsan, her eyes becoming clearer to him by the second. Elsan cracked a smile at her beauty, but it quickly faded as reality again settled in. Another man, matching Mora's long-sleeve black shirt, black khaki pants, and black boots, stood several feet away.

"My name is Sairin Storm," he greeted. "I'm Mora's brother. Pleasure to meet you, Elsan."

"What happened?" Elsan said, lying flat on top of a silver platform, rubbing his eyes and glancing from side to side. "Where am I?"

"We set up a trap," Sairin began with a slight grin on his face. "It was supposed to be for the guards that might make it this deep in the sticks. We weren't expecting you, but what an exciting surprise you were, Elsan."

"How do you know my name?" Elsan asked with narrowed eyes, lifting his back off of the platform and resting on his elbows.

"Your parents," Mora said. "They have quite the presence here, even when they aren't physically here with us all. Riklin and Tera are two of our leaders. Riklin and one other man founded our group several years ago."

"What group?" Elsan pressed. "You're telling me you know my father?"

"You have a lot to learn," Sairin said, turning toward the doorway of the small room that was enclosed by a steel ceiling, steel floor, and steel walls. "Maybe we should introduce you to the rest of the group and talk things through. We all know your father, some more than others, and we can all speak for him."

"Will one of you please just tell me what is happening here?" Elsan asked, raising his voice a bit.

"We call ourselves the Guild, our members wrights, especially inside the city walls, where we need to be discreet," Mora said, placing her hand upon Elsan's shoulder and locking her eyes onto his. "We're rebels against the Republic. Your parents are as well. Now, please follow us."

7

Elsan stared blankly as Sairin and Mora walked out of the room and into the hallway, so as to lead Elsan into a nearby room, though they did not even turn to see if he was following behind them. Placing his hand on the side of his shorts, Elsan realized that Tera's tablet was taken from him. He jolted forward.

"Hey!" Elsan yelled, springing to his feet and chasing after Mora and Sairin as they walked into the narrow hallway with openings to other rooms. "What do you think you're doing? That tablet is my mother's, and now it's mine."

"Relax, Elsan," Mora replied, continuing forward alongside Sairin.

"No, I will no-"

"Relax!" Mora interrupted, spinning around to stare Elsan in the eyes, causing the fevered young man to stop immediately. "We'll give it back. We're on your side, your parents' side."

Elsan nodded, sensing a genuine nature in Mora's eyes. Subdued, he continued behind Mora and Sairin through the hallway. There were massive bedrooms with over one hundred beds on either side, as well as a room with a large battery, a colossal kitchen, multiple giant bathrooms with dozens of showers and toilets each, and a door at the end with a fingerprint protected lock. Mora and Sairin turned into the kitchen, followed by Elsan hunching in fatigue.

"It could use a little charge," Mora said, holding up Tera's tablet before attaching it to a wall-mounted charging station in the dining area.

Elsan froze at the sight of more people in black khaki pants, black boots, and long-sleeve black tops. Some wore black brimmed hats to match. They ate along four kitchen tables that stretched parallel to a freezer, a cooking area, and a small food production room. As he realized that the people he was observing were all recruited by his father, or someone who followed his father, he stood upright, astonished. He then refocused as Mora turned to speak to him.

"Everyone here truly admires your parents," she said. "You must trust us."

"It's hard to know who to trust," Elsan said.

"Well, we're lucky to have found you," Sairin interjected. "These documents you brought to us are very important."

"Why is that?" Elsan asked.

"They're proof of things that Zanoma residents don't seem to know about or never wanted to believe," Sairin answered.

"Your father got the opportunity he was looking for. Lealan Wiske trusted him," Mora said. "Please, join us at the table, Elsan. We'll get you some food."

Elsan was caught between capitulating to paranoia and placing trust in the Guild. He joined the table of men and women from the ages of his generation to Riklin's generation, all different heights, weights, skin colors, hair colors, eye colors, and temperament, at least that which was apparent in their body language. As he approached two adjacent open seats, the nine closest wrights turned and stared.

"We heard you're the coveted first catch," a man with a long brown beard said, a sneer on his face.

"Apparently," Elsan responded with his eyes fixated on the table.

"So, you're Riklin's son, aren't you?" a young, blonde woman asked.

"Yes," Elsan answered.

"He's a great leader," the woman said. "A great man. Handsome too, for an old man."

"He's taken," Elsan said, cracking a smirk while continuing to stare down at the table.

"I know," the woman said. "Tera is very important to all of us here as well."

"And what exactly are you all here to do?"

"We're fighting to overthrow the ignorant rulers that squandered our resources and hoard those that remain," Mora said, sitting down in an open seat next to Elsan, staring at him with slightly narrowed eyes, absorbing Elsan's attention with enough gravity to blur those around them. "We're fighting to bring people together while those rulers try to tear us all apart. Violence isn't accompanied by hatred as much as it once was. It's starvation and desperation that turns us into the animals we are deep inside. The Guild is here to expose those who made the world what it is today, to create hatred for them so anger is directed where it should be, instead of at each other."

"You must have heard something from your parents," a slightly aged and bearded Macrum said, breaking Elsan's focus on Mora.

"Not yet, Macrum," Sairin said, placing a small tray of heated beans and vegetables in front of Elsan. "They kept him safe as long as they could."

"What are you talking about?" Elsan asked with narrowed eyes.

"You have a lot to learn," Mora said.

"The anger you speak of," Elsan said, staring back at Mora. "That anger should be directed at dead men, the men who led Ainkia. Should it not?"

"We have men and women from Ainkia who would refute that," Sairin said, pointing his hand toward Macrum. "Ainkia's allies, and even Zanoma's too."

Elsan's eyes widened as he stared at Macrum. He turned his head toward Sairin, who simply nodded his head slightly while staring back at Elsan. Mora placed her hand on Elsan's forearm.

"Elsan, take your lunch and come with me," she said. "Let's talk about this in the other room."

Elsan picked up his plate and followed Mora outside of the kitchen and across the corridor, where there was a small nook with several circular tables. They sat at the first table on the right. Elsan pushed around his food with his fork, staring down at his plate without saying a word.

"Els-" Mora began.

"You're in bed with the enemy," Elsan said. "An enemy everyone in the city thinks is finished, but you're working with them."

"Their government is finished," Mora said, speaking softer. "All governments are finished, but not everyone they governed. You need to understand what we're fighting for."

"Well, I know what I'm fighting for. In fact, I think it's about time to go back and fight for my parents the right way."

"What happened to your parents?"

"I'm shocked you don't know already. You seem to know everything about my family."

"Are they in trouble?" Mora asked, eyes expanding. "I assumed they sent you to us. They spoke about telling you."

Elsan inhaled deeply, sighed, and replied, "Some guards came to my house to question my father. They started to get violent with both of my parents before I escaped with the tablet that my mother gave me."

Mora's chin stiffened and she tightened her jaw before saying, "We need to tell the others. I'll tell the others after you get settled."

Elsan held a long silence before looking up at Mora and asking, "What is this place? Why are all of these people here?"

"We're in an abandoned training facility," Mora began. "There are two others, one south of the city, and another west. Many wrights are from Zanoma, especially South Village, and many are from around the world, not just Ainkia. Tibs and Nap talk about restoring order in other territories, but they're conquering them. They don't have production facilities yet, so the Republic provides food from the Sustenance Sector that the people of Zanoma don't know about. People in South Village starve when there are no more rations, and so do these survivors. The Republic provides them with protection from anarchists in nearby provinces, the anarchists that the Black War created as governments collapsed. Guards aren't allowed to speak, but they don't care. Some think like Tibs, some fear Tibs, some think they're doing good for the world, and some just care for their families and nothing else, but they're putting more power into the wrong hands. The survivors have no leverage for independence, except when operating in the dark, so many came here. Your parents trust them. We trust them. You must trust them too."

Elsan again took a deep breath, so as to suggest that his denial was waning, and said, "I saw the data from the Sustenance Sector. They're lying."

"Yes," Mora replied. "There's never been enough to go around, but it's been disguised as shortages, thefts and acts of anarchy for a decade."

"How so?"

"When the poor don't get their rations, it's because of a *theft* of the Sustenance Sector, which is then blamed on the poor, so there's no sympathy," Mora said. "Or it is because of a supposedly unavoidable shortage. Before the Black War, there were enough resources for everyone, but the leaders of the world were concerned with the preservation of wealth, and now that the world's resources are scarce, the leaders of Zanoma want to ensure that the animals within them never need to be released. We need to expose them as the scared creatures that they are. They aren't gods. The fates of others shouldn't be in their hands."

After a brief pause of reflection, Elsan replied, "Nor should it ever be."

Mora smiled and said, "Now you sound more like your father."

Elsan finished his food, so Mora offered to give him a tour of the cramped, underground facility that housed over one hundred rebels. To start, the two walked toward the entrance. It was at the opposite end of the hallway from the locked door. A ladder led up through a vertical conduit, a square passageway to the surface of the forest.

"This leads up to the center of a giant patch of junipers a bit deeper into the forest than you've been," Mora said. "It's camouflaged at the top."

"How long have you been sleeping in these bedrooms?" Elsan asked, stepping inside an expansive room, near the ladder, filled with beds with white sheets, white pillows and small black blankets.

"Sairin and I have been here for two years," Mora answered. "He worked for your father at Wrexon's End Distribution Center. Your father recruited him and me to come here after our parents passed on to the next realm."

"I-I'm sorry to hear that, Mora."

Mora stared at the ground, took a deep breath, and replied, "They won't have died in vain."

"If you don't mind me asking, what happened?"

"Our father was killed by some guards," Mora began, looking up at Elsan, a numbing tone in her voice. "He exposed something about Chancellor Tibs and Commander Nap. Macrum can explain that more. Our mother had bone cancer and died before she could get the medical attention she needed."

"That's terrible," Elsan said. "I'm so sorry."

"Thank you, Elsan."

Elsan took a deep breath. The two continued back into the kitchen, where the others were cleaning up after themselves. Mora showed Elsan the large cooking area, which had many refrigerators, stovetops, and ovens. Through another doorway at the end of the cooking area was a room with rows of hydroponic vegetables, potted fruits, trellised bean plants, and more. Blinding lights hung from above. Through a larger, more tightly sealed door at the end of the food production room was a freezer with preserved food from the base.

"Is this enough?" Elsan asked.

"We find a way to manage, but we need to pull from the city sometimes," Mora answered, before leading Elsan out of the kitchen and into the battery room. "We could use your help in here."

"I can do my best."

Elsan followed Mora away from the black, floor-mounted battery and out of the room. They passed the bathroom, which was shut with silver sliding doors. Nearing the heavily locked door at the end of the hallway, Elsan swallowed an empty air bubble and inched forward behind Mora's back.

Mora placed her finger upon the identification pad. The locks on either side of the door were released from their clamps and slid out of the way of the door. Mora twisted the wheel-shaped knob in the center of the silver door and thrust her elbows back.

The door creaked open, exposing a faint cyan and a back wall of mounted guns. Elsan and Mora entered the room. Each wall was covered with sleek, seemingly untouched guns illuminated with arctic blue from underneath. With the Zanoma military symbol, a simple anchor surrounded by a circle, along the barrel, they were identical to those of Zanoma's guards. They had large barrels, small muzzles, and blue-tinted ejection ports.

"Will I be expected to use these?" Elsan asked in concern.

Mora smirked, though it quickly faded, and said, "I can't say for sure, but you will learn. Davlin! Come give Elsan some beginner's training!"

"I'm not sure if I'm quite ready for combat," Elsan said, waving his hand from side to side to suggest that Davlin hold off. "I've never shot a gun before."

"You don't have a choice, Elsan. Everyone in this base must be prepared for the rebellion."

"Rebellion?" Elsan queried, his voice rising in volume. "What kind of rebellion is going to come out of this base in the middle of the forest, with a bunch of novices like me learning to aim at targets."

"Wars can be won with intelligence and with the support of the people," Mora replied in a more soothing tone. "The Republic's authorities believe that they're more intelligent than they truly are, and we can beat them if we get the people, and the right people, on our side. Besides, we don't have much of a choice."

Elsan had no reply as a blonde man a bit older than him entered the room and said, "Elsan, it's very nice to finally meet you. My name is Davlin. I know your father. He's a great man."

"Nice to meet you, Davlin," Elsan replied with an uneasy tone.

"Follow me."

Elsan followed Davlin as he neared the right wall of the weaponry. There was a single gun at eye level, with no gun below it and no gun within five feet from above or either side. Davlin lifted the gun. The wall it was mounted on sunk forward and slid to the left.

"This is how we get into our training room," Davlin said. "If there's no gun on the wall, the room is being used and it isn't safe to enter. There is another one of these on the side wall to our left."

"I see," Elsan replied, taking a moment to notice the same arrangement on the adjacent wall.

Elsan stood still as Davlin entered the training room, so Davlin turned back and said, "Are you coming in or not?"

Nodding with an awkward shrug, Elsan followed. The training room was lined with the same metal as the rest of the facility. There were only two lights mounted on either side of the entranceway. Directly in front of Davlin and Elsan was a square shooting box with glass bordering the nearest side and the two adjacent sides. The open end faced, on the opposite side of the room, a caliginous space.

"So, how do we begin?" Elsan asked.

"I'll show you," Davlin replied, pressing a small black button beneath the right-side light. "The back wall is several feet thick, so it can sustain gun shots from this distance, but we don't use real ammo in here. We only use laser cartridges. This is called dry fire training. So, remember, save the real ammo."

A vibrant blue plane appeared seconds later, extending from the corners of the floor and walls to those of the walls and ceiling. A concentration of white light moved randomly around the plane. It was like nothing Elsan had ever seen before.

"What is this for?" he asked.

"This is what we use to train our wrights," Davlin explained. "We aim for the white lights when we fire at the surface. We don't have the capability of producing the type of armor that the guards have, so accuracy is most essential. If we are able to hit the exposed areas, such as their faces, or necks, or creases in their armor on the sides of their legs and arms, or even other parts of their body as their armor is worn down, then we have a chance to defeat them in battle. This is how we practice with the goal of achieving that level of accuracy in combat."

"The men we would battle have been training to shoot guns for years. What makes you think we can do it better, and without armor?"

"We have no choice."

"We can choose to live," Elsan mumbled.

Davlin turned his shoulders to face Elsan and said, "Your father was a man of immense pride, Elsan. I presume you are as well?"

"I guess so."

"By any means, a man of immense pride will see no other outcome than for the good of the world to prevail. We must make sure of that. Life isn't promised to us anymore. Don't you understand?"

Elsan stared at Davlin with no words to speak. He took a deep breath and ducked his chin to his chest. After a moment of reflection, Elsan nodded his head as he tilted it back up.

"Good. Let's begin," Davlin said, entering the shooting box with the gun. "Watch closely."

Before taking aim, Davlin examined the gun at all angles and said, "It's important to make sure your weapon is in top form. We stole parts for rifles, some coil guns and machine guns, and we put them together ourselves. It's best to check before using."

"Won't we be fighting against superior weapons to these?" Elsan asked.

"Yes," Davlin began. "Sometimes grenade launchers, more machine guns and rifles, and automatic weapons like lasers and rail guns."

Elsan gulped, pointed at the rifle in Davlin's hands, and said, "Well, how is it?"

"This one is just fine. The outer shell is intact. The muzzle is perfectly cylindrical."

Elsan nodded.

"Do you see this piece?" Davlin asked, pointing at a hinged steel piece covering the ejection port. "This is a magazine. It feeds cartridges into the chamber to be fired. This weapon is sufficiently loaded with laser cartridges. A fully loaded weapon can account for many more shots than you might think. If you have one-hundred percent accuracy, you could do a lot of damage with just one round of ammunition."

"Surely, not all guards are deserving of such a fate," Elsan said with a deepening tone.

"No, they aren't, but they're defending evil, whether they're aware of it or not," Davlin replied. "To let them get away with the things they've done would be to let our children and gradchildren live in the same world we've lived in. Use caution. Attempt to contain guards and confiscate their weapons before shooting. Violence against guards should only be in defense."

Davlin shut the flap and rested the barrel of the gun atop the edge of the training box. He wrapped one hand from below the end of the barrel closest to him. The other hand rested by the trigger.

"Make sure you hold your guiding hand firmly around the barrel," Davlin began before bringing the side of the gun up to his cheek. "Bring your face here so the end of the gun follows your eyes, and when you prepare to shoot, maintain a steady grip so the gun also remains steady."

Elsan watched as Davlin fired the first laser magazine at the target plane. The lasers were far quieter than actual bullets. Ten shots struck the surface of the plane, zapping the concentrated white light nine times. The last did not.

"Well, I missed one," Davlin said. "But I used to hit it less than half of the time. Now, it's your turn."

"Sure," Elsan said with jittery hands.

As the two switched places, Davlin said, "Give me ten shots."

Elsan wrapped one hand around the barrel, placed the other on the trigger, took a deep breath, and mumbled, "Here it goes."

He pulled the trigger, time after time. Not a single shot made contact with the white target. Elsan sighed and turned in the direction of Davlin.

"That was only nine," Davlin said. "Focus. Take a deep breath and fire just as you finish exhaling. Follow the target like you know where it will go next. Accuracy only comes when you have a clear target."

Elsan turned back toward the target plane. He brought the side of the gun up to his cheek and focused his vision through the end of the gun. After a deep inhale and a soft sputter of an exhale, he pulled the trigger. The laser struck the white target. Elsan cracked a quick smile but retracted it immediately. He stood to his feet, left the shooting box, and handed Davlin the gun.

"I'll end on that," Elsan said before pressing the exit button and walking out of the training room.

8

In the evening, Elsan stepped out of a shower in the base's bathroom after some time to himself and a quick cleanse. The bathroom was expansive like the bedrooms were, with countless stalls and bathing areas. The water was cold; the water pressure, low. With a rub of the eyes, the bathroom brightened and Elsan's jaded mind was revitalized.

With a towel around his waist, he walked through the hallway to the bedroom that was assigned to him and many others. Sairin dropped a pile of black wright attire onto Elsan's bed. There were black cloth shirts, pants of stalwart black khaki, and briar pitstop boots.

"Wear this," Sairin said.

"Thank you," Elsan replied.

"Do you have any clean clothes?"

"No."

"We'll find you some extra pairs of pants and shirts. I don't want to smell those rancid clothes you've been dripping sweat in for the past two days. We can take care of those."

"Will the guards recognize this?"

"They know nothing yet. This is just what we wear around here. It's what we've been able to smuggle past Zanoma's borders."

"What if they catch on?"

"You're starting to ask questions," Sairin said with a smirk. "I like that, but just put the clothes on and come to the kitchen."

"What's in the kitch-" Elsan started to ask, but Sairin left the room before he could finish another question.

Elsan dropped his towel and dressed himself in the black garments. The clothes appeared ragged, unlike the sleek shine of the suits in Zanoma. The material was otherwise warming and soothing to the skin.

The bedroom door opened after Elsan pressed the small black button on the right wall. He walked toward the kitchen. As he entered, he stumbled backwards at the surprise of over one hundred wrights shouting his name.

"Elsan! Elsan! Elsan!" the rebels chanted with wide smiles on their faces, their echoes projecting off of every wall of the kitchen.

"What's going on?" Elsan asked, a slight smile forming on his face.

Sairin approached him, laughing, as he wrapped his arm around Elsan's shoulders and said, "We don't celebrate too often, Elsan, but your father has been the leader for our cause, and you're the heir to his throne. We couldn't help it this time."

"It's still my father's throne," Elsan replied.

"It is," Sairin said as all of the wrights attentively watched. "But you're a special addition to our group. Let's get you a drink."

"Sure," Elsan answered, surprised that the atmosphere of the rebel base had come to this point after such a grave greeting earlier in the day. "With all of the effort spent smuggling materials out of Zanoma, you managed to smuggle liquor too."

The other rebels began separate conversations as Sairin led Elsan to a refrigerator and replied, "Of course! The people making this world worse celebrate their successes, so why shouldn't we?"

"Fair enough," Elsan said as Sairin mixed him some vodka with carbonated water.

"Here you are," Sairin said, handing him the cup. "It isn't much, but then again, no one is spoiled here."

"Thank you."

Mora approached Elsan and Sairin as Elsan took his first sip. She grinned at Elsan, sparking an instinctual glimmer in his eyes. He quickly calmed himself, looked at his drink, and looked back up at Mora as if her grin suggested something wicked.

"This isn't going to knock me senseless, is it?" Elsan asked, lifting his drink in front of his face and pausing before taking another sip.

"Don't be so paranoid, Elsan," Mora said as she mixed her own drink. "Go on and drink up."

"Come on," Sairin said, tapping Elsan on the chest. "I'll introduce you to some of the others."

Elsan followed Sairin and Mora as they approached a circle of wrights.

"Everyone, as you know, this is Elsan Amaranth, son of Riklin Amaranth," Sairin said. "Treat him as you would his father. And Elsan, meet some fellow members of the Guild. There are people from Zanoma, Cronen, and Goacao all in just this circle."

"Nice to meet all of you," Elsan said, calmer than when he had met Macrum earlier, as the other rebels nodded in greeting.

"Your father is a very courageous man," a bald man with blue eyes said.

"Thank you," Elsan said. "I know."

"What were you doing before we caught you?" a short woman with red hair asked.

"I-I was just wandering, worried about what I would eat, what I would drink. I didn't know what I was looking for, or where I was going."

"Where did you go?" the bald man asked, the other heedful rebels to his side.

"Well, I found the swimming hole nearby," Elsan answered. "Then, I ventured to the northern shores, but I didn't stay there long."

"The northern shores?" the red-haired woman asked with widened eyes. "Ornaia?"

"I think so."

"Did anyone see you?"

"I-I'm not sure, but I think if someone did, they would have tracked me down."

The rebels stared at each other, and the red-haired woman replied, "You must be more careful, Elsan. If they knew someone was watching them, they'd likely know to check their abandoned facilities, like this one and the others we're occupying."

"I understand," Elsan said.

"You grew up in Wrexon's End, correct?" a brown-haired man asked.

"I did. I *live* in Wrexon's End," Elsan retorted.

"I lived in South Village, just around the bend," the man replied. "I can't say that I still *live* there."

"Oh, I se-" Elsan said, though he was interrupted by Mora.

"Elsan!" she shouted, waving him over to her and a tall man with short, black hair.

"It was nice to meet you all," Elsan said as he took a swig of his drink and approached Mora.

"Elsan, this is Paxtus," Mora said. "He was a guard before being ridden of by Commander Nap. He is a good friend of your father."

"Pleasure to meet you, Elsan," Paxtus greeted.

"You as well," Elsan replied, feeling a rush from the alcohol that numbed his heavy heart. "Your name actually sounds familiar. Maybe I heard my father say it in the past."

"That's probably because it was all over the ductway monitors a few years back."

"Why?"

"The other guards were becoming suspicious of me as I was helping your father steal clothing and other items from the Republic. They suspected me of stealing weapon parts from one of their storage facilities as well. I escaped before they could do anything about it, but they did as they always have to dissenters. I was on every monitor with the labels 'thief' and 'traitor' below my picture."

"I'm sorry to hear that," Elsan said.

"That's alright. I guess it was technically true," Paxtus said, causing Elsan to chuckle for a second. "I wanted to meet you so I could tell you something, Elsan. All hatred in the world will be directed at your father for this. They will lie, and you cannot believe them, nor can you lose your composure as they attempt to tarnish him. He's my friend and a good man."

Elsan nodded and replied, "I understand. I know he is. They can't take my love for my father away from me."

Paxtus smiled, placed his hand on Elsan's shoulder, and said, "Good man. Now, let's drink and enjoy the night."

"Let's drink," Elsan replied, nodding in agreement before finishing the rest of his drink.

For all of the inebriated wrights, time accelerated. Elsan stood constantly swarmed by rebels rhapsodizing his father, wringing Elsan dry of what he thought he knew about his father. He poured drink after drink to ease his discomfort.

His body eventually rejected a sip, so he placed his cup near the sink of the kitchen and leaned against the wall. Scanning the room, he stood completely still, still mystified by the people he was with and the shelter he found himself in. He was suddenly drowning in a daydream of the life he once thought to be his own. Stupefied, he continued to be approached by rebels eager to meet him, eager to speak of their appreciation of Riklin and Tera.

Elsan found himself sinking into thoughts of his childhood. He recalled a time prior to the Black War, when Riklin planned to take he and Tera to the other end of the world and back, though after the destruction, travel was no longer possible. The love of his parents kept Elsan warm when the world became cold, but he was suddenly without them. He was surrounded by strangers. The surface of Elsan's eyes became glossy and his chin quivered, but before he could begin to cry, he was approached again.

Mora walked toward Elsan again, this time alongside Macrum. He was taller than he looked sitting down. He reached out his hand.

"My name is Macrum," he said while shaking Elsan's hand with Mora's hand on his shoulder. "Your father is an incredible man. He had a special talent for gauging people just by looking them in the eyes and sensing their body language. That's how he got our early recruits, and the Guild expanded exponentially ever since."

"I see. Well, I remember you from earlier. Nice to meet you again, Macrum," Elsan said in a reserved stance. "You came from Ainkia."

"Macrum came all the way from Ainkia near the end of the Black War," Mora said with a confirmatory nod. "My family housed him for a short while to keep him safe before he escaped to come here. He blended in, but we had to cut our rations smaller at the time."

"For that I'm forever grateful," Macrum said, turning his head to look at Mora before looking back at Elsan. "Without the Storm family, I never would have been able to tell my story."

"What is your story?" Elsan asked.

"Maybe it would be better told on another day," Mora said to Macrum.

"No," Elsan said. "I want to hear."

"Go on, then," Mora said to Macrum, who nodded, took a deep breath, and turned back toward Elsan.

"It's true what they say, the radical *theorists* that Chancellor Tibs undermines," he began, engrossing Elsan as Elsan thought through all of the accusations made against the Republic's government officials over the years. "I was a guard in Ainkia. The stories about Tibs are true. It was him who ordered the murder of Medrik Malva. It was Commander Nap who commited it, in Zanoma's embassy. Total control—that's what Tibs wanted. When the murder was blamed on Ainkia, Malva's death gave him that, though he got in over his head. The malevolence of the fictional villains you read about as a child—that type of evil truly exists in this world, within Tibs. He's a paranoid man, quick to crush anyone who curbs him. I escaped Ainkia with surveillance footage and made several attempts to bring Tibs down, but it never worked. Mora's father lost his life helping me, and I don't see a way to release the footage now. It would be blocked and discredited very quickly, and I would be found faster than I could say the name, Chancellor Tibs, again. The rulers tell the tales of our world, and we need that power before the truth can be told."

Elsan's cheeks became red. His vision began to fade as his stomach turned. Abruptly, he turned toward the kitchen doorway, placed his cup on a counter to his right, and began stumbling away.

"I need to rest," he said. "I don't feel well."

Mora looked at Macrum in concern before following behind Elsan, who was exiting through the kitchen doorway. Once in the hallway, she spotted Elsan entering the bedroom.

"Elsan," Mora said, chasing him into the bedroom. "What are you doing?"

Elsan sniffled, sat on his bed, cleared his throat, and answered in a raspy tone, "I just need some time to myself. I'm sorry."

After a pair of tears trickled down Elsan's right cheek, Mora said, "You're overwhelmed."

Elsan nodded. Mora watched as he dug his face into his hands. She stepped toward him, slowly, and sat beside him.

"Elsan," she began. "I understand the shock you feel. When I first came here, I couldn't believe where I was, what I was doing, where my life had taken me. This wasn't part of my plan, and I know how small it can make you feel."

Elsan wiped his face with his shirt and said with a clearer voice, "Tibs has my parents. I worry that I'll never see them again."

"We will free them," Mora said firmly, placing her hand on his forearm. "They're far too valuable of a source of information. They won't be harmed."

"I hope you're right."

Mora stared into Elsan's eyes as he looked up at her, placed her hand on his knee, and asked, "Do you want to go back to the dining area?"

"I should get some rest."

"May I stay and talk with you as you wind down?"

"Yes."

"How do you like your new clothes?"

Elsan smirked and replied, "My father never had a sense of style."

Mora snickered and said, "Well, you look good in black."

"Thank you," Elsan said, his cheeks flushed, heart racing as he sunk deeper into Mora's eyes.

She pressed her lips against his. An alleviating rush filled the air between their aching hearts before Mora left Elsan to sleep. Elated, if only for a moment, Elsan drifted into the evanescent night.

9

Several years after the Black War ended, on a morning with a lambent sunrise, Chancellor Tibs and Morin Malva descended from the suites of the Zanoma Tower in the private elevator. Morin was a late teenager whose widowed mother spent most of her time in their suite, and much of that sleeping, especially on such a dreary day. He prayed before his father's spirit in the Forum every morning, but this was the anniversary of Medrik Malva's death. Tibs offered to join Morin in visiting Medrik's cast stone statue, holding his hand over Morin's shoulder while they bowed their heads and closed their eyes. Morin whispered some words.

After Morin finished, Tibs stepped in front of him, between Morin and Medrik's statue, and said, "I just want you to know that your father taught me everything that I know about being a leader. Whenever

I'm faced with an important decision, I wonder what Chancellor Malva would have done during his reign. As Medrik's son, it's in your nature to lead as well, and you're in a position of great influence, which is why I want to talk to you about something today. Let's speak more in my office."

Tibs walked with Morin under his arm back to the private elevator, continuing to mumble to him. They arose to Tibs' suite near the top of the tower and the elevator opened directly into the common area. Tibs led Morin into his office to the left, where the woman from the Communications Sector stood by the camera. Commander Nap stood with his arms folded and chest protruding in the shaded corner behind her, where his eyes could barely be seen.

"Take a seat," Tibs said, holding his hand out in front of a chair opposite his desk.

"Sure," Morin said, staring back at Nap timidly as he approached the chair.

"Morin," Tibs said, followed by a sigh as he sunk into his desk chair. "We've lost thousands of lives over the past four years. Cancer. Starvation. Malnutrition. Anarchy and all of the violence that comes with it is on the rise too. If it weren't for the consistency and stability of the Republic, Zanoma, all of humanity, could have collapsed entirely by now."

"I agree," Morin said. "It seems like the Republic has been the only thing keeping the world together through the Black War until now. What does this all have to do with me?"

As Morin listened closely, Tibs gave a soft smile and continued, "We would certainly be better off with your father, and I hope you don't give any credibility to those baseless and offensive accusations about me and your father, because I truly wish he was here today. He would be very proud of our officials."

"Lies spread easily in the modern world," Morin said, nodding. "You were always loyal to my father. My mother and I never had a chance to see that video, and we never wanted to. It doesn't matter anyway, because there wasn't any credibility to it. It would just upset us."

"Thank you, Morin," Tibs began. "Well, to continue to the purpose of this conversation, a change in administration is supposed to occur next year, but we don't believe that Zanoma can handle the instability and inefficiency that comes with such a change at this time. For that reason, we plan to repeal the process and extend my administration indefinitely. We believe that your father would have done the same, and we'd like your support. After your father's death, Evarand has essentially taken over the role of Vice Chancellor in terms of critical decision-making, though he is truly the Military Commander. In your father's spirit, we'd like you to join us to fill in the administrative responsibilities that Commander Nap doesn't have the time for. You can be the Chancellor's Assistant. How does that sound?"

Morin stared blankly at the surface of Tibs' desk before nodding his head and saying, "You have my support. I think the people will be very happy to allow this administration to continue to lead, and it would be an honor to represent my father's legacy as the Chancellor's Assistant. Thank you, Chancellor Tibs."

Moments later, Morin was guided to the side of the camerawoman by Nap. Chancellor Tibs set his posture at his desk. The camerawoman began filming, and within the hour, the recording played on every monitor and every tablet in the city.

"Good people of Zanoma," the recording of Tibs began. "Over the past four years, we've fought through many tragedies. Cancer. Disease. Starvation. Violent anarchist attacks. Fortunately, we have had outstanding government officials to lead us through these challenges. What our world needs now more than ever is stability and consistency. We can't afford to risk the future of humanity as we rebuild. For that reason, we see a change in administration as a serious risk to the momentum we've built over the past four years. We plan to repeal our traditional political process and extend our administration's tenure indefinitely. We understand that residents of Zanoma may have significant concerns with breaking from tradition. However, this is only temporary and we ask for your cooperation as we continue to move forward from the Black War. Additionally, to bolster the legacy of Medrik Malva, we've decided to bring his son, Morin Malva, into the administration as the Chancellor's Assistant. Morin would like to say a few words."

Morin stepped into the screen, standing next to the seated Tibs, and said, "Thank you all in advance for allowing me to support the Republic through this strenuous time. My father would be very proud of this administration, and of me for carrying his legacy in any way that I can. I hope that we have your support in continuing to fight for our future. Thank you."

· ·

Elsan awoke with a damp shirt and droplets of sweat sinking into his sideburns. The blankets of all of the other beds in the room were pulled back, the room empty. Elsan's throat was so dry that he could barely breathe without cracking his lips further, so he rose to his feet and made his way to the kitchen.

"Good morning!" Sairin greeted Elsan as he walked into the kitchen. "Here's some water. We have beans, barley, and some fruit."

Elsan would have eaten nearly anything so long as it filled his stomach and absorbed the alcohol. Before he could eat or even barely speak, he quaffed two cups of water and filled another. He gasped for breath after finishing a third cup.

"Why don't you take it easy today, Elsan?" Sairin said. "I'm sure you could use a day to rest."

"How can I rest?" Elsan said. "My parents were taken from me and for all we know, they could be out to find us as we speak."

"We all thought that way when we got here," Sairin replied, grasping Elsan's shoulder. "But they tend to count those that are missing as being dead. You should do whatever you can to relax. It will help more than anything else right now."

Elsan took a small portion of each food option, sat alongside the six rebels remaining at the dining table, and greeted, "Good morning."

"Good morning," all six replied, some mumbling as they chewed their food.

The television projected onto the center of the wall beyond the long tables. It was turned on for the first time that Elsan had seen. On the screen was the Zanoma Morning Report.

"On this day," Amon Sarato began from the Communications Sector facility by the central receiver. "We celebrate the life of one of the greatest war heroes in Zanoma's history. His name was Waldon Biggs. Biggs was a leading air fleet commander in the Ainkia attacks that gave Zanoma ultimate leverage to end the Black War. When there was a threat against Zanoma's security, Biggs acted both quickly and intelligently, allowing us to defeat our enemy. Biggs represented all of us here in Zanoma. He allowed us to celebrate our lives to this day, as people united in rebuilding our world. In honor of Waldon Biggs, we shall keep him firmly in our hearts, cherish the days that he has allowed us to have, and dream of the future he has allowed for our children and grandchildren."

The wrights remained silent. Elsan remained quiet too, focusing on the food under his nose.

"Another interesting development has come to our attention," Amon Sarato continued. "Hundreds of pounds of various foods have been stolen from the Sustenance Sector. It is believed that the thieves were a group of anarchists from Tocano who made it past our walls during the Black War. The theft is under investigation and will hopefully be resolved shortly considering the fact that we all rely on this food to nourish us and our children. More is to come on this story."

"Lies," the brown-haired rebel said, nudging Elsan while pointing at the screen. "That's what they do. They deflect blame for food shortages onto the poor and the outsiders, while Chancellor Tibs and everyone under his wing stock up on their reserves to control the other territories of the world."

"Are the stolen files what we base these theories on?" Elsan asked.

"We have men on the inside. These aren't theories. They're facts. Besides, knowing what we know already, we've learned to see motive in the media, in addition to the story itself."

"In other news, a tragedy at a local Zanoma home," Amon Sarato said as Elsan continued to focus on his breakfast. "Living in the home were the couple, Riklin and Tera Amaranth, and their son, Elsan Amaranth."

Elsan immediately dropped his fork and stared at the television with eyes wide as the open air. His heart stopped. In a whirlwind of anger, excitement, and agony, he glued his eyes to the screen.

"After receiving a call from Zanoma's leaders two days ago, guards left to the Amaranth home to investigate what the leaders reported to be an incident of theft, but not the theft we are used to seeing in Zanoma. Riklin, believed to be mentally ill, was suspected of stealing the personal devices of Zanoma's leaders while serving as the Assistant Head of the Energy Sector, so the guards' efforts seemed to be warranted. When the guards arrived, Riklin was holding a firearm. Tera Amaranth and her son hid in a nearby bedroom. Riklin refused to hand over the devices and began firing at the Zanoma guards when they approached him. Tragically, Riklin was killed when the guards fired back in an attempt to neutralize him. No charges will apply to the guards as Commander Nap and his team simply followed protocol. Tera Amaranth was arrested while defending Riklin's actions and hiding the devices. Riklin's and Tera's son, Elsan Amaranth, fled the home in horror, guards described. There have been no reports of Elsan's whereabouts since the incident. If anyone has any information regarding Elsan's location, please send it to the Zanoma Emergency Center. Tera Amaranth, also potentially mentally ill, remains in isolated imprisonment until the investigation is carried out."

The rebels glanced at Elsan, his hands curling to fists. A single tear trickled down his cheek to his quivering bottom lip. Blood boiled beneath his flesh, his cheeks scarlet red.

"Here is Chancellor Tibs in response to the devastating events that took place," Amon Sarato continued, signaling the screen to switch to a view of Chancellor Tibs in his office.

"Riklin Amaranth," Tibs began. "Hard working energy specialist, yet deeply troubled on the inside. He was believed to be a proud member of the Energy Sector. However, Riklin's knees buckled under the pressure of our re-developing world. It seems that he became paranoid and lost trust in our leaders. Many of us in government worry that the ideology of the anarchists is being adopted a bit more as of late, but we will fight against it to keep our people safe. We must remember the progress we have made in re-developing our war-torn world. We must continue forward on our path toward sustainability and true freedom, rather than falling into the depths of our fears like Riklin Amaranth did. Regardless, this incident is truly demoralizing and requires our strength as a community to overcome. Please, send your best wishes along to Elsan Amaranth and those that knew Riklin dearly. Tera Amaranth will be imprisoned indefinitely as we investigate any potential ties to anarchist groups."

Elsan sprung to his feet and flung his plate at the wall where the television was projected, shattering the plate on impact. He turned toward the kitchen door and walked swiftly and stiffly with his tightened fists at his sides. The rebels, including Sairin, followed closely after him.

"Elsan!" Sairin yelled, but Elsan continued walking toward the ladder at the entrance of the base. "Elsan, where are you going?"

Elsan did not respond, so Sairin and the other wrights continued to follow him. Mora entered the hallway from the weaponry and scanned all of the concerned faces. She spotted Elsan at the opposite end of the hallway, placing a hand on one of the ladder bars and a foot on another.

"Elsan, stop!" Mora yelled. "You can't go out there alone!"

Elsan lifted his hand from the ladder, turned toward Mora, and shouted, "You told me we would free them!"

Mora remained silent. Elsan walked toward her, past the wrights watching, speechless, from outside of the kitchen. His narrowed eyes glared into Mora's, his jaw jutting out.

"Well, now my father is dead! Dead!" Elsan screamed with lunacy in his eyes before looking around at the other wrights. "I'm done with this place. I'm going to free my mother by myself."

"Elsan," Sairin said as Elsan turned back toward the base entrance. "Don't leave. You have no idea what you would be getting into."

"And why should I believe you?" Elsan yelled, swinging back around to Sairin. "Why should I believe anything any of you say? Why should I believe anything anyone says anymore?"

"Elsan, they'll put you in prison too. Inside those walls, anything is possible. Keep yourself safe. Stay with us and we'll do whatever we can to free her."

"Anything is possible? Torture?" Elsan said, his voice beginning to tremble, tears forming in his eyes. "Will they torture my mother? Will they kill her too?"

Elsan fought back the tears, marched rigidly back toward the entrance ladder and started to climb up. Sairin and some other male wrights ran after him and grabbed him by the arms, legs, and waste. Tugging him off the ladder, the rebels held Elsan's limbs as tightly as they could while Elsan wailed and weeped. His eyes were forced shut, squeezing out tears as his echoing howls filled the hallway.

The rebels loosened their clasp, and Elsan's legs lost will. Elsan's back fell into the wall to the right of the entrance ladder and slid down until he sat on the ground, panting. His chin collapsed to his chest, his torso twitching as he cried some more, and he wrapped his hands atop the rear of his skull.

The rebels stood speechless around Elsan. They looked at one another, hoping one would have something uplifting to say. There was nothing to say, nor were there promises anyone was willing to make after seeing the shocked look in Mora's face.

The brittle air persisted until Sairin knelt beside Elsan and said, "I'm sorry, Elsan, but we can't let them win. We must move forward."

Sairin waved the other rebels away, so they dispersed to different areas of the base. With his hand wrapped around Elsan's tricep, Sairin lifted the distraught young man to his feet. Elsan's neck drooped and his knees wobbled as he followed Sairin back into the kitchen for some water.

Though there were a few dents in the wall where the screen lit, the Zanoma Morning Report still played on the far wall. Elsan ignored the dialogue, but was suddenly captivated by the sound of a familiar voice. It was Ermin speaking to a reporter, a staggering sight for Elsan having never been in the spotlight before.

"It seems that you knew Riklin well," the reporter said. "It must be very difficult to comprehend how this happened. How do you feel about the events that have occurred?"

"It's tragic," Ermin began as Elsan moseyed toward the screen with dazed eyes. "Not only the death, but knowing he was involved in such things. I saw him as a good man, an admirable man, for all of my life, but my view is different now. I just hope Tera is proven innocent in this and released quickly. I hope Elsan is safe, and I hope the two of them come to the side of the Republic without resistance."

"Evidence seems to suggest that Tera was an accomplice to the theft in that she tried to hide the evidence," the news reporter stated. "Were you aware of that report?"

"Yes."

"If that is true, do you still believe she should be released by the Republic?"

"I hope that it wasn't her idea and that she was a victim of the situation," Ermin responded.

"I see," the reporter said. "And what about your friend, Elsan? He may have had no knowledge of his father's actions, but we do not know because he is still missing. What would you say to Elsan if you were able to reach him?"

"I would tell him to come back home to help rectify this," Ermin said.

Elsan walked, snarling, toward the projector. He lifted his arm to turn the projector off and turned back toward the hallway. Sairin and many other wrights looked at him, awaiting his word, but Elsan said nothing.

"Don't let what you see on that screen get to you, Elsan," Sairin said. "It will only poison your mind."

"Then why do you all watch it?" Elsan asked.

"Because we can use it to predict their next move. At least some of it is true."

"And what's their next move?"

"It seems that they may know about our group. They wanted you to see that, return to free your mother, and turn over the Guild. Soon, maybe they'll know about the base, assuming your mother eventually speaks. We must be prepared for that too."

Elsan picked up his cup of water and left the kitchen. Sairin followed in fear that he would actually leave the base, but Elsan turned in the opposite

direction and walked toward the weaponry. He entered
the weaponry, where there were over a couple dozen
wrights. The wrights quickly directed their attention
toward Elsan's bloodshot eyes.

"I'd like to train for a little while," Elsan said. "If
that's okay with all of you."

"Go right ahead, Elsan," a tall, skinny bald man
said. "The training room is open."

"Thank you," Elsan said with a cold stare at the
wall in front of him.

Elsan lifted the gun guarding the entrance and
the training room doorway was revealed. He entered,
turned on the target plane, and stepped inside the
training box. Without hesitancy, he shot repeatedly at
the white concentration of light. Not a single bullet hit
the mark, so he took a deep breath and bombarded the
plane with another round.

Again, none showed great aim. Elsan pounded
his fist against the transparent walls of the training box.
Before another round could be fired, the bald rebel
entered the training room.

"Is everything alright in here, Elsan?" he asked.

"Yes, I'm fine. I'll be fine. Please, let me continue
for a while," Elsan said.

"Sure," the man said before turning with
hesitance back toward the weaponry.

Elsan refocused, rested the bottom of the gun
atop the training box wall to reload, and wrapped his
hand firmly under the barrel of the gun. As he inhaled,
he pulled the side of the gun up to his cheek and

imagined his father's head being smashed against his kitchen table. As he exhaled, his target became clear.

A rapid fire of ten strikes expelled from the gun. With each shot, Elsan held the gun tighter, his eyes focused on the white circle. Although not to his content, four of ten hit the target. The more the mourning man pulled the trigger, the more accurate he became. The more he thought of Riklin, the clearer his target became. Fury growing within him, Elsan continued his training seemingly without end.

.·.

For three days, Elsan had spent a majority of his time in the training box. Addicted to the explosive outbursts, he itched for improvement with each round. After the first day, any less than seven out of ten made him clench his fist and clobber the translucent walls of the training box. After the second day, any less than eight out of ten would do the same. By the third day, nine out of ten. Tunnel vision had trapped Elsan in the training room from dusk to dawn, with an occasional break to eat and drink while others took their turns in the training room.

On the third day, Elsan was in the training room firing yet another round at the target plane. For the first time, he was a perfect ten for ten. Placing the gun against the training box wall, Elsan stepped back from the opening. His narrowed eyes leveled.

The training room entrance opened and Mora walked in. Her glossy eyes showed concern and fear in approaching Elsan after he had screamed at her days before. Elsan turned his chair toward the doorway and stared at Mora through the training box walls.

"Hi, Elsan," she said. "I-I just wanted to check on you, to see how you're doing."

"I'm fine," Elsan said with an apathetic expression. "No need to worry."

"I-I also wanted to apologize. I'm sorry for everything that's happened."

"There's no need to apologize."

"Well, I want you to know that I'm going to fight as hard as I can to find justice for your family."

"Thank you, Mora. As will I."

*   *   *

Tera sat with shaking hands inside a priority prison cell in the Zanoma Detention Center, just north of the Zanoma Tower. Prods were attached to either hand, a stun belt wrapped firmly around her waist. Her widened eyes were vulnerable, seemingly open for the interrogators to invade.

"Please," Tera pleaded, turning her fatigued head slightly from side to side. "I've given in. Please tell me what you've done with Riklin. I've given you information. Please, tell me he's alright."

"I'm sorry, Tera," a guard said sarcastically. "But the information you've given has yet to be confirmed. Not to mention, you haven't given us all of the information that we require. There's more we need from you first."

The guard placed his thumb on a button on a small black cube of metal. Nothing was physically connected to the cube, though it was wirelessly connected to the prods and stun belt, capable of inflicting extreme pain within each fiber of Tera's muscles. In atrophy, Tera stared hopelessly at the button as if she expected the guard were about to send another signal to the stun belt and prods.

"What else do you want to know?" Tera asked, her weakened shoulders starting to slump. "I've told you everything I know."

"We know there's more," the guard began. "Riklin must have had a great depth of information about Zanoma and Chencellor Tibs in order to get a hold of the information that he was able to steal. He must have had some help."

"I told you already. I don't know of anyone else involved in the theft."

"What about your son, Elsan?"

"He doesn't know anything. We left him out of this his whole life."

"Maybe we can ask him ourselves. Do you know where we can find him?"

"I just told him to run. I don't know where he ran to. I truly don't know."

"We know Elsan has the files" the guard began. "We know he has your tablet. We also know after some further exploration into Riklin's communication networks that Riklin had a connection to many who have been missing from Zanoma for years. We're going to find out where those people are, and where your son is. Perhaps they're in the same place. You can make this far easier than you are. Now, I'll ask you one more time. Where did you tell him to go?"

"I already told you, I ju-"

Interrupted by a sudden shock, Tera rattled in her chair and fell to her side. She groaned with her fists tightened, her veins bulging against her skin, her hair follicles erected. The guard smirked and shook his head from side to side.

"You stupid, stupid woman," the guard said. "Must you be so stubborn? Or, will you start to cooperate? The sooner you give me the information I need, the sooner this will all be over for you."

"You'll pay for this," Tera mumbled with her cheek pressed against the polished concrete floor.

"Excuse me?" the guard retorted, standing to his feet, strolling toward a helpless Tera, kneeling down, and grabbing her face with his left hand. "Do you know what we're capable of?"

Struggling to breathe, Tera whispered, "The good will prevail. You will not win."

The guard let go of her face and again pressed the button. Tera's body vibrated against the floor and her teeth clenched hard enough to chip away at the edges. The guard returned to his seat, leaving Tera pouting on the floor, wincing, as her muscles remained stiff.

"Don't make this harder than it needs to be, Tera," the guard said. "The longer this takes, the harder this will be for you. The longer this takes, the harder we will come down upon your son, and anyone else you're connected to. Our forces are fully prepared for whatever pitiful attempt at a rebellion your little friends make. If you allow that to happen, your friends and your son will be wiped out. Innocent people in Zanoma will die. Do you really want to be responsible for that?"

"If I had more information to tell, and I told you, what would be different?" Tera said.

"Your son and your rebel friends will be captured, thrown in jail, and kept until we decide they can be freed. Their lives will be spared."

"Why should I trust you?"

"You have no choice. Your plan will fail. Your son will die, and we'll start to experiment with some torture tactics in the meantime."

"I promise, you will pay for this."

The guard pressed the button again. He walked towards Tera, holding the button down as he approached her, allowing her to agonize on the floor for longer. Once he stood over her, he released his thumb from the button. He placed one hand under Tera's shoulder and wrapped the other around the top of the chair.

Lifting Tera and the chair upright, the guard said, "You're not helping anyone, Tera. You'll end up alone in here for the rest of your life, without a single visitor. You won't even have living friends or family to visit you in the first place."

"I'm not saying anything more until I see that Riklin is alive and well," Tera said.

"One moment," the guard said.

Tears surfaced in Tera's weary eyes as the guard left the room. Her hands began to shake. All of her muscles throbbed, and she suddenly squinted her eyes as tears spouted out. While her torso convulsed, her heart pounded against her chest.

Within minutes, Commander Nap entered the room. Panicked, Tera stared at Nap as he approached. He knelt in front of her.

"You have no leverage, Tera," he began, staring directly into her eyes. "Let's be clear about that. Do you feel powerful demanding to see your beloved partner? We have more ways of pulling information out of you. We've been gentle so far. So, here's the truth. Riklin is dead. He resisted, right down the hallway in another cell, and we shot him. We shot him right in his heart, and we watched him bleed out on the floor. Unfortunately, he's already been cleaned up, so I can't show you the mess. I can't let you say goodbye. What I can do, Tera, is give you time to think about your son, to think about the things you can tell us that would save his life, and yours. It would be a shame if he lost you too."

Tera sat, sickened, staring into Nap's eyes with ire and shock. She opened her mouth, desparately searching for something to say to release the deep pain in her heart, but she could hardly breathe. Nap smirked, stood upright, and backed away as Tera's cheeks and narrowing eyes turned a fierce red.

10

A brisk morning came about in Ornaia, six years after the Black War, as Chancellor Tibs, Commander Nap, and Shylo Cob stood a distance from the landing strip near the headquarters, where their military aircraft rested, ocean waves rolling behind it. Breathing clouds of cold air, they each stood with their arms folded, looking into the skies in the direction of Zanoma. Their pilot, a guard of the Republic, stood on the balcony of the headquarters, peering through the peephole of his gun toward the surrounding lands.

"They should be arriving any minute," Nap said. "So long as they're operating on time."

"Well, do either of you have any news to share while we wait?" Chancellor Tibs asked.

"Fydel tells me that birth rates are up," Shylo said. "I guess the people are seeing more hope for their children nowadays."

"The world is still mad," Tibs replied, shaking his head. "It has been for decades. That's why I never had children even before the Black War."

"Is that why? I assumed you didn't have children because you were just too mad yourself," Shylo said with a smirk.

"Careful, Shylo," Tibs said with a smirk of his own. "You may be right, but I'm your boss, whether I'm mad or not. Besides, we both know that I choose officials who think like me."

Three more military aircrafts descended and stopped beside the aircraft that was already there. The doors of the aircrafts opened and a platform folded to the ground. Guards with large packages strapped to their backs walked down from the aircrafts and toward the Ornaia headquarters. Shylo Cob stepped ahead of the guards and led them toward the entrance of the headquarters. One by one, the guards got a nod from Tibs and Nap as they walked by.

The basement of the headquarters contained freezers and other food storage rooms, where packages were ordered and stacked according to the directions given by Shylo Cob. Holding a tablet in his hands, Shylo typed rough data of the packages being stored in each section of the basement. After the guards finished, they ascended to the first floor with Shylo Cob, meeting Chancellor Tibs and Commander Nap in the lobby.

"Very good," Chancellor Tibs said, Nap standing next to him with a stern expression. "Show these men where they'll sleep, Evarand."

"Yes, Chancellor," Nap replied, before signaling to the guards to follow him upstairs.

The second floor of the Ornaia headquarters contained an exit to an expansive balcony, a large office where Chancellor Tibs worked while in Ornaia, and bedrooms with several bunk beds in each. The walls were not yet painted, the beds not yet made. Guards paced through the rooms, back down through the lobby, and outside to board the aircrafts again.

Before Shylo Cob left, he turned to Tibs and said, "We're running out again. We don't have enough for South Village."

"That's quite a shame," Tibs said, turning toward Shylo Cob and grinning, no flinching in his eyes. "But our men will be prepared again."

*   *   *

Languid mothers and fathers lined up in the South Village Sustenance Center. One by one, they were handed their rations for the week. Guards stood by each pick-up window and by the entrance to the building, a few-story building on the edge of South Village nearest the Industrial District, as the anxious parents gathered food for their children.

An older woman with sallow skin approached a pick-up window with a forced smile and said, "Hello. How are you doing today?"

The woman across from her turned to her colleagues, turned back toward the older woman, and said, "I-I'm sorry. We've run out of rations for the time being."

"B-But my family is overdue," the older woman said. "We finished our last rations yesterday. We've kept it longer than we needed to... a-and that was less than we normally get. What are we supposed to eat?"

"I'm sorry," the Sustenance Sector employee said. "I don't have an answer for you. We are working to refill rations as soon as possible. Production has slowed a bit lately."

"This can't be," the older woman said, her eyes appearing angrier and more fearful both at once. "My grandchildren are just growing. They need to eat."

"I'm sorry," the employee said before she and her colleagues at the other pick-up windows shut the gates over their windows and left the resident-facing room for safety.

Chatter spread through to the back of the lines. The older woman looked around at the other furious and distressed residents of South Village who suddenly found themselves in a precarious position. Their children, their grandchildren, whose bones already protruded from their skin, were to be without food for an unknown amount of time, until new rations were to be packaged.

One man toward the back of the line that the older woman was in turned his shoulder as the last resident to receive rations walked by with their packaged food in hand. He snatched one container from the resident's hand, inspiring other hungry residents without rations to lunge toward the entranceways in an attempt to chase down residents who did receive rations before there were no more. Guards immediately stepped in front of the entranceways with guns drawn, so the residents inside of the South Village Sustenance Center stepped back, weak, frail, and defeated, eyes bloodshot and glossy, while their neighbors made their way home to feed their families.

Eventually, the guards allowed the disappointed residents out of the South Village Sustenance Center to return to their homes to break the news to their families, though the guards patrolled the streets, especially close to the tower blocks, which appeared more decayed than any year since the Black War. Broken windows were removed and not replaced. Concrete was blotched and metal railings were thickly rusted. The asphalt streets below were cracked all over, void of vehicles, trash scattered around. The South Village Slums reminded all of Zanoma's residents of the poverty-stricken regions of the world that they never needed to acknowledge. In their new world, the suffering and the resulting violence was inescapable.

Some fathers folded, holding no hope for their starving children. Others organized outside of the Sustenance Sector in the Industrial District, waiting for a word from Shylo Cob, but he never appeared. The men were too restless to wait around any longer.

Instead, they spread toward Milbon Hill and Wrexon's End, where the Amaranth family watched from their windows as guards pointed their guns at the fitful South Village residents. It was no secret that they had come to steal food from the government employees who were never denied their rations, including residents who supported the Republic no matter what happened, so long as their rations were filled every week. All residents in Milbon Hill and Wrexon's End locked their doors and watched closely, even young eyes like Elsan. Some men rushed the guards, seemingly asking to be shot down, and they were. Zanoma's army of guards was stronger than any other year since the Black War, having become an appealing way for men from the slums to move their families to Milbon Hill or Wrexon's End, as the Republic never seemed to hire enough of them. No man was able to raid a home like in years prior, when the Amaranth family watched their neighbors get robbed of their rations by knife-weilding residents of the South Village Slums.

Riklin placed his hand on Tera's shoulder as they watched the commotion from the window of their home. Elsan, who had grown nearly to his father's height, stood beside them, still a bright-eyed child despite entering adulthood in a world that required rapid maturity. Even as a child, he had seen such bedlam too many times to be shaken by it. He wanted to make sense of it all, but he grew frustrated as he could not, so he walked to his bedroom to lay down.

Riklin leaned into Tera and said, "I can't bear to watch this happen anymore. We're protected—Elsan is protected, but by that gang. The men who put Zanoma and all of the world in this position are sitting up in that tower with the world in their hands, the world they took by force, while the rest of us fight amonst each other."

"We need a change," Tera said.

"We need a change," Riklin agreed.

"We can't organize here. We need to find a way out, for us and many more."

"I've had some conversations. I've found someone who can help us get started."

Nights later, after all of Zanoma had gone to sleep, Riklin left the first level of his tower block with a tablet in hand. He met Paxtus, who had spent the day patrolling in the Central Node, behind the most southeastern tower block in Wrexon's End. Paxtus stood leaning on a crowbar with another small tool in the other hand.

"The electricity is running," Riklin said. "Ready?"

Paxtus nodded and said, "We must be careful. If we see anyone, we're done."

Riklin nodded and replied, "Agreed."

"What did you do with Elsan?"

"He thinks I'm working a full day tomorrow. That'll buy me time."

The two men walked casually yet swiftly to the ventilation shaft structure on the abandoned lot north of the tower block. Riklin peaked around the sides of the shaft and turned his neck in all directions as Paxtus tampered with one of the grates. Paxtus detached the grate and placed it on the ground. Riklin ducked through the opening and Paxtus placed the grate tightly back into position, removing his hands slowly to ensure that the grate did not fall.

"That should do it," Paxtus said. "When you come back, be careful with the grate, and remember, the facility is over a half mile into the forest, past the swimming hole, under a large, open patch of junipers."

"I'll remember. Thank you, Paxtus," Riklin said, beginning to turn toward the ladder leading down the ventilation shaft.

"Riklin," Paxtus said, causing Riklin to turn back around. "Be safe. You have a son here."

"I know," Riklin replied with an unsettled expression. "I'll see you soon."

The entranceway to the hyperloop station in Tocano had collapsed a bit during the Black War, so Riklin shifted dirt and debris as he escaped out to the surface. He hiked over the Tocano Mountains, as he had done many times before, though this was the first time he had done the hike with only the light from the tablet and the moonlight from above. Sickened by the state of the lands outside of the City of Zanoma, yet thrilled in leaving the city for the first time since the Black War, he carried on.

As he passed over the crest of the Tocano Mountains, he noticed some relatively lively forests to the southeast, where the swimming hole was, so he set forth. He bustled through the forest, along a narrow path that had remained remarkably cleared and intact. The prop root net he used to rest upon had fallen apart a bit, so he attempted to fix it from a large branch that part of the net clung by, grabbing some torn prop roots and re-tying them to what remained of the net. Suddenly, there was a rustle of leaves.

"Who's there?" Riklin said, perched many feet from the ground.

Macrum walked out from the woods, his beard grown full, on the opposite side of the swimming hole from Riklin, and said, "My name is Macrum."

"W-What are you doing here?" Riklin asked, holding one hand up, palm facing away, as Macrum hovered his hand over the gun strapped to his side.

"What are you doing here?" Macrum retorted. "How did you get here?"

Riklin paused to take a breath and answered, "I couldn't stand being stuck inside those walls any longer. I'm an outdoorsman at heart. I needed to see that the world I loved still existed, at least to some extent."

"Do you support your Chancellor?" Macrum asked, touching his hand to his gun.

"Not one bit," Riklin replied. "I assume you don't either."

"He isn't my Chancellor," Macrum said with a softer tone, removing his hand from his gun and standing more upright. "I came from Ainkia. I was just fixing some defenses around an abandoned military training facility built before the Black War, then I went to scoop some water from a stream just north that hasn't killed me yet. Why don't you follow me? I'll show you the base."

"That happens to be what I came to look for."

Macrum led Riklin to the underground facility, an investigative and training facility that Zanoma's people were never exposed to. Riklin descended down the ladder after Macrum, who turned on the lights of the main hallway. Riklin stared in all directions in astonishment, his mouth slightly ajar.

"How did you know about this?" he asked.

"I was a guard in Ainkia," Macrum answered. "We had grown more and more suspicious of Zanoma over time, though we learned that Zanoma's issues were beyond Medrik Malva. We built a few of these ourselves in areas that weren't travelled around the City of Ainkia. Luckily, this one that your military built was all set up for me to take it over after leaving Zanoma many years ago. I was too afraid to communicate over Zanoma's networks so I commited myself to survival here; that is, until something, or someone, comes about that shows me that it's time to rise from these depths."

Through the years following, Riklin and Macrum worked together to establish the base as a new home for recruits, dissenters prepared to do whatever was necessary to resist the Republic's agenda—untracked residents of South Village who had been running out of options for survival, foreigners forced to split rations with those who had access, government employees, and even some guards. Macrum stayed in the base, gathering any food from the forests that he deemed healthy, growing what he could under heat lamps, and sourcing water to purify, as well as instructing Riklin, including by pleading to him to find Sairin and Mora Storm. Riklin did the recruiting, discovering new ways to gain and sense trust in people through speech and subtle eye movements, as well as the coordinating of smuggling food out of Zanoma and to the base.

Escape routes were established through hyperloop pathways south and west of Zanoma, leading the rebels to two other underground bases. The Republic grew suspicious of growing numbers of missing residents of Wrexon's End and Milbon Hill who permanently resided in an underground base, and eventually gave their government positions and homes away to South Village residents who were upgraded by the Republic. Yet, the Guild became stronger and stronger, the wrights on the outside hiding well, and the wrights on the inside hushing around those that they did not yet trust.

. .

"I just never thought I'd see them this way," Ermin said, sitting at the kitchen table in his home with his umber-haired parents, Daemyn and Moriah Muttin, whose grimaces accensuated their round faces. "I don't want to see them this way. Elsan is the last close friend I have. They were a second family to me."

"We know," Daemyn said. "We had a lot of respect for the Amaranth family. They were always very good to you."

"They were, and we did have a lot of respect for them," Moriah concurred. "But sometimes people can surprise you. They always seemed to do right by the Republic, but it was all a performance, I guess."

"Don't make assumptions about Elsan based on his parents' actions," Ermin said. "I know Elsan. He wouldn't take part in anything that defies the Republic. He's a good man."

Daemyn and Moriah nodded and looked at each other in concern as Ermin rose to his feet and walked to his bedroom, which looked much like Elsan's, like the bedrooms of most tower block homes. On a shelf in his bedroom was a framed picture of him, Elsan, Riklin, and Tera at the peak of the Tocano Mountains, with the City of Zanoma in the background. As he stared at the picture, Ermin sunk into his memory of that day.

It was a summer afternoon, hotter than any day became after soot clouded the atmosphere. Ermin and Elsan were not yet teenagers, but growing. In the opposite direction of Tocano and the City of Zanoma were the clefts and troughs of the cerulean ocean, splashing into the cliffs of Ornaia. South of Ornaia, the forests were fruitful, emitting a bright green. The air was rich, rejuvenating the mind with each breath.

Ermin recalled looking over and smiling as he spotted, between some pines on the vegetated peak of the Tocano Mountains, Riklin placing his arm over Elsan's shoulders and pointing toward Ornaia. He remembered feeling blissful and excited, especially after Tera wrapped her arm over his shoulders and pointed out the path down to the swimming hole.

As he returned to the present, Ermin's warm heart suddenly turned cold. Ermin lifted the framed picture to look at it once more, staring closer at the faces of the Amaranth family, which appeared benevolent, unassuming, genuine. Yet, he turned the frame face-down onto the shelf and walked away.

Elsan and Mora gaited through the forest as juniper branches pulled on their pants with each step. Creeping sunrays brightened the complexion of Mora's face, though the downcast Elsan was drawn to the soil under his feet. Each step sounded a crunch of crisp, dry leaves, fallen branches, and bundles of sticks, sending chills up Elsan's spine.

Just a bit further! Elsan imagined his father saying, as if he were a boy again, rummaging through the shrubs to the swimming hole with Riklin, Tera, and Ermin, the chatter of wildlife all around.

Isn't it beautiful? Elsan imagined Tera asking, having incited a nod from Elsan and Ermin. *Don't take these things for granted, boys.*

Fading into vision, Elsan diverted his mind in an attempt to stay present, saying, "What about the grains by the swimming hole? Can't we just eat those?"

"That's an emergency stash," Mora answered. "If we had taken from that, you may not have made it to our base. When people get lost, the swimming hole is where they stop."

"I see," Elsan said.

"Here's a possible source," Mora said, placing her hand behind a leaf on a low-hanging branch. "This is a white oak. The lobes of its leaves are rounded, which usually means its acorns are sweeter."

"Acorns?"

"Yes, the acorns are edible, but it isn't worth it to scavenge through these, even though the taste would be much better than most. It's much more prolific to find beech trees with chestnuts."

"Isn't that one straight ahead?"

"You're a natural gatherer," Mora said with a smile.

"I spent a lot of time in the woods as a child," Elsan said with a slight smile of his own. "My mom taught me quite a bit."

"She's very smart," Mora said.

She led Elsan through several oaks in order to reach the beech tree. Elsan awaited Mora's next lesson as she circled the trunk of the tree. She kicked away the leaves and sticks blanketing the roots, before turning away from the tree and distancing herself.

"This won't work," Mora said. "We should keep looking this way."

"Why won't it work?" Elsan asked.

"These forests survived the war, but some of it is home to radiotrophic fungus. There are some black mushrooms growing around the base of the trunk, and the bark is blacker than brown. The husks of the chestnuts don't look right. This tree isn't safe. We should move on to others."

"How hard will it be to find a healthy one? We can't do this all day."

"We have before. In plus, it's good to know how to gather in the wild, especially in this world. Macrum never thought he would need to do it, but he figured it out for five years until your father showed up. It's a miracle that he survived. The chances of him starving or becoming sick were high. We know of an area a bit further, though. I'll show you."

"What about those berries over there?"

"Those berries are orange. We should be looking for a deep blue. Also, the more plentiful the plant, the greater chance it's healthy to eat."

"I see."

"Elsan," Mora began, turning her shoulders to face him. "If you don't mind stopping for a minute, I want to say something."

"What is it?" Elsan asked.

"I-I feel really guilty about the things I said the other night. I shou-"

"Don't apologize. I understand, and I'm sorry for shouting at you."

"I really enjoyed spending some time with you, Elsan, a-and I just wanted another chance before it became too late."

"Too late?" Elsan said.

"Anything can happen on any day," Mora began. "It's impossible to know."

"I enjoyed spending time with you too. Don't worry. The rest is history."

Mora stepped toward Elsan, nearly touching the tips of her boots to his. She placed her hands on his shoulders and rose to her toes. As a flood of doubt and dismay drowned Elsan's fragile mind, Mora kissed him, and Elsan's lips were still.

Grabbing her by the arms, he released her grip of his shoulders and said, "Now isn't a good time, Mora. I-I'm sorry, I-"

"I'm sorry. I shouldn't have. I-" Mora replied, but she was interrupted.

"Don't apologize. Please. I-" Elsan began, though he was interrupted as well.

There was a strong tug of a branch deep in the other direction, far too clear to the ear to have been a natural breeze. Elsan stepped behind a white oak and peaked around the side. In the distance was a guard hanging by the ankle, flailing his free leg and arms as his gun and other equipment fell to the ground.

More guards rushed over to him, through some outlying trees. Elsan could not hear the words they yelled, but they were manic. Mora waved a wide-eyed Elsan toward her, though Elsan was hesitant to crackle the forest floor with his boot.

"We need to return to the base and warn the others," she whispered. "Follow me."

Mora and Elsan swiftly weaved between tree trunks and shrubs. The base was equidistant from the guards and their location, so they elongated the route to be more elusive. Elsan no longer stared at the ground with each step, sacrificing caution as his primitive instincts took reign.

Elsan touched the tablet in his pocket, believing that all of the guards had come for it. He clutched the tablet even though it was held firm by his pants pocket. However, the grasping of his pants was slowing his pace, so he removed his hand and ran faster.

The guards successfully cut the cord of the Guild's trap and helped the freed guard to his feet. They began peering through the peepholes of their guns. Sending a shock through Elsan's body, he saw one guard align his gun in his and Mora's direction. The guard waved the others over and picked up his pace.

"Faster," Elsan anxiously whispered between deep breaths. "I think they see us."

Mora and Elsan scurried to the base entrance and lifted the hatch. With one last glance, Elsan spotted the guards, who started to sprint toward them. He turned his attention to Mora, who had already entered the conduit down to the base.

"Hurry!" one guard screamed.

"Prepare to fire!" another hollered.

Hopping down the ladder to the base hallway, Mora repeatedly shouted, "Gather your weapons! Gather your weapons!"

Elsan alighted onto the base floor and chimed in, "Guards are approaching!"

The wrights flocked to the weaponry, grabbing a gun off the walls, or to the bedrooms, grabbing a gun from under their bed. A stirring aura filled the base. Sairin, the first to attain a firearm, neared the ladder, so as to lead the Guild's defense.

As the hatch door creaked open, Sairin took aim and several bullets were shot down into the base. He fired one shot back and retreated two steps as another shot struck the floor beneath the entranceway. Jumping forward, Sairin fired another shot. A guard fell from the entranceway. His head hit a rung, flipping his body as he crashed to the base floor with a fatal laceration in his neck.

Elsan fought his way to the weaponry in terror at the glimpse of gore greater than he had ever seen. His hands shuddered vigorously, and he suddenly remembered to breathe. After finding a gun, he followed some of the other wrights into the hallway to form a front line behind Sairin.

"Elsan!" Mora screamed. "Stand back!"

He did not acknowledge her, and instead lifted his gun. Two guards perched on a rung above the corridor ceiling and pointed their guns out, firing haphazardly at the crowd of rebels. One wright was struck in the thigh, his flesh ripped open where the bullet pierced.

Sairin and Elsan jumped forward to shoot down the two guards, causing Mora to hold her shortened breath. Both managed to kill a guard with a shot to the neck. The two bodies dropped on top of the already deceased guard on the base floor.

Macrum yanked Elsan back, saying, "Are you crazy or stupid? Get back!"

Mora shoved her arm between the front line and grabbed Elsan by the wrist. She pulled him through the wrights as rapidly as she could, though the base hallway was teeming with them. Discerning himself as the enemy truly for the first time in his life, Elsan allowed Mora's pull in disarray.

"They have my mother," he said to Mora as he attempted to collect himself, trying to dehumanize, in his mind, the man he killed, burying tears and resurfacing his rage. "I need to fight back."

Mora continued pulling Elsan into the weaponry. She shoved him against the weaponry wall, her narrowed eyes glaring into his. Elsan's eyes were tamed, his chest bobbing.

"Don't be so foolish, Elsan!" she scolded. "They want you most of all."

Mora stepped back into the hallway as four rebels cornered Elsan against the wall. With clenched fists and gritted teeth, Elsan stared each one in the eyes. No one spoke a word, and a constrained Elsan could only stand, tortured by the battle cries.

"Retreat!" a voice bounced from wall to wall, through the base hallway, through the bedrooms, through the kitchen and dining area, and into the weaponry. "Retreat!"

The four men who surrounded Elsan paused their safeguard and peaked into the hallway. Elsan snuck behind them, poking his head above their shoulders. The front-line wrights lowered their weapons and spun around, besides Sairin, who shuffled under the conduit entranceway.

"They're gone," Sairin said, staring down at the deceased guards by his feet before abruptly turning toward a struggling rebel who was shot, fighting for his life. "Get this man some aid!"

Several others rushed toward the agonized rebel, who was gripping his thigh in fear of exsanguination. A woman applied hemostatic dressing to the wound and wrapped thick bandages tightly around it, using a tourniquet to limit the bleeding. The other wrights watched, though only Elsan appeared traumatized by the gore. Each grazing of the wound ignited shrieks of pain from the injured rebel.

"Go on!" Sairin yelled, waving off the troubled men and women. "He'll survive. We need to prepare for their return."

Most wrights returned to the weaponry, where small bombs and grenades were collected. Sairin entered the weaponry and turned to the left wall, where an isolated gun rested on the opposite wall. It was the entrance to the other training room. He lifted the gun, causing the wall to sink in and slide to the side like the entranceway to the main training room.

"Anyone with a bomb in hand, follow me," Sairin said as he entered the training room with a group of rebels behind him. "This is what we we've trained for. Place them between twenty-five and fifty feet of the base. Do not place them any closer or else our infrastructure will be threatened. Do you all understand, or must I repeat myself?"

The rebels nodded their heads and climbed up another vertical conduit at the far wall, leading to the forest floor. Each had multiple miniature bombs and grenades attached to their belts. With Sairin leading the way, the men and women who followed acted upon his orders exactly how they were supposed to. Bombs were planted between twenty-five and fifty feet of the base entranceways, scattered meticulously in the rare spots of open land where guards could step. It was just a matter of time until a greater fleet of guards would return to match the rebel forces.

The wrights circled Sairin on a strip of fawn land between the two entranceways. All of them gripped their guns firmly, waiting attentively for Sairin's direction and vigilantly for unforeseen danger. A zephyr brushed through the tree leaves and the air thickened. The rebels clutched their guns tighter.

"Take position behind the rear tree line," Sairin began, referring to a row of white pines on the opposite side of the conduit from the planted explosives. "Don't move until the first one detonates."

The rebels followed Sairin behind the row of white pines, anxiously awaiting the arrival of the guards. Elsan remained inside the base, arguing with Mora and some other wrights about engaging in battle. While Elsan expressed his resentment, the rebels were not persuaded by his impassioned pleas.

"It's great that you've trained so well, Elsan," Mora said as two men held him back by the arms. "But you're the most valuable of us all."

"Me, the most valuable?" Elsan asked with narrowed eyes. "Just because my father was the most valuable doesn't mean that I am now that he's dead. I'm not my father."

"If you're caught, your family will be forgotten," Mora said, speaking softer and stepping closer to join eyes with Elsan. "If you're free, you'll still have a chance to turn your father's skeptics into believers."

"Why would they believe in me? They won't trust me. They'll hate me."

"Everyone will be talking about this, Elsan. Those on the inside will spread your father's message, while others will call him a traitor. Your life will be of everyone's concern until one side comes out on top. Not to mention, we owe your safety to your parents, at the very least."

Elsan stared vacously at Mora. After a subdued pause, he sighed and signaled the two men grasping his arms to release him. The men let go of his arms, gauging his sincerity in his stance.

"Eventually, I'll need to fight," Elsan said to Mora with a more relaxed but still assertive stare before leaving the weaponry for the kitchen.

Mora left the weaponry for the battery room, lifted a plastic hatch along the wall behind the battery, and punched the black button on the inside. Wrights in other areas of the base prepared their weapons again. Elsan sat restlessly at the dining table while a fleet of men and women saturated his paths to each escape conduit. Most rebels packed into every room as others climbed to the outside. Eventually, the air became static, and fearful visions filled the base.

You know exactly what we're looking for, scum! Elsan's brain sounded with the memory of the screams of a guard at his father.

The left side of his head throbbed, as if it had been smashed into the kitchen table itself. Riklin's voice filled his ear, though he could not make sense of the words. Elsan sunk deeper into his chair, like the news of his father's death into his moldable mind.

After extended moments of empty silence, a fork on a dining table rattled for merely a second. Elsan looked down at the fork, and back up at the men and women standing in front of him. They all stared back at Elsan as if he had moved the table, causing the floor and the fork to vibrate, though he had not.

"What was that?" Elsan asked.

"Prepare your weapons!" Mora yelled from the weaponry. "The first bomb has gone off! I repeat—the first bomb has gone off!"

"Prepare to fire!" Sairin shouted from behind a white pine in the forest, the nearby wrights shifting their weapons from their belts.

Another bomb detonated within Sairin's line of vision, and an army of guards came into sight. His eyes widened at the approaching force and his heart pounded at the cognizance of impending combat, though he kept a steady aim. He and his army of rebels rested their fingers on the triggers of their guns.

"Fire!" Sairin bellowed.

Bullets pierced the fogging air as another bomb detonated. Some guards laid injured or killed by the explosions, while others marched forward. Many bullets bounced from the armor of the guards, while some pierced their necks and jaws. The guards fired back, some bullets striking the trunks of the fortifying trees and others flashing by.

"Prepare to clear!" Sairin yelled.

Shots darted past one another, several killing the guards, and several others chipping at the tree bark that shielded Sairin and the wrights. The white pine shielding Sairin tilted to the side and fell behind the others, causing the other wrights to spring backward.

"Clear!" Sairin screamed.

The rebels jumped out from behind the row of white pines and took aim as they approached the nearing guards. More bombs exploded as the front line of guards crossed the twenty-five foot offset of the base. Mangled guards cried in shock, while those who survived crept forward with bullets bouncing from their armor or piercing the trees that they hid behind.

The army of guards deteriorated, but still outnumbered the wrights. Men and women on the Guild's side started to fall, dropping dead over patches of ferns and bare soil. Sairin lowered his gun, slid behind a nearby boulder, and scanned on either side of his shaking shoulders. The front line was crumbling, and he began to see no hope to win the battle on the forestland against the greater number of guards.

"Back to the base!" he ordered, and the rebels remaining in the front line descended inside after him. "Move! Move! Move!"

Two more wrights were killed before they could attain cover in the conduit, while those who survived stood with the rest within the base, taking aim to the imminent invasion of guards. Merely for a moment, the base was silenced, but an ellipsoid of metal suddenly dropped from the entranceway. In a flash, the base hallway filled with brume, followed by the kitchen, battery room, bedrooms, and weaponry.

It was a tear gas grenade, dropped from the conduit. Guards in protective masks infiltrated the base, while front line wrights fired desultory shots in the direction of the entranceways. Rebels were disarmed, though none were even willing to use their weapons given the chance of striking one of their own while they coughed uncontrollably and their vision faded. Without their sight, they were defenseless.

"Surrender your weapons!" a guard shouted as more and more wrights had their guns ripped from their hands. "Surrender them now!"

The guards disarmed the blinded rebels in the weaponry, in the bedrooms, in the battery room, and lastly, in the kitchen. Rebels surrendered left and right, while Elsan sat at the dining table with only murky, gaseous air in his line of sight.

"Elsan Amaranth," a guard said with a vile undertone. "You're coming with us."

Elsan was pulled between rebels in the kitchen who had dropped to their knees and through the base hallway. Guards with weapons in hand each climbed from the cloudy base to the forest floor.

"Go up," a guard ordered Elsan, placing his hand on the nearest rung and poking a gun into his back.

Elsan climbed from rung to rung as sunrays blended into the dissipating gas. A guard met him at the top, grabbing him by the armpit and pulling him out of the conduit. Mora, Sairin, and several wrights followed from beneath with a guard in between each.

Elsan scanned the forest floor, grimacing at the mutilated bodies of dozens of rebels and guards. A lone tear trickled from his eye as fury rushed through his body like the blood in his veins.

"Do you really think you're keeping Zanoma safe?" Sairin said as three more guards restrained him by the arms and began pulling him away from the rebel base, along with Elsan, Mora, four other men, one other woman, and more arising. "You're defending evil!"

A guard clouted Sairin in the stomach with the base of his gun, "That's enough out of you. Keep it quiet until we get you where you need to be."

Black cloth was wrapped around the eyes of each rebel. Sairin's words were suddenly muted as more cloth was shoved into his mouth. The whimpers of other rebels were muffled as well. Elsan opened his mouth to speak, but a piece of scrunched cloth was forced into his mouth and taped over.

12

Elsan, Mora, Sairin, Davlin, Macrum, Paxtus and several other rebels were shoved forward without an idea of what laid ahead, while most of the wrights from the eastern base were transported to the Zanoma Detention Center for questioning, and in some cases, sentencing. Guards separated Elsan from the group and led him to a different room within the top story of the Republic's shelter on the Ornaian shores. Blindfolds were removed from all of their eyes, but only for Elsan appeared a unique first blush.

Sitting at a spectacular desk of glazed bocote wood was Daiton Tibs, the Chancellor, wearing the same prestigious black suit with the Z on the chest. Standing on either side of his burgundy chair were two guards, completing the encircling of Elsan along with the two guards behind him. Beneath the desk was a luxurious rug designed with branching burgundy patterns within a brown background. Surrounding the rug was a cream tiled floor, leading to the auburn walls, which were decorated with artificial plants anchored by wooden slabs. Tibs sat eerily quiet for a moment, back against the burgundy chair with a roguish grin on his face, before suddenly flinching forward to speak.

"Welcome, Elsan," he greeted, garnering no movement from Elsan's gritted mouth. "Although your presence here in Ornaia is a result of force, I must express my deepest appreciation that you're here today. You truly are a gift. Guards, please let go of his arms. Let him loosen up."

Elsan was released from the guards' grasp and the guards stepped a few feet back. He glared into Tibs' eyes as the Chancellor stared back with a smug smile. His charcoal hair enhanced his wrinkled face and his white teeth, while his bloodshot eyes seemed to branch closer to his pupils. After a deep breath, Elsan's blood began to boil.

"I never wanted to be here," he said. "Not with filth like you."

"Filth?" Chancellor Tibs said in a mordant manner. "That's quite harsh, Elsan."

"Is excrement more fitting?"

After Nap and the four guards each raised their guns and pointed them at Elsan, Tibs simpered and said, "Don't be foolish, Elsan. You're a smart man, just like your father once was."

"Don't you dare speak of my father," Elsan retorted, remaining composed despite a homicidal fantasy to put an end to Tibs where he sat.

"I apologize if I offended you, Elsan," a caustic Tibs said. "I simply wanted to express that, aside from our disagreements, I do admire your father's work."

"You murdered my father," Elsan said, still scowling at Tibs.

"I did no such thing," Chancellor Tibs said. "Your father didn't play by the rules."

"What rules did he break?" Elsan asked, and after Tibs opened his mouth, Elsan continued before Tibs could speak. "Did he starve his own people? Did he order the murder of Chancellor Malva only to watch the world fall in flames?"

Tibs paused for moment, staring at Elsan with piercing eyes and a slightly gaping smile, before he snickered and said, "Your wit is impressive, Elsan, and you've done your research. I admire that."

"You admit it?"

"I admit it, and I would do it again. It makes no difference for you to know; you mean nothing to the people, and even if they believed you, they would know what we're capable of. There's no place for weakness in Zanoma. Malva was weak. The world's resources were depleting, and he wasn't prepared to fight. Do you truly believe that the other leaders of the world were planning for peace? None of us would be alive if it weren't for me, if it weren't for our forces."

"People across the planet would still be alive if it weren't for you," Elsan said, seemingly a bit surprised that Tibs spoke so openly, yet beginning to understand Tibs' nature as he spoke. "All of the world's forests, oceans, lakes, would still bear life if it weren't for you. The Black War may never have been if it weren't for this fallacy. You're nothing but evil."

"Evil is a far too simple concept, don't you think?" Tibs said. "We all want to live well, and sometimes ugly things need to happen to make life the way it is meant to be."

"You painted my father as a paranoid man, but you're the one who's paranoid. You've always been afraid, afraid to lose control. That's why you killed Chancellor Malva and wiped out everyone who opposed you. That's why you killed my father."

"Your father didn't play by the rules," Tibs said, a wry smile on his face. "My rules."

"My father had the courage to expose your war crimes, and your crimes against our people."

"Courage? I call it idiocy."

Chancellor Tibs arose to his feet as a furious and fearful Elsan glared back. The three guards standing behind Elsan stepped forward and pointed their guns at his head. The two guards standing beside Tibs aimed their guns as well, targeting Elsan from both angles. Tibs paced around his desk, narrowed his bloodshot eyes and jutted out his puckered chin, stepped in front of Elsan, turned, and stood eye to eye with Elsan, their faces only inches apart.

"If you ever want to see your mother again, there's one thing you must learn," Tibs muttered as the guards again grabbed hold of Elsan's arms. "You are powerless unless I give you power. Do you understand me? I say what I want to say. You can as well, unless *I* have something to say about it. You think your words have power. They don't. Unless you publicly condemn your father's behavior, you'll never be seen within the city walls again, and you'll be considered a traitor into the future, just like your father."

"My father's words had power," Elsan said. "He had followers, many of them."

"Well, unfortunately for his followers," Tibs began, inching his shrewd eyes even closer to Elsan's. "Their infamous leader is dead."

Immediately after Tibs closed his mouth, Elsan thrashed his upper forehead between Tibs' eyes. The Chancellor collapsed into his desk and to the ground, groaning on one knee with one hand keeping balance. The guards clamped Elsan's arms and tugged him off of the rug toward an open area of tile.

"You're vermin!" Elsan screamed as he grappled with the guards. "Vermin!"

As one guard catered to Chancellor Tibs, the other four pulled their black bats from their sides. Elsan opened his mouth to shriek again, but was clobbered in the upper back by a bat, slumping him forward to his knees. Another blow to the back thrust him face first into the tile floor, where he laid with drool dripping from the corner of his mouth.

Tibs cringed as another guard approached and helped him ascend back to his feet. He rubbed the space between his eyes with his thumb and index finger, eventually opening his eyes to a squint to see Elsan being beaten senseless. Cudgeled again and again, Elsan's body flailed like a fish on land. He curled his knees to his head and covered his head with his hands, but the guards' bats continued to bash his sides, legs, and rear.

"That's enough," Tibs said as one more strike to Elsan's side left him gasping desperately for air. "We don't want to kill him just yet. This is an important man we're dealing with. We could use him. Confiscate his tablet and get him out of here."

Two guards stood in front of the entrance to Chancellor Tibs' office, one guard took Tera's tablet from Elsan's side, and the other two guards spaced from Elsan's feeble body. Wheezing helplessly, Elsan remained on his side. His blurred vision cleared as a sudden inhale kept him from asphyxiating in anguish.

"Cover his eyes and leave him with the others for now," Tibs ordered the guards.

One guard blindfolded Elsan as two others lugged him from the ground. Elsan's knees buckled, so the two guards dragged him by the armpits out through the office door with one guard walking in front and the two guards who were blocking the door following from behind. Tibs' lips lifted to a smirk as he wiped the water in the inner corners of his eyes with the white cloth from a pocket beneath the Z on his chest.

Elsan was propelled outside, into another building nearby, and into an unknown room, where he was shoved into a cell and stabilized by unknown hands. As the blindfold was removed from his face, he realized that the hands were Mora's. Sairin and the other rebels pushed off of the grey walls they leaned against and surrounded him, each raising a hand to support a woozy Elsan.

"Are you alright?" Mora asked with brightened pools in her eyes, her hands stroking Elsan's arms in solace. "What have they done to you?"

"I'm fine," Elsan answered, his shoulders raised by his stiffened back. "I need to sit."

"What happened?" Sairin asked as Mora helped Elsan slowly lower to the ground.

"He insulted my father," Elsan said, bowing his head and taking some deep breaths as he spoke. "He belittled my father, so I head-butted him."

"You head-butted the Chancellor?" Sairin asked with a quick laugh.

"Yes," Elsan said with a slight smirk of his own, though it quickly fell as he winced in pain, holding his side and leaning onto the opposite elbow. "I'm sure you can guess what happened next."

On one knee, Mora rubbed Elsan's back and softly said, "I know it can be hard to keep composure, but keep them happy for now. We'll get out of here eventually, and when we do, we'll make them all pay for this."

"These are powerful men," Elsan said, lowering his voice after Mora gave him a cautioning signal with her eyes. "How do you expect to do that?"

Mora peered up at a camera in the corner of the wall, turned back toward Elsan, put her mouth closer to his ear as she continued to rub his arm, and whispered, "Help is on the way."

Elsan gazed up at Mora to gauge her confidence, though he doubted her promises. He twisted his torso to see what was behind him. A transparent wall stood between him and an open room of dark grey walls, polished concrete flooring, and a white ceiling. An identification pad was on the door on the opposite wall. The room extended farther to the left of the section that the wrights were in, though Elsan did not know what was in the unseen area.

"What's on the other side of this wall?" Elsan asked, pointing to the left wall.

"There's an interrogation room on the other side," Mora answered. "Paxtus is in there right now. He's being questioned by two of the guards. They're taking us in one by one. I think the rest are in other cells in the building."

Sairin walked toward Elsan, knelt down, and mumbled, "These aren't normal guards, Elsan. They'll do anything to get the information they want. Anything. There aren't checks to their power in Ornaia, not like in the city. Besides, there's no need for secrets anymore. When they bring you in, tell the truth."

A perplexed Elsan sat in silence, looking around with his mouth slightly opened. Sairin stood upright and leaned against the left wall where Macrum stood, giving Elsan a confirmatory nod, though Elsan was still unclear of the message he was trying to send. Mora and the other rebels spread about the room, standing and sitting against the four walls. Elsan, Mora, Sairin, Davlin, Paxtus, and Macrum were joined by Noland, a somewhat dark-skinned man with a narrow jaw, Sabil, a pale-skinned, short, muscular man with dark hair, and Frewine, a tall man with peach skin and brown hair.

The seven wrights bided for some time, standing stoicly in silence. Eventually, Paxtus was escorted back into the cell by the two interrogators. One held Paxtus' arm while the other actively carried his gun. The gun was pointed into the cell as the transparent, hinged door was opened.

"Sairin Storm, you're next," one guard said after jostling Paxtus into the cell. "Nobody else move, or we'll shoot. Is that understood?"

The rebels nodded their heads as Sairin exited the cell, escorted by the guards to the next room over. Elsan's alert eyes scanned the room expecting to sense concern in the other wrights' eyes, but the others simply stared into their laps. This confused Elsan, as he could not help but wonder how the rebels remained so composed. Yet, he took a deep breath and leaned his back against the transparent wall. He rested his head against the wall and forced his eyes shut. With another deep breath, his rapid heartbeat slowed.

The interrogators soon returned to the cell with Sairin and said, "Elsan Amaranth, come with us."

Elsan stood to his feet, his heart anomalously calm. A gun was pointed at his head, but he did not acknowledge it. He followed behind one guard while the armed guard followed from behind him. With hope engrained in him by the unwavering confidence of the other wrights, Elsan walked toward the interrogation room void of fear.

"Take a seat," the leading guard said after opening the door to the adjacent room, signaling Elsan toward a black metal chair along one side of a black metal table while the other guard entered from behind, standing over Elsan's shoulder.

The dimly lit space laid a saffron layer atop the table. As one guard sat across the table from Elsan, his face entered the glow. The other guard stood in the shadows of the corner, with the whites of his eyes more prominent than the grey tint of his face and neck. Both the black guard uniforms and the black rebel uniform blended with the emptiness behind their backs.

The seated guard pressed the screen of a tablet rested on the table in front of him. Elsan watched his insipid expressions as the other guard tucked his gun into his belt. The standing guard kept a hand on the smaller gun to his opposite side.

"So, Elsan," the seated guard said. "You are the son of Riklin and Tera Amaranth, the greatest threats to the Republic since the stampede of outsiders after the war or the man who released that footage. They had a strong following; I'll give them that, but they're all detained now. Well, maybe not all of them. There must be more. I presume you're aware of some others that you can tell me about."

"You're in on this too," Elsan said. "You knew about the murder all along."

"Chancellor Malva needed to be escorted to Ainkia by many guards," the guard said. "Commander Nap couldn't do that alone. I'm confident you wouldn't believe me if I told you lies, so let's get to the point. If you ever want freedom, you'll need to publicly denounce your father's actions, and if you don't, the people have heard all of the theories before and they're not going to trust an enemy of the Republic anyway. Maybe you and I can build some trust today and work toward your freedom. First, we need some names. Who were your parents involved with? It could be friends, family, colleagues… anyone. Who did you see them with the most? This is an easy question, Elsan. We're not asking you to implicate anyone, just list those closest to your parents."

"I-I don't know many names besides the ones in the cell with me. I don't even know the names of a few of them. I stumbled upon them when I was lost. This all fell upon me when I was eating dinner with my family. I didn't know anything about the group before that. My parents didn't tell me."

"Whether you're new to the group or not is of no matter to us. The rebels in that base will be dealt with and their names will never mean a thing again anyway. Who do you know inside the city walls?"

"I know a lot of people inside the city walls. We'll be here all night."

"Don't be smart with us, Elsan. You won't like the path that will take you down."

"I just don't understand where to start."

"You know what we want, just get to it and stop wasting our time. You'd be a fool not cooperate with us. A fool, just like your father."

"Don't speak of my father."

"Or what?" the guard taunted as the other guard took aim at Elsan with his pistol. "Your father was a *fool* for starting this treasonous group. He never stood a chance against the Republic. Does that make you angry, Elsan? Am I bothering you now?"

Elsan glared into the guard's eyes for a moment before responding, "What do you think I know? My father may have started the group, but I wasn't aware of it until your men brutalized him. I didn't know anything about the group or anyone involved."

"You don't seem to be listening to me, Elsan," the guard replied. "Tell us who your father knew on the inside, who your mother knows. Give us some names like your friends in the other room did. Who did you see them with recently? Who did they talk about from their work? Who came to your home most often?"

"They didn't talk about anyone at work, and we haven't had any visitors recently."

"Is that so?"

"Yes, it's true. They kept me in the dark."

The seated guard stood to his feet, strolled around the table, and stood behind Elsan. He pulled a rope from his belt as the other guard stepped closer with his gun still aimed at Elsan's head. The rope was wrapped around Elsan countless times, constricting his chest, waist, hips, thighs, calves, and feet, as his ankles were tied tightly together. Elsan sat in disturbed stillness, no longer void of fear, struggling to think of a name that would protect him as he was distracted by the guard's actions.

Once the rope was knotted, the guard pulled an electrical prod from his belt. Attached to it were several electrodes, which the guard stuck to Elsan's temples, pectorals, and obliques, causing Elsan to tremble, knowing what was to come. The guard holding a gun retreated as the other returned to his seat.

"Do you want to help us now?" the guard asked, holding up the button on the opposite end of the table.

"I-I" Elsan stuttered, unable to collect himself before the guard pressed the button and shocked him to his core.

A cringing Elsan shook violently in his chair with a clenched jaw, the chair rattling over the ground. The guards watched with blank stares. The torturous moment seemed to last an eternity for Elsan, though it eventually came to an end. He breathed heavily after having held his chest tight.

"How about now?" the guard asked. "Who have you seen your father spend the most time with in the past three years? Anyone, Elsan. Just say the first people you can think of. Again, this is very simple."

"W-Well, we were very close to a neighboring family," Elsan muttered with a grimace and a weakened neck. "Their surname is Muttin. My friend's name is Ermin Muttin, the mother's name is Moriah Muttin, and the father's name is Daemyn Muttin, but I don't know of any involvement by them in the rebel group. Their family has always been the lawful and obedient type. They didn't question their authorities; at least, I never witnessed it."

"I see," the guard said, typing the names into the tablet. "Who else?"

"I-I don't kno-"

The guard electrocuted Elsan again, causing Elsan to convulse within the constraining rope. Elsan's hairline glimmered in perspiration while the guards grinned, glowering at his squinted eyes. After the button was released, Elsan breathed heavily as his neck wilted like a dwindling daffodil.

The seated guard again stood to his feet but walked toward the back corner of the room, where a television projector was perched within the walls. Alongside the projector was a camera. The guard turned on both devices, causing light to emit from the projector onto the opposite wall while the camera recorded the room.

Elsan shuddered at first sight of the television screen. Appearing on the screen was Tera, in the same situation as Elsan. A gun was pointed to her head while another guard sat across from her, holding the prod attached to her temples, pectorals, and obliques.

"Leave her alone!" Elsan screamed, wrath in his eyes as he attempted to lunge forward despite being tied to the back of his seat. "I swear, I don't know anything! Leave her alone!"

The armed guard forced Elsan back into his seat as the other guard said, "Are you sure you want to stick to that story, Elsan?"

"It's true!"

"That may be so, but your mother was as much a part of the rebel group's formation as your father was, and she isn't being very cooperative."

"Don't you dare hurt her."

"We don't plan to hurt her anymore."

The standing guard stepped toward Elsan and pressed his gun against Elsan's head. Unfazed by the gun, Elsan watched the television screen as his muted mother cried, also staring in the direction of the screen.

"We have no need for you, Elsan," the guard said. "You're merely a hostage to us now. Let's see what's more important to her, the anarchist group or her only child."

*   *   *

In Zanoma, Ermin, Daemyn, and Moriah Muttin were hauled from their respective workspaces and dragged through the ductways, toward the Zanoma Detention Center. Bemused, the family questioned the guards' actions, but the guards disregarded them. At Elsan's word, the Muttin family was, for the first time, in defiance of the forces of the Republic.

13

"Let me talk to her," Elsan pleaded to the guards as he peered up at his mother's face, which was projected along the opposite wall. "Please."

"Why should I do that?" the guard opposite Elsan retorted.

"I can convince her to talk."

The guard nodded at the other, who held his gun tightly. The armed guard let go of his gun and turned toward the camera to unmute it. He sent a message to the guards interrogating Tera through a tablet of his own. The message was an order to unmute their camera as well. A moment later, Elsan could hear Tera's whimpers through a faint static.

"Mom!" he yelled. "Can you hear me?"

"I can hear you, Elsan," she replied. "Everything is going to be alright. Do you understand?"

"I understand. I love you, Mom."

Elsan's chin began to quiver. His eyes watered as Tera's chin began to quiver as well. Tears forming in her eyes, Tera opened her mouth to speak.

"I love you too, Elsan."

"Get to the point or I'll mute it again," the guard sitting across from Elsan said.

"Mom, you can tell them," Elsan said. "Tell them what they want to know."

"I-I don't know anything, Elsan," Tera responded. "I was barely involved in this, but they don't believe me."

"You gave your tablet to your son before he escaped," a guard in the Zanoma Tower with Tera said. "We aren't stupid. It's in our possession."

"Mom," Elsan said. "They'll kill me if you don't speak. I'm useless to them otherwise."

"No, they won't, Elsan," Tera said. "They won't because I know nothing more."

"Do you want to place a wager on that?" the armed guard in Ornaia said with snide cruelty in his voice, pointing a gun at Elsan's head.

"Mom," Elsan began. "Please, just tell them what you know. I already told them everything I know, and they know you were involved. Save my life, Mom. We will see each other again."

"They wouldn't allow that," Tera responded. "Why would they allow us to be free to see each other again? Why would they ever take their eyes off of us? Why would they not kill us anyway?"

"If you tell them what they want to know, there is, at least, a chance."

Tera settled her eyes on the table in front of her. The guard standing behind Elsan pushed his gun deeper into Elsan's head. Elsan watched Tera's face on the screen as she inhaled.

"Alright," she said, her eyes a pool of crystalline spirit. "Alright, I'll speak."

The projector Elsan watched was shut off as it appeared that Tera would continue to be questioned. Elsan clenched his jaw, staring at the blank wall as the gun was taken away from the side of his head.

"Well," the armed guard said. "I don't think we need you anymore at the moment. You're free to return to your cell with your pathetic, little friends. We may need you again if we need to convince your witch of a mother to speak again, though."

Elsan scowled at the guard as the other guard untied the rope that restrained him. Homicidal fantasies again overcame Elsan's mind as the guard smirked in smug apathy. After being lifted to his feet, Elsan was led by the guards back to the cell of wrights.

*   *   *

In the city, Ermin, Moriah, and Daemyn Muttin were led into an interrogation room of their own within the Zanoma Detention Center. The large room had a door on each wall, three of which led to smaller interrogation rooms. Unlike the Amaranth family, the Muttin family was handled delicately. The guards that took them into questioning did not know anything of the family's relationship to the Amaranth family, and they did not want to fuel any hatred toward Zanoma or the forces that maintained it. Still, the Muttin family was offended by the suspicion.

"Why have you taken us?" Moriah asked with vigor in her voice as six guards entered the expansive room from behind with a tranquil demeanor. "You must tell me, you know. It's against the law to be held in custody without reason."

"We understand," one guard said. "But it's important that we didn't say anything in public."

"Why is that?"

"Because the situation is classified in order to prevent civil unrest," the guard said, his soothing tone calming Moriah a bit. "You're affiliated with possibly the greatest threat to Zanoma's security in the post-war era, the Amaranth family."

"We're just as surprised as you are by this," Ermin said. "We aren't affiliated with their treachery. We're innocent."

"When was the last time you spoke to Elsan?" the guard asked Ermin.

"I spoke to him the day he went missing, but there were no signs that something like this would happen. I never expected this. I-I just want to know if he knew what Riklin was doing or not. He may be innocent. I believe he's innocent."

"That may be, but we have yet to find him, so that much is not clear yet. Additionally, if he has left Zanoma somehow, the chances of him surviving are slim. We just need to gather as much information as possible until we're able to find him."

Ermin's chin stiffened and his eyes watered slightly as Daemyn said, "Please understand. This is all a big mistake. My family feels betrayed by the Amaranth family, just like the rest of the residents in the city. We have always supported the Republic. We oppose anything that threatens to impede Zanoma's progress, even if it turns out to be our friends, who we blindly trusted for so long."

"We do understand," the guard replied. "But we're trained to take caution. Our protocol is to take each of you into separate rooms for questioning. So long as all of your stories of the recent past are consistent, you will be free to return to your home."

The guard's tablet rang with an incoming message. He was told by another guard to meet within his office immediately, so he tucked his tablet back into the side of his pants. The Muttin family watched, puzzled, waiting for the guard to speak.

"I'll be back," the guard said before turning to the other guards in the room. "Watch over them for just a few minutes."

Several minutes passed and the guard had not returned. The Muttin family stood awkwardly, occasionally staring at the guards that watched over them. Droplets of sweat surfaced below Daemyn's hairline.

"This is stupid," Ermin said, staring at each of his parents. "Look at what Riklin is putting us through. We had no part in this."

Ermin's parents glanced at him, but their focus shifted as the lead guard walked back into the room. The other guards placed their undivided attention on the lead guard in anticipation. The Muttin family eagerly awaited the lead guard's words.

"It was nothing too important," the lead guard said, turning toward the other guards as he spoke. "We'll speak about it later in Commander Nap's office. Separate them for final questioning and let them go so long as all of their stories are consistent."

Ermin, Moriah, and Daemyn were each led by two guards into separate small interrogation rooms, much like the one in Ornaia, with two lights slightly illuminating the room. No gun was withdrawn from the belts of the guards. The Muttin family was entirely cooperative. No force was inflicted upon them.

The Muttin family was questioned individually for nearly a half an hour. Guards asked about the past week, including the places they had gone, and the timing of different events. They asked about their last contact with Elsan, Tera, and Riklin.

As the questioning neared an end, the guard interrogating Ermin asked, "Before you go, I must ask one last question. If Elsan were to appear in Zanoma, would you inform the authorities?"

"I-I can't say," Ermin answered. "I would need to hear his story first."

"You would let him go if his story was justified?" the guard asked. "What if he lied?"

"Why are you under the assumption that Elsan is guilty? Elsan is not his father."

"It's a hypothetical question, Ermin."

"Yes, but why must you paint him as a traitor when we don't know if he is or not?"

"I-"

"I would ask him about his involvement. I have known Elsan all my life and have trusted him all my life. If he can look me in the eyes and tell me he's innocent, I still may not believe him, but I wouldn't turn him in without being sure, especially knowing that the guards have a bias against him. Besides, he has nowhere to hide in Zanoma. You wouldn't need me."

The guard remained silent for a moment before saying, "Well, Ermin. That's all I have for now. Let's go out to the lobby and wait for the others."

At about the same time, Ermin, Moriah, and Daemyn were taken into the lobby. They looked at each other in concern, but their eyelids sunk, knowing in the deepest state that all in their family were innocent. The guards nodded to one another before turning back toward the Muttin family.

"Please take a seat while we review," the lead guard said to the Muttin family.

After several minutes of silence, Daemyn chuckled. Moriah and Ermin joined, as the family had finally found amusement in the absurdity of the situation. The atmosphere of the room became timid, soothing the volatility in their defensive minds. Ten more minutes passed as the Muttin family discussed their individual conversations with the guards. The six guards reentered the room one by one.

"You are all free to return home," the lead guard said. "We apologize for the stress we have put on your family today. I hope you understand our purpose, and we thank you for your time."

"We understand," Daemyn said with a nod, speaking on behalf of his family. "We support you and wish we could help you get to the bottom of this, but we have kept to ourselves much of the past few years."

"Many of us do these days," the lead guard said. "Work, eat your rations, maybe catch up on some news, then go to sleep. We forget what the date is half the time. That's the life we live for Zanoma."

"Well," Daemyn began. "I tell my son every day to dream of a day when the world goes back to the way it was. Dream, and someday, it will happen."

The Muttin family was released from the Zanoma Detention Center and led out of the building by the lead guard. They walked to Wrexon's End Ductway and stepped onto the transporter, their shoulders settling at their sides. As they returned home, Tera remained in isolated imprisonment several stories

above. She sat on the floor in somber silence, yearning
to hug Elsan once again.

*   *   *

With Mora by his side, Elsan thought of his
mother, feeling the warmth of Tera's heart within his
cramping chest. The rebels sat quietly, while only one
guard was still present in the room, besides those
observing through the security cameras in the corners of
the walls and ceiling.

One of the guards that interrogated the wrights
left the room minutes earlier to speak with the others,
his chest protruding arrogantly as he paced out. The
guard that remained had his weapon tucked within his
belt, his fingers removed from the trigger. As the rebels
sat in silence, the door to the detention room suddenly
swung open. Another guard sprung through the
doorway toward his confounded comrade.

Through the insulation of the wrights' cell, not a
word could be translated from the chatter of the guards.
Elsan focused his eyes on their mouths, but he couldn't
read their lips as he hoped. The two guards hustled out
of the detention room and slammed the door shut,
sending a jolt through the room. Elsan flipped his head
around, hoping to hear an explanation from one of his
fellow wrights. Connecting eyes with Mora, his
inquisition kept him from blinking.

"They're here," Mora whispered with an austere expression.

The imprisoned rebels could not hear the whistling bullets ricocheting off of the building's concrete exterior, but they waited in hope that their message had reached those elsewhere. As they listened anxiously, an army of wrights from the other bases approached the Ornaian Shores from all angles of the surrounding forest.

A small group of men, previously guards, led the attack, having been recruited to the side of the rebels by Riklin and Paxtus during the first year of the Guild's creation. Spread across the horseshoe shaped front line, they positioned their counterparts, a fleet of all backgrounds grinding their teeth in preparation of an invasion.

"Take shelter after each shot!" each of the rebel militia's leaders hollered. "Fire!"

Wrights pulled their triggers as they aimed at the scrambling guards of Ornaia. They hid behind boulders and a dense stretch of coastal tea trees as the guards fired back. Swarmed by six guards, Chancellor Tibs was swiftly escorted toward the military aircraft on the seaside airstrip.

"Fire at the north side!" one of the Guild's leaders screamed.

One shot struck the leg of a guard, but Tibs was able to secure a seat in the military aircraft, alongside one pilot, before any damage could be done to him. Weapons were aimed back toward the Ornaia headquarters' courtyard, but all of the guards rushed inside. Guild leaders raised their weapons into the air and looked to those on either side.

"Go!" they shouted.

The infantry of spirited insurgents stormed toward the building, holding the barrels of their guns in one hand and balancing with the other. Guards scattered throughout the building, positioning strategically in preparation of shooting anyone who came through their doors. The imprisoned rebels dug their foreheads into their folded hands until the floor beneath them vibrated, rattling the suddenly unoccupied security cameras.

Infiltration began as the Guild's militia used laser devices to unhinge the headquarters' doors, as well as the doors to the detention building, dropping them to the ground. A shiver was sent through the floors and up through the spines of the guards. Unlike the guards, Mora, Sairin, and the other imprisoned wrights in all of the detention rooms enjoyed the savage sound.

In the headquarters, one wright in the militia was struck in the leg, but his simultaneous shot struck the neck of the guard who injured him, killing him within seconds. Several more bullets deflected off of the rebel armor, redirecting to shatter picture frames and pots holding phony plants. Three more guards were quickly killed as the rebel militia swarmed the first floor of the building.

"Surrender!" a wright ordered the guards. "Surrender, and your lives will be spared!"

The dozen remaining guards rested their weapons on the floor. Three rebels approached each guard, confiscating their weapons and forcing them to lay flat on their front sides. Remaining rebels searched throughout the building for hidden guards, as well as the imprisoned wrights in the other building.

Guards on the second floor of the headquarters were controlled by some of the remaining rebels, while all guards in the detention building were as well. Eventually, Elsan, Mora, and the other imprisoned rebels jumped to their feet as the door to their detention room was opened. The remaining rebels released them from their cell, consoling them like abandoned children, including Elsan, who they only knew through Riklin's and Tera's many stories.

"We're alright," Sairin said. "We're all fine. Where are the others?"

"They're in another building," one of the other rebels answered. "The guards have been contained, but Tibs escaped in an aircraft."

"Bring all of the guards to the other building. I want to have a word with them."

Elsan and the other previously imprisoned rebels stomped into the headquarters and onto the cream tiled floor, which was lined with a long burgundy, brown rug, identical in design to the rug in Chancellor Tibs' office. There were shards of glass stuck between the bristles of the rug. Black boots crunched them deeper as the wrights entered the building. The cream tiled floor of the first story had a tint of orange from the setting sun, which shined through the polyethylene windows.

"Good evening, friends!" Sairin clamored, his voice projecting throughout the expansive lobby, aiming to penetrate the ears of the detained guards. "It's a long fall from the top, isn't it? Yes, a long fall, indeed, my friends. You see, every action has an equal and opposite reaction. That's what we've all learned in our schools growing up, at least. Isn't that right? After more than a decade of acting on the side of evil, on the side of truly insane men, on the side of entitlement, deceit, and cruelty, you are now witnessing the reaction, and this is just the beginning, my friends. This is just the beginning of your downfall. However, I do believe in redemption. I truly do. So, you can cooperate with us and your lives will be spared, or, you can claim loyalty to Chancellor Tibs, Commander Nap, and the Republic, and we'll paint this floor red. What will it be?"

"W-We'll cooperate," one guard uttered with his face to the floor. "Please don't kill us. We have families back in the city. We have children. We'll do anything. Just tell us what to do."

"Good choice," Elsan said with a strong, steady tone, sparking a pleasant smirk from Sairin, who nodded for Elsan to continue. "If only you made that choice to begin with. You've betrayed the people of Zanoma! You've helped to oppress your neighbors. You've put your children in danger. People would be afraid to leave the city even if they were allowed, but you cling to the riches of the biggest traitor of all, out here by the ocean.

You've done a great job restoring Ornaia; I can't deny that, but a selfish man is a worthless man. You are worthless men. Sairin is right, though; that can change, so long as you cooperate."

"Store these pawns in the detention cells until we decide how to use them," Sairin instructed, still staring at Elsan with a smirk, so as to suggest surprise by Elsan's sudden ascent.

*   *   *

Ermin worked tirelessly in Zanoma for the rest of the day after his interrogation, distracting him from the thoughts of Elsan that were racing relentlessly through his mind. Nearing the end of his shift, he decided to leave a bit early since he had taken care of all of the tasks on his schedule.

Ermin packed his bag with empty food containers, tucked his tablet into his side, and stood to his feet. Pacing through the hallway of the third floor of the Zanoma Tower, he glanced at each face that passed him by, trying to get a glimpse of their true beings, but he dodged their eyes whenever they looked back. Murmurs from within Lealan Wiske's office diverted Ermin's attention as he walked by Wiske's partially cracked office doorway.

"Cold storage is all we would want to keep running while they occupy Ornaia," Commander Nap said to Wiske. "What can we control?"

Ornaia? Ermin mouthed with narrowed eyes.

"We can control all of it," Lealan said. "Or none of it. We can't control small parts."

"We should speak further with Tibs. Join me in his office."

Ermin scurried away from Lealan Wiske's office, knowing that he and Commander Nap would soon exit. His narrowed eyes were stuck in place, hedging between his confusion, his unavoidable worries of Elsan, and his nostalgic memories of joining Elsan in the Amaranth family's adventures. He felt neither betrayed, afraid, nor empathetic, but rather, he became vehemently curious.

*   *   *

Followed by several wrights, Elsan marched into the single detention room that they kept the smaller number of guards in. When he entered the detention room, the guards pushed each other around in a fight toward the back of the detention cell, fearing Elsan's intentions.

"Please, don't kill me!" the guard in front of the detention cell doorway yelled as he was shoved into the translucent wall of the cell.

"You all know that in the eyes of Chancellor Tibs, you're dispensable," Elsan began. "Don't you?"

The guard whimpered and said, "Please, spare us. Please."

"Why should I?" Elsan said with wrathful eyes. "Why should I spare the lives of men who have sold their souls? Why should I spare the lives of men who support the killing of my father and the imprisonment of my mother?"

"Please. P-Please, give us a chance."

"You want a chance? Now, you want a chance, after all that you've done?"

"P-Please understand. W-We wanted only what was best for our families."

"That may be so, but look where it got you. It got you locked up in a cell, just like you were trying to do with all of us. Your sad excuses aren't enough to repay the damage you've done. You've spent years guarding your wealth. Yet, your worth has been reduced to rubbish. You truly are dispensable, but maybe there's a way you can redeem yourselves."

"Just tell us how."

"Join us," Elsan began, projecting his voice to the other guards in the cell. "Join the rebel group and redeem yourselves for all of your wrongdoings. Fight against your faint-hearted leaders. Fight against their power to decide all of our fates."

"They'll kill our children," another guard said. "They'll kill them if they find out that we've betrayed the Republic."

"You're on the other side, now. You're imprisoned, disarmed, and powerless, just like the rest of us will be if this regime isn't defeated. Join us, and together we can find a way to reunite you with your children before anyone is lost."

The guards all looked at one another, most nodding their heads, before one said, "Alright. We'll join the rebels."

"You're making the right choice. It's about time you all made the right choice."

Elsan turned away from the guards, leaving the cell door shut. His eyes remained narrow, as the instinct to preserve the power of the Guild emerged. He aimed to proliferate the guards that were on his side, which were far more valuable in combat. Yet, he remained humbled by the heartache of losing his father and by his fear for the life of his mother. The other wrights followed Elsan as he walked back toward Chancellor Tibs' pristine office, Sairin just a step behind him.

"You know," Sairin said, a smirk forming on his face. "You're starting to sound like your father."

"He was a great mentor," Elsan, a restive soul, replied with a slight smile of his own, though it quickly faded. "But I'm not my father."

14

The hardest choices a leader must make are the ones that offer a benefit for taking the lives of others, a memory of Chancellor Tibs' most famous speech surfaced in Elsan's mind as he drifted from dream to reality. *War, though tragic, has been a necessary part of humanity throughout history. We can only hope that the Black War leads us toward an age of eternal prosperity, once and for all.*

Elsan never forgot that day, in his early teenage years, when he, Riklin, and Tera sat astounded in front of the television projector in their home. They believed that the attack on Ainkia would be necessary, as most of the Republic of Zanoma believed. Although they were lied to, wrights held onto some regret of this stance. As an adult, Elsan experienced the same change of thought in the span of just a week.

When he awoke on the rug of Chancellor Tibs' office, he rose to his feet and walked through the upstairs hallway. Stepping over nearly a dozen sleeping wrights, Elsan made his way toward the balcony, where the rising sun illuminated the cream-colored tiles. A long shadow trailed Davlin as he patrolled.

"Has there been any cause for concern thus far?" Elsan asked Davlin as he stepped onto the balcony, his eyes squinting at the unsparing morning sun.

"There hasn't," Davlin replied. "It would be difficult for them to take their men out of the city so quickly with so much happening there, but we should be wary of that. We should move quickly."

After a brief moment to breathe in the morning air, Davlin turned away from the warming sunrise to face Elsan and said, "When I first learned about Medrik Malva's murder, I almost attacked Tibs myself—a crime of passion, in a way. That sentiment made me realize that the rebellion needs to stay organized. When people see what Tibs and Nap have done, what some of their guards have done, the lies that led to the planet's downfall, they'll go mad. If we can tame the madness, our army will become stronger, and theirs weaker. The Republic is nothing without their people. Do you understand?"

"I understand."

"Good, because while we need to move quickly, we also need to be smart."

"Do you worry about air strikes?"

"I can't say for sure, but I doubt that they would destroy Ornaia. There's quite a bit that's stored here."

"I see," Elsan said with a nod. "I'm going to check on the others."

He walked back into the building and turned toward the stairway. In his peripheral vision, he spotted Mora standing in Chancellor Tibs' office looking frantically from side to side. As he walked back over the sleeping wrights in the hallway, Mora turned around and saw him. Her concerned eyes calmed as Elsan entered the office and shut the door behind him.

"I was worried about you," Mora said. "I knew you slept in here and I didn't know where you went. I thought something might have happened to you, but here you are."

Elsan smiled and said, "I appreciate your concern. I'm doing just fine. I was checking in with Davlin on the balcony. We're clear."

"That's good. It's unclear if we'll be able to stay for long, though."

"Why is that? We can protect ourselves here. There's food here."

"That's not my concern. We're not here to defend ourselves. We're here to defend the people of Zanoma. They're still in the city being preyed upon. We must protect them, and share this food with the people who need it most, in the slums."

"Then we need to go back. But when?"

"Let's gather the others to come up with a plan."

As Mora was walking out of Chancellor Tibs' office, Elsan reached for her shoulder and said, "Wait, while we have a moment to ourselves, I want to say something that I've been thinking about. It would be best before the others wake up."

"What do you mean?" Mora asked as she turned to face Elsan.

"I want to apologize, Mora. I-I keep thinking about how I treated you when I found out about my father. It was wrong and thoughtle-"

"Please, don't apologize," Mora interrupted. "We can't help how we react in times of tragedy."

"I know," Elsan said. "But you didn't deserve that. It wasn't your fault."

"Thank you, Elsan; I understand what you're going through."

"I do have a bone to pick with you, though," Elsan said with a smirk, revealing a large bruise just below his hip. "From the day we met."

Mora laughed and responded, "Our traps are quite forceful. It won't happen again."

As Mora again turned to exit Chancellor Tibs' office, Elsan grabbed her arm, spun her around, and kissed her. Violent thoughts vanished into the cool air as they wrapped their arms around each other, kissing away the armor over their hardened hearts. The hairs on their arms arose as Mora allowed Elsan to lay her back onto the bocote wood desk, their breaths deepening between each kiss. Gravity held no weight.

Abruptly, the door to Chancellor Tibs' office creaked open and the two sprung upright. It was Sairin, with a cowlick protruding from the right side of his head, rubbing his waking eyes as he walked in. After an extended yawn, he blinked his eyes.

"How did you two sleep?" he asked. "I slept like a baby, believe it or not."

Mora and Elsan smiled before Mora replied, "I'm glad to hear that, brother."

"Well, we should see what food they have in storage," Sairin said, turning around as Mora and Elsan smirked at each other. "I don't know about you two, but I'm getting hungry."

Elsan, Mora, and Sairin searched through the Ornaia headquarters' kitchen, which they found to be in the basement. Several wrights woke up and followed, all eager to settle their aching stomachs. Inside the storage freezer were shelves of all sorts of frozen foods. There was lettuce, kale, tomatoes, sprouts, wheatgrass, avocados, bananas, and much more.

"Where do we begin?" a male wright said, already salivating at the sight.

"Keep yourself under control," Sairin said. "We must save as much as we can."

"But we've missed meals."

"Relax. We need to sacrifice," Sairin said while tapping the hungry rebel on his gut, causing the rebel to snarl back.

"We should transport some of this back to the slums," Elsan added.

"Yes, we should."

"What about the guards?" Mora asked. "Should we give them some?"

"We can feed them in their cell," Sairin said as the wrights gathered the bare minimum amount of food necessary to sustain the ferocity and focus of those in Ornaia. "I don't trust them yet, not enough to let them eat with us. We must only reward them once they've proven their worth."

"Sairin," Macrum said, signaling for Sairin to step aside to speak with him in private, and Sairin did. "Maybe it's time we reach Morin Malva."

*   *   *

In the late afternoon, the poor of the South Village Slums and the homeless, those typically labeled as thieves and bandits, slogged toward the Sustenance Sector facilities in the Industrial District. Many had bloodshot eyes, as well as protruding cheekbones, casting a shadow over their malnourished, pallid skin.

As the crowds continued to grow larger, Shylo Cob walked through the sliding doors of the largest facility and to the edge of an elevated platform with a guard on either side and six guards following from behind. The guards lifted their guns in front of their bodies as Shylo Cob adjusted his suit top. Pelted by the gazes of thousands of hungry people, he took a deep breath.

"I understand you all must be extremely concerned with the recent thefts of the Sustenance Sector and the shortages as of late," he said. "That is why I have agreed to reveal and discuss an ongoing investigation with you today. We have been scanning through surveillance footage and have searched for DNA within our facilities. Unfortunately, though our agencies have done a great job, there have not been any significant leads—at least, for now."

"Liar!" a woman yelled as uproar ensued.

"This is your security failure, not ours!" a man shouted.

"You must sacrifice too!" another man hollered, as many began to chime in.

"Liar!"

"Traitor!"

"We want justice!"

"Ladies and gentlemen," Shylo Cob began. "I understand that these circumstances are devastating, and we are working tirelessly to hunt down the culprit or culprits. We wish that we could provide the typical rations for the time being, but we can't. We've been through this several times already, so you must already be aware that we need to distribute rations according to the protocol established after the Black War. Government officials and employees, as well as the city's workforce, will be first to receive their rations. Remaining rations will be distributed through the South

Village Sustenance Center, and will be handed out according to due dates of residents."

"There's never enough!" a woman yelled from the middle of the crowd, inciting all of her starving neighbors to heckle Shylo Cob as well.

As the guards raised their guns, Shylo Cob raised his voice and said, "Although this shortage is devastating, we must remain patient and intact. Until further notice, this theft is under investigation, and will remain under investigation. We will remain vigilant, but our jobs only become more difficult without the support of our people."

"Coward!" a man yelled over the rest of the crowd's chatter.

"Please remain patient as the investigation continues," Shylo Cob said. "Remember, it is compassion and sacrifice that will carry us through such strenuous times."

Furor followed as Shylo Cob walked back into the facility with the guards. Most people trudged toward their respective homes, or makeshift dwellings, but a cluster of the hungry horde chose to climb the stairs of the Central Node nearby. An outraged group of young and middle-aged men fortified in front of the Zanoma Tower Ductway.

After allowing several employees through, the group of men spotted Shylo Cob as he walked out of the main entrance of the Zanoma Tower. He approached the men with the same eight guards surrounding him, stopping just feet away.

"Please, excuse us," Shylo Cob said. "Please understand that we are doing everything we can. I must make my way to the distribution centers."

"You're lying to us," a brown-haired man in front said. "I can see it in your eyes."

"I assure you," Shylo Cob said. "I am being completely transparent about this investigation and I am just as frustrated as all of you."

"Frustrated? You aren't the ones with starving children at home," a dark-haired man said. "And we don't believe you."

"Well, you don't have the basis to say such things and I don't have the time to convince you, so please, move aside," Shylo Cob said, sticking his hand between two of the men at the front of the group.

The brown-haired man impulsively and aggressively grabbed Shylo Cob's arm and gripped his wrist with pressure. A shot was fired by one of the guards, just feet away, striking the man in the stomach as another man reached for Shylo Cob as well. Many of the group started to flee, while the second man to pursue Shylo Cob was shot in the stomach as well. One man remained, horrified by the rush of blood.

"What have you done?" the man cried. "You've killed them!"

The last remaining man was then interrupted by a shot to the stomach—dead within seconds. Shylo Cob stared at each of the guards and rushed back inside of the Zanoma Tower with two of them. On the third floor of the Zanoma Tower, Ermin watched with

widened eyes and a fallen jaw as the bodies of the
victims bled out, as confused passersby cringed and fled,
as oblivious men and women moseyed back toward
South Village beneath the ductways.

15

Rebels packed into the common area of the first floor of the headquarters in Ornaia. Standing and sitting shoulder to shoulder, they stared in silence, all in the same direction. The television projector was on, displaying the Zanoma Morning Report and Amon Sarato, who discussed the events of the previous day.

"Such a troubling occurrence, it was," Amon Sarato said. "These thieves have taken far more than our food. They have taken a bit of our sanity, a bit of our trust in one another, and love for one another. These thieves have caused good, innocent men to lash out against Zanoma's leadership as they attempted to investigate. In times like these, we must remember that the true enemies are the anarchists behind such crimes. Our greatest threat is the fragmentation of our people. Unity is of utmost importance.

Yesterday's tragedy must not be forgotten. Yet, as the investigation continues, we must protect the brave, virtuous guards and head officials who are constantly fighting to protect all of us as well. Thank you for viewing today."

Sairin shut off the television as the wrights looked at one another. The room remained silent, stymied by an unspoken anticipation of the events to come. Elsan took a deep breath of the room's sultry air and rose to his feet, attracting the attention of his stagnant counterparts.

"It's time," Elsan said. "If we wait, they'll continue to rally the residents against us. They'll bomb us here or pin the food that's stored here on us."

After another moment of silence, Sairin stood to his feet and said, "Elsan is right. Let's move."

As the wrights in the room nodded in agreement, Elsan said, "Start packing."

Most rebels followed Sairin to the basement, where they gathered insulated containers to carry the food. One by one, the containers were filled with as much food as possible. After each container became full, they were strapped to the back of a rebel to be hauled back to Zanoma.

Meanwhile, Elsan walked upstairs alongside several wrights to the detention room, where the cramped Ornaia guards waited restlessly to be freed from the confines of their cell. As Elsan approached the transparent wall between them, the guards turned with torment in their bloodshot eyes.

"Are you men ready to redeem yourselves?" Elsan asked.

"Yes, Elsan," the front guard responded as the others nodded their heads, Elsan examining their eyes to sense loyalty.

"Good. You will be given the task of distributing food from the basement of this building to the hungry people of South Village. You will be unarmed and several rebels will accompany each of you at all times. Once your duties have been completed, you will be free to return to your families within Zanoma. Should you choose to rejoin the Republic at that time, we can no longer try to protect your safety."

"You have our support," the guard said. "So long as none of you harm our families."

Elsan nodded and the unarmed guards were released from the detention cell. Elsan led the mixed group of armed wrights and, for at least a short time, newly appointed rebels toward the basement, where wrights lined along the walls, waiting to be strapped with a container of food.

The Guild was ready for a return trip to Zanoma, a route including a trek through the coastal forests, a hike over the bordering Tocano Mountains, through the desolate valley of Tocano, and through the hyperloop.

The army of wrights marched through the forests and up the edge of the marigold mountains with the morning sun striking their path. The backs of their heads blocked the rays from their unfazed eyes, their faces still warmed with harnessed fury. Elsan looked back, only for a moment, to watch the beams of light bounce off of the ocean waves and creep over the sawtooth tree line of the Ornaian forests.

Over the mountain peak, the Guild descended down the shaded slopes with the containers of food bringing momentum to their burdened backs. No military aircrafts were in sight. The Tocano Mountains blocked the valley from the morning sun in its entirety, the air far cooler on the western side. Crusted soils became firmer with each step.

Tromping between the collapsed Tocano tower blocks and industrial buildings, the steadfast men and women stared ahead with tunnel vision. As they neared the edge of Tocano, and the entrance to the hyperloop, the morning sun peeked over the mountains as it neared its midday position. Wrights climbed down into Tocano's hyperloop entranceway while Elsan looked back once again.

He was drawn to the sun, which grew more assertive throughout the long trek as it ascended over a mountaintop. A soothing sensation calmed the thumping of his chest as he kept his eyes on it. After a deep breath, he entered the hyperloop entranceway.

Another long trek through the hyperloop led the Guild to the ventilation shaft in Wrexon's End, but they chose to continue to the primary hyperloop entrance in the Industrial District due to the weight on their backs. They paused for a moment to catch their breath, the containers of food challenging their condition. They continued forward, nearing the primary hyperloop entranceway shortly after their break. Elsan's heart began to race as the idea of returning to Zanoma, where he was a wanted man, finally settled in.

"We need to keep you hidden, Elsan," Sairin said within the dimly lit tunnel. "We'll bring you to a wright's home for hiding."

"Sairin, now is not the time for me to hide," Elsan argued. "I need to help. I ne-"

"Elsan, please listen to me," Sairin interrupted, expanding his eyes and lowering the volume of his voice. "You will show your face in Zanoma, but it needs to be in the right way. The people are not ready, Elsan. Not like this. You'll see. Trust me."

Elsan took a deep breath before responding, "Alright, but what if someone sees me along the way? You told me rebels could only travel into and out of Zanoma at night."

"Today, we risk everything. Put on these sunglasses."

Elsan placed the pair of sunglasses over his ears and the cleft of his nose and said, "Do you actually think this will be enough?"

"Yes," Sairin answered as the rest of the wrights put on pairs of sunglasses as well. "No one is identifiable without their eyes."

As a group, the rebels walked around the curling hyperloop passageway, coming into the sight of three guards stationed at the entranceway. The guards heard the footsteps and spun around. They picked up their guns but their stance was timorous.

"Drop your weapons and get down!" Davlin shouted as the Guild got closer.

The guards lowered to their knees, placed their guns on the ground, and put their hands behind their heads. Several wrights confiscated the guns and watched over the guards as the rest of the wrights climbed up and out of the hyperloop, quickly merging casually into crowds of people, though their all-black attire and food containers caught the attention of some. Wrights started to attract the stares of some nearby residents, though it was of no matter. They wanted to be seen.

Heart pounding, Elsan followed Sairin and Paxtus as they separated from the Guild to go toward the border of Wrexon's End and the Industrial District. They arrived at the ground level of a tower block, where there was a mainentance door leading inside the back of the building. In one rapid movement, the door slid open and Elsan was pulled inside before he could even see the face of the person taking him in.

The rest of the Guild continued toward the South Village Slums, avoiding guards stationed on their route from the Industrial District. Dispersing throughout the narrow streets and passageways of the slums, the rebels garnered the perplexed stares of many more Zanoma residents who were concerned with the strange containers strapped over their shoulders. Still, the rebels started going from tower block to tower block, complex to complex, leaving packaged food within the compartments that the Republic used to deliver not rations but other goods and necessities such as home maintenance tools, clothing, and even medicine—anything that the resident needed to bring about a bare minimum standard of living, besides rations and purified water. The Guild was the first to deliver food.

People passing by watched the wrights drop off the food, floor by floor, unsure of whether the acts were made with good intention, unsure of what exactly was being placed into the compartments. Chatter spread throughout the slums, but no one attempted to put a stop to the unexpected acts.

Guards circled and patrolled within South Village, as the most hostile borough of the city was becoming more and more hostile each year, and at the time, each week, each day. They noticed residents of South Village jostling and talking amongst themselves more than they typically did. Eventually, some guards spotted rebels in their black outfits, with the food containers over their shoulders. Several guards approached a small group of wrights as they exited a tower block.

"Excuse me," one guard said. "What are you all doing? You don't appear to be from around here. What's in those containers?"

"I apologize," a female wright said, attempting to look calm, as if the wrights were innocent saviors of the slums. "We're just trying to help some people in need. We'll leave now."

She stepped around the guard, followed by her fellow wrights, the guard sneering at her and the other wrights as they passed. The guards approached the tower block and entered its small courtyard, an open-air central area surrounded many stories high by home entrances, a feature uncommon in most of the city's tower blocks. Along one side of the courtyard were the compartments for the first floor. One guard stepped closer to them. It took him only a second to notice that one compartment was loose. He glanced inside the compartment to see some packaged food.

"Stop right there!" the guard shouted as he spun around, simultaneously pulling his gun from his side. "Stop what you're doing immediately!"

The wrights were already distant from the tower block, running away, weaving between the many hungry people roaming the streets. Frightening the innocent, the guards sprinted after the rebels. Crowds of people gasped in fear and cleared to the sides of the streets and corridors, allowing a path for the guards to chase down the rebels.

Eventually, one male wright was struck in the leg by a guard's smoking gun. Screaming in agony, the wright laid on his side along the cracked pavement in the middle of the street as the other wrights continued running. Residents swarmed the scene.

"What's happening? Why are you detaining this man?" a woman asked in a panic as the guard wrapped the wright's arms behind his back, but the guard remained silent.

Throughout the streets of South Village, more and more wrights were being chased and detained.

Residents followed each pursuit in both fear of the rebels and indignation toward the guards. Rumors spread of the food distribution throughout South Village and all of Zanoma as wrights were forced toward the Zanoma Detention Center with their hands behind their backs. Hordes of people followed the guards and the detained rebels to the entrance of the Zanoma Detention Center, yelling in confusion, aggravation, and desparation.

Wrights were jammed into cells, and there were no Guild members left in the bases to rescue them. Guards returned to South Village to confiscate the food that the rebels delivered. As they approached each tower block, enraged residents blocked the guards from the courtyards and lobbies.

"Please move to the side," a guard at one of the tower blocks said to the people standing in his way, several other guards standing behind him. "We need to get through. Please move to the side."

"Not without answers," a black-haired man said. "What's happening?"

"We have reason to believe that these men and women are the thieves we've been looking for. The food can't be trusted," the guard said, nudging forward. "Please move to the side."

"Why should we believe you?" the man retorted, he and his neighbors sticking out their chests.

"You have no choice. Move aside."

As the guards raised their weapons, the residents split to the sides reluctantly, watching skeptically as the guards dug through the compartments, confiscating the food and hurrying out of South Village before hungry residents could act on animalistic impulse. All across the South Village Slums, guards confiscated food and carried it to the Sustenance Sector in the Industrial District. Conversations between residents carried on as the people of Zanoma searched for answers, answers that they feared they would never find.

Within Chancellor Tibs' suite, Commander Nap informed Tibs of the rebels' imprisonment as Morin Malva listened. They stood by the polyethylene glass walls to look over the street and ductways as commotion ensued. Tibs peered up at Nap from his desk on the verge of enraged excitement.

"Has Elsan Amaranth been captured?" Tibs asked Nap, grinding his teeth after speaking.

"There's been no sign of him," Nap said. "We're not sure where else to look."

"Question the rebels until you find out where he is. Find out at all costs. Make examples of them if you need to. Do you understand?"

"Yes, Chancellor."

Commander Nap retreated from Chancellor Tibs' office and paced swiftly back to the private elevator. The guards prepared their weapons and lined up along the cells in which the wrights were forced into. After leaving the Zanoma Tower for the Zanoma Detention Center, Nap entered the scene.

"All of you, listen! And listen well," he demanded. "I'm going to make myself perfectly clear.

We have scanned all of your fingerprints and confirmed all of your identities. One of your most prized possessions, Elsan Amaranth, is nowhere to be found. We'll ask you all kindly to disclose Elsan's location, or lives will be lost. It's that simple. Now, we'll get the process started. Who would like to volunteer?"

Commander Nap walked slowly along the transparent walls of the many cells that the wrights were packed into. Each disarmed rebel gave empty stares to Nap as he walked by. At one cell, Nap stopped, turned, and stared Mora into her narrowed, yet frightened eyes.

"How about you?" Nap said, signaling the guards to remove her from the cell.

The guards opened the door to her cell, grabbed her by the arm, and tugged her to the center of vision of the other cells. Two guards aimed their guns at the back of her head. Sairin pushed to the front of a far cell, eyes expanding at the sight of his sister.

"So, young lady," Commander Nap said, stepping face to face with Mora. "Do you know of Elsan Amaranth's location? And don't lie to us. You won't like what happens when we catch you lying."

"No," she said. "I don't know where he is. I wasn't told anything."

"Fair enough. I may actually believe you, but someone in this vicinity must know, right?"

"I-I don't know. He could have wandered for all I know. I truly don't know where he is."

"I'm not so sure I believe that one," Nap said with a grin before turning toward the cells. "Does anyone else know of Elsan's location, or does anyone else know who is aware of Elsan's location? One of you must know. He was with you in Ornaia. Speak now or this young lady's life will be taken from her. I would surely hate to end this beauty's life so early."

Sairin gritted his teeth and clenched his fists, face burning red. He watched as Commander Nap paced cell-by-cell, waiting for an answer. The air in the hallway was still as Nap glared at the front rows of wrights, so he walked back toward Mora, lifted his pistol, and pressed the muzzle against her pulsing temple.

"No one knows?" Nap asked the rebels once again, resting his finger on the trigger of his gun while looking cell by cell for a motion. "It seems difficult to believe that the son of Riklin Amaranth is out there all alone after being in Ornaia with all of you, but I guess no one wants to speak up."

"I'll speak," Sairin said, raising his right hand in the air.

"It's good to see that someone cares about this young lady's life," Nap said with a sadistic smirk as Mora, dismayed, shook her head slightly from side to side at Sairin. "Now, where is the young Amaranth."

"Don't!" Mora cried to Sairin.

"He's hiding in Wrexon's End," Sairin said. "He wouldn't say where. He didn't want us to know. Just like the leaders of the Republic, our leaders don't arm us with much information to share."

"Not the perfect answer, and I don't appreciate the mocking of the Republic," Nap said, gritting his teeth a bit more between words. "But it'll work for now."

Guards shoved Mora back into one of the many cells full of rebels and veered toward the elevator. Mora's cheeks cooled to her normal complexion as several rebels consoled her. Sairin, in a separate cell, took a deep breath.

"You're lucky to have drawn so much attention to yourselves," Commander Nap said to the Guild. "You've spared your lives. Congratulations, but we won't spare you all. If I'm not mistaken, many of you are technically missing, and many of you are foreigners. No one would know the difference. So, get comfortable, and we'll see each other again very soon. Until then, I don't want to hear a word coming from this hallway. Is that understood?"

The rebels did not flinch, so Nap simply smiled and walked away. The Guild was left to be watched over by twenty guards. Within minutes, many other guards raced through Wrexon's End Ductway.

Barraged by the questions of countless observers regarding the imprisoned rebels and the food that was distributed, the guards held their weapons close. The people of Zanoma ultimately maintained composure, as they had been accustomed to secrecy behind such investigations, as well as such cruel acts. For the unseen power of the Republic engulfed them all.

Not far away, Elsan stood with his back against the wall of the maintenance room on the bottom floor of the tower block he was forced into, his scuffed arms folded. The guard in his defense, Garik, a bulky but old, grey-haired man, shuffled about the room in a guard's uniform. After tucking a tablet into his pocket, he approached Elsan abruptly.

"Are you ready?" Garik said.

"What if I wasn't?" Elsan asked.

"Well, I guess I wouldn't give you much of a choice. Let's go."

Garik secured Elsan's hands behind his back, removed the sunglasses from his face, and quickly guided him out of the tower block. Residents of Wrexon's End turned their heads, recognizing Elsan's face from television. Within Wrexon's End Ductway, residents formed a canal on the transporter for Garik to quickly bring Elsan to the Industrial District and to the Zanoma Detention Center.

"Traitor!" many yelled.

Many others shouted obsceneties at Elsan, and many others remained silent, instead staring at Elsan, wondering what the young man had done, if anything, to further his father's agenda. Most guards were in the Zanoma Detention Center after wrangling wrights from South Village, but some remained in the streets, ductways, and Central Node. They joined at the sides of Garik and Elsan to ward them from restless residents.

Observers followed the scene as Garik walked Elsan into the Central Node, down a stairway to the streets below, and toward the Zanoma Detention Center. Zanoma was becoming a territory clouded by curiosity, even more than it had been, with frustrated residents fervently returning to their televisions after Elsan was taken in.

Unaware, many other workers remained focused. Ermin strolled along the third floor of the Zanoma Tower, but was suddenly halted by the sight of a familiar face in the streets below. He paused and leaned against the translucent wall.

"Elsan," he whispered to himself, eyes wide open, mouth gaping.

Ermin rushed to the Zanoma Detention Center as fast as he could, where countless residents clogged the area outside of the visitor's entrance. He pushed his way to the front of the crowd and leaned over a temporary rope that blocked the residents. A guard approached him within seconds.

"You need to step back, young man," the guard said to Ermin.

"I want to see my friend," Ermin replied. "I want to talk to Elsan Amaranth."

"I'm afraid that isn't possible," the guard answered. "Not during an ongoing investigation."

Garik processed Elsan and placed him in an empty room of only dark grey walls, a dark grey celing, and concrete flooring. Elsan settled against the far wall as Garik instructed some guards in the hallway to join him in retreiving Chancellor Tibs and Commander Nap. Many guards defended the entrance to the Zanoma Detention Center. The people of Zanoma were becoming impatient, beginning to lose faith in the fabric that bound their home.

Several guards left for Chancellor Tibs' suite alongside Garik. Tibs, already aware of Elsan's imprisonment, sat at his desk with his hands folded. Morin Malva watched while the Communications Sector employee prepared to operate the camera in Tibs' office, though Tibs stood up at the sight of Shylo Cob, who stood in the common area. Tibs walked into the common area to speak with Shylo Cob in private.

"It appears we have a scapegoat," Tibs said softly.

"It appears so," Shylo Cob replied.

"Spike the water with whatever works."

"Yes, Chancellor."

Residents sat on the couches of their homes and stood within the ductways, awaiting a story from the Zanoma News. Ermin hurried home to tell his parents about Elsan. Daemyn and Moriah were preparing dinner with the rations that residents of Wrexon's End were supplied, so Ermin led them to the common area of their home to watch their projector.

"Good evening, good people of Zanoma," Chancellor Tibs began after appearing on every screen in Zanoma. "As you may know, some very strange events occurred today. Hundreds of men and women were detained after distributing packaged food to residents of South Village. It is believed that these men and women are connected to Riklin Amaranth. It is also believed that this group was involved in the recent theft of the Sustenance Sector. The food has been confiscated and is being tested for contamination. We fear that they have gotten their hands dirty in other ways, so we hope that you will report anything suspicious that you may see. We must stay strong in defending the Republic of Zanoma against anarchy."

"They got Elsan, too," Ermin said, causing his parents to hover closer in concern.

Ermin stared blankly at the projector, sitting between his parents, until his chin quivered and his eyes closed. Squalls of heavy breaths caused his torso to convulse. Tears squeezed out of the corners of his eyes as his parents braced his trembling hands.

Within Chancellor Tibs' suite, Commander Nap stood in the common area. As Tibs walked into the common area, Garik and the other guards entered the suite through the private elevator. Nap and Tibs turned toward them as they approached.

"Elsan Amaranth has been detained," Garik said. "He's been processed. I thought you two might want to handle the rest yourselves."

Chancellor Tibs grinned and said, "Thank you, Garik. Let's go see Riklin's son."

"I'll stay and watch Morin," Garik said. "He can't be left alone."

"Very well," Nap said.

Chancellor Tibs, Commander Nap, and the other guards entered the private elevator to descend to the ground floor and walk to the Zanoma Detention Center. Morin Malva sat in Chancellor Tibs' office after the Communications Sector employee shut down the camera and left. Garik entered the office.

"Hi Morin," he said, walking slowly toward Morin. "I know you're used to it, but I hope you don't mind some company."

16

Ornaia guards were processed and released from the Zanoma Detention Center. They returned home to their families within the Zanoma Tower suites to live in discomfort, no longer having trust in the Republic to protect them, nor having yet earned the trust of the Guild. Meanwhile, Elsan sat in an interrogation room. Three guards walked in as Elsan lifted his face from resting upon his clenched fist. He looked each guard in the eyes, waiting for one of them to speak.

"Elsan," the guard in the middle said. "You're being transported."

"To where?" Elsan asked.

"You'll see when you get there," the guard responded as the other two guards tied Elsan's hands behind his back, taped his mouth over, and placed a black cloth over his face.

The men were silent as they lifted Elsan by his underarms and led him out through the doorway of the interrogation room. With images surging in his mind of the enormities that could follow, Elsan's heart walloped his chest. He breathed heavily as the four men zigzagged from corridor to corridor, toward the center of the Zanoma Detention Center. After climbing several sets of stairs, walking through a hallway, and entering a room, the guards removed the cloth from Elsan's head, untied his hands, and ripped the tape off of his mouth without mercy.

Elsan was brought into a heavily guarded cylindrical cell within an expansive room with a ceiling two stories high. The walls converged to a rounded peak, lined by twelve columns of celeste lights. The guards gathered on the second of the two stories, within a soundproof watch-room, to speak with Chancellor Tibs and Commander Nap. Eventually, they turned away from Tibs and left the watch-room to stand around Elsan's cell from all angles.

Chancellor Tibs looked at Elsan from within the watch-room. He grinned and walked slowly toward the transparent wall of the watch-room. When he approached the wall, there was a metal post up to his waist. A button was on top of the post. He sat down in a chair in front of the post and pressed the button, sending a faint static through the room around Elsan's cell.

"Elsan Amaranth," Tibs said, smirking a bit more after his voice projected throughout the room below and caused Elsan to look back up at him. "It's a pleasure to see you again. Last time we saw each other, I should have had you killed for what you did to me. Fortunately for you, your friends came to save you, but now we have them too. Who will save you now? The people? Is that what you hoped for with this scheme? Fortunately for you, your face was seen in public, but the people will forget about you soon enough, and we can come up with a story for you, and your mother, once they do. We can come up with a story, just like we did for your father."

Elsan gritted his teeth and started to scream at Tibs, slapping his hand against the transparent walls of his cell, but the cell was muted, so Tibs continued, "I'm sorry to anger you, young man. We never wanted to treat you this way. You and your parents had roles in the Republic and a better life than most in Wrexon's End. Yet, your parents chose not to play by the rules, and here you are, following in their footsteps. What a shame that is. What a great contributor you could have been. For now, we'll give you some time to think ab-"

Suddenly, a screeching alarm sounded. The celeste lights turned red and flashed on and off. Chancellor Tibs sprung to his feet within the watch-room as the guards turned to face him and froze. From Elsan's view, Tibs appeared to signal for one of the guards to join Commander Nap to ensure his safety. Tibs, Nap, and the guard exited through a private elevator just outside of the watch-room. The other two guards stayed in the room, watching over Elsan, who was confused, gawking from wall to wall, face to face.

On the floor in front of the many cells previously occupied by the Guild were several guards on their knees with guns held against their heads by double the amount of their guard counterparts. These counterparts were Garik's recruits, and their comrades in the Guild were funneling out of their cells toward a private exit that one other guard held open. Garik's recruits disarmed Commander Nap's men and took off behind the Guild.

A group of four guards emerged near the section of isolated cells that Elsan and Tera were in. They freed Tera, who was not being watched over at the time, before approaching Elsan's cell and containing the corrupted guards in the room on their way. Elsan's eyes narrowed in fear and bewilderment as the guards rushed around the cell. He raised his hands in the air, but hesitantly lowered them as he saw his mother. After the guards opened the cell door, Elsan approached Tera, cautiously, with a stunted smile.

"You've come to save me," Elsan said, turning toward the guards as he spoke. "You've saved my mother. Thank you."

"We work with Garik," one guard said. "Unfortunately, we're some of only few that he could wrangle, but it was enough to set you all free."

"The Guild is all free?" Tera asked, the guard nodding in response.

Tera jumped into Elsan, hugging him and kissing his head repeatedly. Tears fell from her eyes as she pulled her face away to look into Elsan's eyes. Elsan quickly settled Tera to stand flat on the ground and held her by the shoulders, smiling as he stared at her. He pulled her close again and consoled her. He squeezed his mother tightly as both knew the other was thinking of Riklin, and they mourned together for the first time, though Elsan abruptly held her out in front of him again with a suddenly resolute expression.

"There's no time, Mom," Elsan said. "We need to leave immediately."

After the corrupted guards were disarmed, Elsan, Tera, and the four new recruits hastened to escape through the Zanoma Detention Center's western exit stairway. As they hustled down countless stairs, the guards covered them in front and in back, keeping a watchful eye out for Commander Nap's men. It appeared that Nap's guards that were in the building had fled, whether to chase after the scarpering wrights or to find safety from the Guild.

People in the Zanoma Tower quickly learned of the escape as guards rushed to defend the entranceways and the Forum. Frightened workers fled the Zanoma Tower, surging through the Zanoma Tower Ductway and through the Central Node, where many other guards gathered. With panic in their eyes, the workers swept up pedestrians along their route home, as if they were under attack. Chancellor Tibs' guards that were stationed elsewhere in the city hurtled to the area

surrounding the Zanoma Detention Center after
receiving orders from Commander Nap.

Garik's recruits, with Elsan and Tera between
them, reached the ground level of the Zanoma
Detention Center. They tiptoed toward the exit door, so
as not to discount the possibility of guards standing on
the other side waiting to pin them down. After opening
the exit door, they found themselves justified. Two of
Nap's men were waiting outside. They attempted to lift
their guns, but before they could take aim, Garik's
recruits intimidated them into handing over their guns.
The guards dropped to their knees with their hands
behind their heads.

No more of Nap's men were in sight, so the six
wrights, including Graik's recruits, sprinted toward
Milbon Hill. The group hid in stealth behind a concrete
support beam before continuing through the more
condensed areas of the Industrial District between them
and Milbon Hill. In the distance, in the middle of a
hexagonal grouping of tower blocks over the border of
Milbon Hill, were ten guards seemingly in intense
conversation, pointing fingers in all directions. In the
opposite direction, toward the Zanoma Tower, was a
similar group of guards doing the same.

The group crept from wall to wall, slow enough
to remain quiet, yet swift enough to remain unseen. As
the group ventured closer to a ventilation shaft in an
abandoned lot in Milbon Hill, they took a last look
around. It did not appear that they were being followed,

so they removed a loose grate and continued down into the hyperloop. They veered west, toward Treton.

On the surface of the City of Zanoma's streets, guards gave up on the larger group of wrights as they were unable to get enough guards to the Industrial District in time to stop them before they stormed the hyperloop entranceway, despite the wrights being unarmed. The search for Elsan and Tera continued, but eventually, they gave up on finding them as well. The Guild had escaped. After scouring the Industrial District for quite some time, guards returned to the Forum, where Chancellor Tibs and those in his defense waited for reports from Commander Nap and his closest followers.

"Chancellor Tibs," Nap said, approaching Tibs within the Forum. "Maybe we should bring men back from the other territories."

"We can't do that," Tibs said, his jaw starting to jut out farther. "Some people in those territories might sense weakness in our ability to protect them, and some might become a bit too hopeful for my liking. Besides, that won't be necessary if you have our men here prepared. Can you do that?"

Commander Nap nodded and joined several leading guards gathered behind Chancellor Tibs, who was standing in front of the cast stone statue of Medrik Malva. Chatter filled the room as more and more guards filtered in. Chancellor Tibs waited patiently, with his arms behind his back, until all doors were closed and all sounds to the open air of Zanoma were blocked.

"Silence!" Tibs screamed, causing Commander Nap and the hundreds of guards to turn toward him and watch heedfully for his next words. "It seemed we had won the war, men, but suddenly we are more vulnerable than ever. Some of our men have turned against us and have joined the rebel group, allowing them to escape the city untouched. We must not succumb to their anarchist ways! We must not abandon each other! We must not abandon our Zanoma brothers! Nor should we stop hunting these anarchists down. We will destroy their image, making sure that their group doesn't grow any larger, and then we will destroy them with the people behind us. We must search for them, considering all possibilities. We will send at least three military aircrafts to fly overhead immediately, and they will shine their lights on the bordering lands. We will do the same in the morning. We will use overwhelming force. We will separate the rest of you and give you orders when the sun rises. Promptly arrive here at dawn, and be ready to relentlessly hunt these deranged anarchists. We have come too far from the Black War to allow them to set us back. We, the true pioneers of the new age, will not be defeated!"

The audience of guards roared and waved their weapons above their heads. Chancellor Tibs scanned the impassioned faces, his scattered vision flickering in paranoia, though he cracked a quick smile, satisfied by the aggressive cries of his men, though some blending into the crowd were hesitant. Guards left the Forum to return home, some through the Zanoma Tower and others through the ductways.

*   *   *

Within the hyperloop, Elsan, Tera, and the four rebels reached the hyperloop entranceway in Treton, where the rest of the Guild was standing, waiting. Catching their breath, the six of them hunched over, placing their hands on their knees. Elsan and Tera stood upright and gave each other a warm look rather than paying mind to the other wrights.

"I thought you might be dead," Tera said as tears again spilled from the corners of her eyes. "I thought you might be dead and there was nothing I could do about it but sit in that awful cell and cry."

"I worried about you every second," Elsan said, wrapping his arms around his mother. "But we're back together again and we need to move forward, for Dad. I-I have so much anger inside of me. We need to avenge him at all costs."

"We will," Tera said, placing her hands on Elsan's shoulders and holding him in front of her. "Anger is a truly great emotion if you use it the right way, Elsan. Control it. Your father knew how."

Elsan nodded and said, "Yes, Mom."

He wrapped his arms around his mother again, the two spreading the warmth of their love through each other's grieving hearts. Tera peered over Elsan's shoulder. Garik was standing not too far away, admiring the Amaranths' renewed connection. Tera looked at him, released Elsan from her grasp, and approached him.

"Garik," she said, stepping closer. "You left the city."

"Yes," Garik replied. "It was time to carry out my duties and get out."

"He knows?" Tera asked with soft eyes as Elsan stepped beside her.

Garik nodded and said, "I think, deep down, he believes, but he never wanted to admit it to himself, or cause any trouble for himself or his mother. Hopefully the whole city will believe soon enough. Now, we should continue to the base."

After Garik gave a signal, wrights started to climb up and out of the hyperloop entranceway in Treton. Tera and Elsan stepped in back of countless rebels. Mora and Sairin stood near the front.

"We must move quickly," Macrum said, standing next to Sairin. "There will be military aircrafts flying over our heads very soon. We must get to the forests before they can track us."

Elsan and Tera followed the other wrights out of the hyperloop entranceway, on the edge of the decimated city of Treton, and onto the barren land west of Zanoma. After all wrights escaped the underground, the Guild sprinted away from the entranceway. While it was nearly too dark to see just steps ahead, Tera knew

that the forests were about a half of a mile west of
Treton, which was hidden in the darkness of the night.

After running for quite some time, over the dead
land and through the silhouettes of broken buildings,
the Guild ran into the petrified tree line of the forest. As
they walked deeper, the forest appeared healthier, and
they were protected more and more by the cover of tree
leaves. Still, the rattled rebels jumped beneath black
locusts and white oaks after spotting a light shining in
the distant sky.

Hearts racing, the rebels looked at each other and
bent down, curling their shaking knees to their chests.
The light of the military aircraft weaved between the tree
leaves as they swayed in the evening wind. Seconds of
trepidation passed and the aircraft hovered away, toward
Treton and the northwestern shores.

"We're almost there," Tera said.

Minutes later, Tera spotted a silver maple with a
chip in its trunk. Elsan and the rest of the Guild
followed closely behind as Tera directed the Guild
toward an open area of junipers a short distance from
the silver maple. She leaned over and lifted a hatch.

"Go," Tera said, signaling for Elsan and the
other wrights to enter.

Tera was the last to descend into the base. When
her face showed within the base hallway, after passing
through the vertical conduit, the rebel militia erupted.
Tera could not hold back a smile as she was greeted with
such respect and admiration.

"Tera! Tera! Tera!" many rebels chanted, clapping and cheering for her return.

As Elsan, Tera, and the rest of the wrights settled into the base, Elsan approached Mora with a smile and said, "You were right all along, Mora."

Mora smiled at Elsan and turned to cheer for Tera. Elsan scanned the packed hallway of ardent rebels, smiling at the heartwarming support they had for his mother. Prouder of his mother than ever before, Elsan turned back towards Tera and clapped along with the rest of the Guild, chanting his mother's name with a tenacious tone.

"Thank you!" Tera yelled over the crowd, causing the wrights to stop cheering and listen closely. "Thank you all for the warm welcome back! But it is not the time to celebrate. They will stop at nothing to destroy us now. At dawn, we will prepare. We must act swiftly. The imminent battles that await us will not be won easily."

17

The warm glow of the morning sun crept over the tidelands and permeated through the petrified tree and rock formations of the once fertile western forests, where years of rain from the evaporating ocean deteriorated life above and below ground. It crept over the walls of the city. It was a musky morning in the City of Zanoma, one with agitated air encumbering those left within the city borders.

Guards departed from the basement of the Zanoma Tower. Some groups stomped around the streets of Milbon Hill, some in Wrexon's End, some in South Village, and many in the Industrial District, particularly near the primary hyperloop entranceway. Some other groups were stationed in the ductways, while the rest were sent in military aircrafts to search through the bordering lands in the daylight.

Shouts were heard from the border of the Industrial District and South Village. Guards sprinted to various homes within the village, where brothers, sisters, mothers, and fathers screamed in shock of the sight of those in their families motionless in their beds, having not woken up from their slumber. Many were blistered and had vomit on their sheets.

Oblivious to the calamities happening in South Village, Morin Malva sat at the kitchen table of his suite in the Zanoma Tower, across from Nena Malva. Nena's eyes were not quite as dull as they typically were. They were wider, brighter with heightened perception, as she knew Morin had something important to say.

"I needed to get you out of bed before I left for work," Morin said.

"Well, it must be important," Nena said, her voice softer than the cool morning breeze, yet hard as the solidified soils. "What is it?"

"It's about Dad," Morin replied, Nena's eyes perking a bit. "He… he didn't die the way we've been told, not at the hands of Ainkia's men."

"Morin," Nena said, shaking her head slightly from side to side. "We've heard this before. There's no *real* evidence, and the Republic and Chancellor Tibs were always very loyal to Medrik."

"There's evidence," Morin said, pulling a tablet from his pocket, the tablet that Garik gave to Morin, that Sairin gave to Garik, that Macrum gave to Sairin before that. "We just never saw it before, and we didn't want to believe that it could be true, but I believe it is now. We need to keep our mouths shut for now, or this evidence could disappear."

"Morin," Nena began. "We shouldn't get caught up in these theories."

"You'll see for yourself," Morin replied, beginning to search through the tablet.

He navigated to the surveillance footage that Macrum acquired from the security center in Ainkia that monitored Zanoma's embassy. The video began, showing the still room with the walkway, rails on both sides, piping and equipment supporting ventilation and heat recovery systems outside of the rails. It showed the man wearing the black suit with the Z on the chest running from around the corner of the walkway, and the other man following in a guard's uniform with a Z on the chest as well. The man in the guard's uniform shot the man in the black suit in his back, causing him to flail to the ground. The man in the guard's uniform stepped over the fallen man and shot him again in the back of the head.

Nena's chin quivered as she stared up at Morin, taking her eyes off of the troubling footage. Morin rewinded the video to when the man in the guard's uniform first entered the screen. Both his face and the man in the black suit's face were visible at the same time, so Morin paused the video.

"That's Dad," Morin said. "And that's Evarand Nap. This couldn't have been doctored, not to look like Dad's face or to mimic the way he moves, or to look like Nap's face. It's real. It's as clear as day to me."

"It's him," Nena said, tears starting to trickle from the corners of her eyes. "I never wanted to believe the rumors, and I never wanted to seek out this footage because I was scared, but I think deep inside, I always knew. I'll never forget that face. We saw him for the last time earlier that day. I'll never forget how he looked before taking off. And that's Commander Nap. There's no doubt that that's Nap."

"Tibs was behind it, Mom," Morin said, speaking quieter but more directly. "One of the guards told me. Tibs saw an opportunity to control the world and ran out of road. He's manipulated all of us. The head officials he appointed as Chancellor—they're just like him—hungry for power, paranoid of being exposed. His men control the central receiver and all of the city's networks. They're conquering the other territories. The men who killed Dad continue to secure more power. We can't keep hiding from this."

Nena leaned back in her chair, pouring tears, clearly overwhelmed, but swallowed and said, "What can we do?"

"Nothing, until the rebels come back. Someday soon, our influence will be crucial," Morin said. "I need to report for work. Will you be alright?"

"I'll be alright," Nena said.

Morin descended several stories to Chancellor Tibs' suite. Tibs stood near the translucent walls, staring down at his city. At the gentle rumble of the private elevator, Tibs looked to his left to see Morin entering the common area of the suite. Morin stepped toward Chancellor Tibs decorously.

"You wanted to see me, Chancellor?" Morin said, as Tibs had requested him that morning.

"Yes," Chancellor Tibs said as Morin stepped beside him, also staring down at the city while some movement came about near South Village. "We need to make a report. It's a bit last minute, so I couldn't get the typical camerawoman here. I'll need you to operate the camera. They'll be ready for us at the central receiver whenever we notify them. Do you remember how?"

"Yes," Morin answered.

"Good."

"What happened?" Morin asked.

"There have been a series of deaths so far this morning, and I fear it will continue," Tibs said, causing Morin's eyes to widen.

"How?" Morin asked. "What happened?"

"The water supply in South Village—it's been poisoned," Tibs began, causing Morin's eyes to widen more for a moment as he fought the instinct to narrow his eyes in anger, knowing that he could no longer trust his leader. "Several of our guards joined Riklin Amaranth's anarchist group. We believe that they contaminated one of the facilities near a grouping of tower blocks in the slums."

"Atrocious people, those anarchists are," Morin said. "Now they have our men, too. It seems like it may never end."

Chancellor Tibs turned away from the city view. He gave Morin a curious look as he was surprised that Morin was so short of words, so cold in his tone rather than being soft spoken like he normally was. Tibs sighed and stepped a bit closer to Morin, who had turned to face Tibs as well.

"Hopefully we can do something to make it end," Tibs said with strong focus on Morin's eyes and a wry grin. "Is there anything else you'd like to say before we begin?"

Morin gulped, shook his head slightly from side to side, and said, "No. These things have happened so many times—I'm just numb."

"As are we all," Tibs replied.

On the public monitors, home television projectors, the projector in the western rebel base, and tablets, Chancellor Tibs gave the early morning announcement, saying, "As you all know, Zanoma has been faced with various forms of chemical warfare in the past, during the Black War by enemy territories and even after by anarchist groups. As we expected, the food that was distributed to the homes in South Village were contaminated, as confirmed by our food scientists in the Sustenance Sector. And that's not all. Within one day of the food distribution, there have already been several reported deaths in South Village due to drinking water contamination. It is believed that the crime is linked to a group of thirteen guards who later released the rebel group. These men are traitors—make no mistake. Residents in South Village reported blistering, vomiting, and for a dozen people so far, a permanent loss of breath, all during just one night. We fear that more fatalities will be reported as a result of this contamination. We urge those living in South Village to join their neighbors in other areas of the city for drinking water, or to find drinking water at public facilities within the Industrial District.

Many of you were likely already aware that the rebel group involved with the food contamination scheme was freed last night. As I mentioned, the same guards believed to have poisoned the water in South Village were also behind the escape. It is strongly believed that the rebels have escaped Zanoma's borders, so we urge all of you to keep a keen eye out for any suspicious behavior. Our guards are working in full force, both within Zanoma and in the air outside of Zanoma, to find the escaped anarchists and bring them back to justice. Thank you all for listening."

Ermin turned off his tablet and placed it on the kitchen table of the Muttin home. Daemyn and Moriah sat beside him and watched his face as he picked his head up. Daemyn sensed his hesitancy, as his shift at the Zanoma Tower started in less than an hour.

"You still need to go to work, Ermin," Daemyn said. "He didn't say anything against that, and we have an obligation to our government."

"Dad, the anarchists are on the loose," Ermin began. "People in Zanoma, people in the South Village Slums… they're starting to become restless. There have been bigger and bigger crowds outside of the Zanoma

Tower and in the Central Node every day. There are riots in the streets and in the ductways constantly, and apparently, our guards aren't enough to keep us safe. How am I supposed to feel safe at work? How am I supposed to feel safe in the ductways and in the streets? Why would you two, of all people, want me to go in on a day like this?"

"The people of Zanoma can't afford a day off," Moriah said. "We can't back down and hide at home all day. We need to perform our daily duties. We can't succumb to these low-life agitators. Their power will only grow stronger if we lose our way of life. More people will go hungry and more people will resort to violence. The Republic needs us, and we need them. Anarchists won't stop that."

"What if the rebels have a greater purpose?" Ermin proposed to his obstinate parents. "What if Riklin was a victim of corruption? What if there are things that the Republic isn't telling us?"

"Don't be foolish, Ermin," Daemyn retorted. "Riklin died because of his violent resistance to the guards, who were just doing their jobs."

"How do you know?" Ermin questioned. "Did you talk to the rebels, or are you just trusting the words of Daiton Tibs? No one saw Riklin being transported from his home. No one saw what happened."

"Chancellor Tibs allows the great spirit of Medrik Malva to live on," Daemyn bellowed. "He stands for the pride that Medrik Malva had in Zanoma. I'm not going to trust the words of lawless people."

"I know Elsan," Ermin said, more subdued, yet stern. "There's more to this than we all know."

"Maybe you didn't know Elsan or the Amaranth family as well as you thought. We've been loyal to the Republic our whole lives. We won't change that now. We want to be a part of the future."

"So do I," Ermin said, pushing his chair back, standing to his feet, clenching his jaw, grabbing his work supplies, opening the door of the Muttin home and slamming it closed behind him.

Ermin walked through the streets, as countless Zanoma residents did throughout the city. Fires blazed within every heart. Some were angry at the rebel militia, in belief that they were truly responsible for the recent food shortage and the poisoning of their neighbors in the South Village Slums. Some were angry at Chancellor Tibs for failing to protect them, and some in belief that Tibs ordered the poisoning of the water supply. Some could not find the crux of their fury, but flooded the ductways blindly, as Ermin had.

In South Village, poor families fled the slums as reports of fatalies continued to come out, further fueling residents to rush the ductways in a panic. More than two dozen more residents of the South Village Slums began blistering, vomiting, and ultimately taking their final breaths. News spread, and the havoc within the ductways intensified.

Ermin paced through the ductways, peering over at different groups forming before his eyes. People surrounded residents speaking out against Chancellor

Tibs. Others surrounded residents, and some guards, speaking out against Riklin Amaranth's rebel following. Residents searched for answers from their neighbors, settling for those that brought any sense to the tragedies and suffering.

"We must maintain faith in the lessons we've learned from Medrik Malva," a man said, projecting his voice over a group of residents as Ermin walked by. "We must protect Zanoma at all costs!"

A bit further, Ermin passed a crowd of residents rallying around another man, who shouted, "We cannot stand idle as they kill our neighbors!"

Moments later, Ermin walked through Wrexon's End Ductway, where a large crowd gathered around a guard, who kept his weapons to his side. It was a guard previously stationed in Ornaia who had been detained and ultimately freed by the rebel militia. Residents surrounded the guard, keeping quiet, appearing more astonished than other groups. As Ermin stepped closer, he could hear the guard speak.

"I was stationed in Ornaia, before the rebel army invaded our facilities," the guard said to the small audience in front of him. "I have seen the severity of the violence that the rebels are willing to inflict on people who get in their way, but the atrocities commited by the leaders of the Republic of Zanoma, before the Black War and after, even today, is unrivaled. They are responsible for more death than any few beings in our planet's history—and I was one of their sheep. My partner and children were protected and enriched, and I convinced myself that that was all I cared about, but I can no longer blindly support men who place such little value on human life. I can no longer support Chancellor Tibs, Commander Nap, or their loyal followers. I can no longer be a member of this depraved family that Tibs built. I will join all of you to fight back!"

Many roared in respect of the guard, while some backed out of the crowd, yelling, "Traitor!"

Chancellor Tibs overlooked the city from the common area of his suite, seemingly detached and devoid of emotion. He watched as his people gravitated toward groups of neighbors with shared views, as crowds warped continuously through the streets and public ductways. He watched as these groups rallied against one another, pushing up against each other within the major intersections of boroughs, the Central Node, and the Industrial District.

Hostile hoards of residents became violent, as many grew tired of hollering at one another to no avail. People swung fists, shoved, and pulled each other's clothing in passion, yet without purity in their motives. Through the chaos, truly confused residents clung to any belief that would give them purpose in the fight for the future of their world.

Guards stationed around all entrances of the Zanoma Tower as enraged groups of residents approached. Residents screamed outside of the Sustenance Sector, demanding more answers from Shylo Cob, but the Head of the Sustenance Sector remained indoors. Residents rabbled outside of the Forum, outside of entrances to other government-controlled buildings, and within the Central Node, demanding more answers from their Chancellor, but Tibs remained in his suite, standing still at his window and staring down at his perturbed people.

Throughout the city, guards spread toward congested areas with the intention of deescalating the tension between wrathful residents. They stood at the edges of intersections and created a ring around the Central Node, many pushing through crowds to pull residents apart and freeze others with fear as they held their weapons in hand. Residents supporting the Republic cheered for the guards. Those supporting the Guild screamed at the guards, but stood back knowing that the guards were quick to pull their triggers when provoked by their own people.

Merged within a group of rebel supporters in the Central Node, Ermin was energized. He was as clear in his beliefs of Elsan's true character as he had been before Elsan's escape from the city. He was trusting of the rebel supporters, and the rebel army, whom he hoped would soon return. Moriah and Daemyn Muttin awaited Ermin's return home, gauging the fear in each other's eyes as concerns for his safety emerged while some aerial footage of the civil unrest played on their television projector.

The ductways were quickly controlled by the guards, causing those in contempt of the Republic to join those rallying outside of the Sustenance Sector. Fearful residents yelled at the guards defending the entrance as death reports dwindled, but continued to come out and spread throughout the city. Residents continued berating the guards, minds in fragments, desparate for answers.

Ermin returned home to Daemyn and Moriah, who greeted him at the front door with open arms. They sighed, relaxed their shoulders, and pulled Ermin in to hug him harder than they had in quite some time. Ermin rested his head on his father's shoulder, his eyes fixated on the ground behind Daemyn.

"I couldn't stay," Ermin said.

"It's alright," Moriah said. "We saw what's happening. We're just happy that you're safe at home again. We're sorry we pressured you to go."

"It's alright," Ermin said, sitting in a chair at the kitchen table with Daemyn sitting on one side and Moriah sitting on the other. "But I can't rest. The people who poisoned the water won't rest, so I can't rest. We can't rest."

"Anarchists have attacked the people of Zanoma many times," Daemyn said. "That is true. But we must trust our guards to protect us and bring them to justice. They've dismantled many anarchist groups over the years since the Black War."

"I wasn't talking about any anarchists," Ermin retorted. "I was referring to Chancellor Tibs, Shylo Cob, Evarand Nap, and their followers."

"Don't tell me you're falling for those preposterous theories," Daemyn said.

"A guard in the ductways spoke out against our leaders. He said he was stationed in Ornaia for years. His family was enriched and protected by Chancellor Tibs. Why would he lie about his own wrongdoings?"

Daemyn sighed, shrugged and said, "Don't be so quick to believe everything you hear, Ermin. Besides, even if this were true, we don't want you getting caught in a violent outbreak. We love you and we worry about you getting hurt."

Ermin took a breath and ultimately cracked a smile, enjoying the warmth of his father's words. Yet, his smile faded, as he knew Elsan and the rebel army required as much support as possible from the residents of Zanoma. He did not want to let anyone down—not his parents, not Elsan, and not his neighbors—but the world needed to be freed of tyranny.

As during any other night, Zanoma residents returned to their homes, though many were uneasy. Families mourned the many lives lost in South Village. They ate their approved rations of food as they hoped within their hearts that justice would soon come for the souls of their poisoned neighbors.

New rations still were not delivered to the South Village Sustenance Center, though even the frailest likely would have ignored them due to losses of appetite. Parents, siblings, children, and friends consoled each other as the bodies of those lost to malfeasance continued to be transported to the Health Sector to be given postmortem examinations. Fydel Cob, Head of the Health Sector, was present, if only to appear devoted to the forgotten residents of South Village.

*   *   *

Twilight came and passed. Within the western base, wrights began resting, at least physically, after spending the day assembling and gathering weapons in preparation of the battles to come. No plan of attack had been made yet, though the Guild believed that they had the necessary time while still being hidden from the Republic with their weapons ready.

Elsan sat beside his mother at a table within the dining area of the base after the Guild had eaten dinner together. Tera rubbed his back as he rested his head on her shoulder. The warmth radiating from their hearts helped to fill the void left by Riklin, if only for a moment.

"Elsan," Tera said, causing Elsan to lift his head from her shoulder and look into her eyes. "I want you to remember something. You're not a soldier. You must stay protected as much as possible. The people will need you after this is all over. Your brains, your affection, your strength—you're becoming more like Riklin every day. The people can't afford to lose both of you."

"I'm not Dad," Elsan said. "I'm just a pair of young eyes, seeing what he fought for and doing my part. I need to fight like everyone else."

Tera took a deep breath, her tired eyes glazed, and said, "I love you, Elsan."

Elsan smiled slightly and said, "I love you too, Mom."

18

The revitalized rebel militia awoke within the western base while it was still dark outside. Elsan, Tera, Davlin and Paxtus tiptoed above the base, peering between tree leaves to scope out the distant skies above the City of Zanoma for military aircraft. After spotting several above the dead lands south of the city, the four wrights looked around at each other and nodded. Elsan squatted to open the hatch door, but was halted by the crack of a bush limb.

He stood up abruptly, stomped around an anxious Tera, and raised his weapon. After a few steps past an evergreen, he spotted a blacktail deer. It appeared healthy, yet fearful of the rebels as it darted in the opposite direction, toward the city. The four overstrung wrights released a sigh of relief.

The Guild ate breakfast in the kitchen, seemingly not worried about an impending attack, savoring each bite of rice and beans. They did not know how long the standoff with the Republic would last, or whether they would be the assailants or the hosts of the brutal battles to come. Food storage would support the great number of wrights within the base for only three days, though the wrights knew their time at the base would be short, hungry or not.

Men and woman, young and old, took a moment to reflect after years of a battle of wills. Some hung their heads in anticipation of a fateful bloodbath, while others prayed for an enlightened world, an age of rapturous hope. Elsan was different. His world transformed in ways he had never thought possible, in a severely short amount of time, so his heart held the strangers who would soon have the same experience, at least as it related to the many unknown truths about the Republic and the many unsought consequences of the Republic's actions. Innocent victims, these strangers were that Elsan empathized with, unaware that their goodness greatly exceeded the evil in the world. For the first time since the Black War, the air outside of the city walls felt lighter, less burdened by the weight of the past.

Elsan muted the mundane clamor of the nearby wrights. He was overcome with a vision, a vision that Riklin had when he chose to form the Guild. An image of a peaceful, fruitful world manifested in Elsan's mind, forming a fog that suffocated him. Within his mind, he vowed that he would carry that vision through each step, each movement, each spoken word. Sitting in silence, he held a spoon with a heap of heated beans steadily in front of his closed mouth.

"Elsan, my son," Tera said, placing her hand over his shoulder and leaning her head toward his. "What are you thinking about?"

"Nothing," Elsan said, staring down at his food and taking a second to breathe. "I'm just tired. My mind is still working to wake up."

"Well, eat your food. We could be surprised at any moment. You need to be ready."

"I will be."

Elsan and Tera were joined by Mora, Sairin, Paxtus, Davlin, Garik, Macrum and two other militia leaders within the dining area, each holding half-portions of beans, barley, and cabbage. The two militia leaders were similar in stature to Paxtus and Davlin. As they sat along the dining table, their avid eyes focused on Elsan.

"Elsan," Sairin began, holding his palm up and turning toward the two wrights. "This is Karum and Heron. Karum is from Cronen. Heron is from Ainkia, like Macrum."

Karum had dark hair and dark skin. Heron had light brown hair and fair skin. Both held the same dour expression, as the other militia leaders tended to.

"Very nice to meet you both," Elsan said as Karum and Heron nodded back in reverence. "Thank you for joining my father's mission."

"Speaking for all of us, your father," Karum began speaking to Elsan before turning his eyes toward Tera. "Your partner, was a great man. We'll fight for his spirit alongside you, and we'll finish what he started. We thank you for continuing to fight as well."

"Well, our next moves are critical," Tera said. "We can't be stagnant. They want to defeat us outside of those walls. We can't let that happen, or else we'll disappear and be forgotten, or be made historically infamous. And whatever we do, we must plan well so we can preserve as many lives as possible."

"I agree, but we aren't prepared to fight them yet," Sairin said. "They'll be ready in full force. They have twice as many guards as we have men and woman, and stronger weapons. We can't just charge in."

"Maybe we can," Elsan said, causing everyone at the table to look over at him.

"What do you mean?" Mora asked.

"There's more animosity toward Chancellor Tibs than ever before, even than when the rumors about his involvement in Medrik Malva's death spread throughout the city, and the Republic looks weaker than ever before. The Republic may be placing blame on us for poisoning those people, they may be rallying their strongest supporters against us as we speak, but the people of Zanoma are starting to pay attention to what we're doing, their fear of the Republic is waning, and their resistance has become stronger every day, despite Tibs' attempts to defame us. They'll continue to kill the innocent and blame it on us, the *anarchists*. We may never have as much support as we do now and people are dying because of it. Our militia may be outnumbered by their guards, but there are many numbers of people more."

"So, what are you suggesting?" Tera asked.

"I'm suggesting that we make ourselves seen, that we force the people to see this battle for what it is, whether they support us or not. I'm suggesting that we don't die in the dark."

*   *   *

The morning skies were brooding, the air laden with incertitude. For the ways of force were finally being challenged. Guards were stationed within the streets and ductways, outside of the Forum and the Sustenance Sector, in Wrexon's End and Milbon Hill, and within the Central Node in preparation of the continued hysteria. Many of the henchmen paced haphazardly around tower blocks in Milbon Hill, Wrexon's End, and South Village. Most others were in the Industrial District, watching carefully in the ductways, in the streets below, at the bases of buildings, and around the hyperloop entranceway. Within the Zanoma Tower, guards stood at tower entrances, against hallway corners, and inside workrooms.

Chancellor Tibs sat in silence at a dining table within the common area of his suite, avoiding the breakfast that was prepared for him. Sipping on a tall glass of purified water, he swallowed reluctantly and smacked his lips. He leaned his head on his hand as his elbow rested atop the arm of his chair. His leg shook rapidly as the metal walls seemed closer than ever before, the translucent walls more tinted with the taut shade from the edges of the planet.

*   *   *

Dew dribbled down the boots of the rebels as they coalesced above the western base in the blue hour of the morning. A battle between the rulers of nightfall would soon begin. Leaders of the Guild stood at the front of their army of vindictive warriors. Chins quivered with the brisk breeze and hands fidgeted with the hounding trepidation. The wrights started to march forward, their focus on the battles that lay ahead, and particularly the skies above.

As the wrights walked further away from the base, the moss blackened, the copper tint of the tree trunks became stronger, and the dancing leaves started to disappear. The rebels were silent, enough so to hear the buzz of a fruit fly as it fed upon nearby plants. Ninebarks and holly bushes started to cover the lands between the trees, though none of these plants had leaves to cloak the rebel army. Wrights kept their eyes on the skies above, knowing that they were exposed for the Republic to attack by air.

After creeping cautiously through the forests, the Guild moved into position at the edge of the desolate wasteland of Treton, dreaming of freeing the people of Zanoma and the future of humanity from the perils of the world. There were partially collapsed tower blocks on either side of the militia. Wrights howled and bellowed, which with fortified integrity tethered the Guild together. Paxtus, Davlin, Garik, Macrum, Karum, and Heron trudged through the northern side of the circle of followers as a small walkway was opened to them. After they reached the front of the rebel army, the circle reclosed, cramming Elsan, Tera, Sairin and Mora to the center. Paxtus waved his right hand, and the Guild began marching behind his lead. Elsan stomped forward, beside his mother, with centered vision, life clutching to the creeping morning sun. For in his mind, the world would soon be in his hands, in rebel hands, to be rebuilt alongside the liberated.

Fractured infrastructure laid on either side of the militia as they continued in the direction of Zanoma. Behind Paxtus' lead, and subsequently the lead of the other rebel leaders, the Guild started to sprint with their sights set in the direction of the hyperloop entranceway at the edge of the abandoned City of Treton. The rebel militia reached a row of disintegrated buildings when they suddenly held still.

A distant hum came to the rebel army's attention and quickly grew louder, so the wrights stopped and stared at the distant sapphire skies. A military aircraft appeared, followed by three more. The wrights started to sprint faster, knowing that their lives may depend on their ability to reach the hyperloop entranceway before the military aircrafts could strike them. The military aircrafts grew larger in the sky, and the purr of their motors resonated through the rebel militia.

"Hurry!" Heron hollered to the rebels behind him. "Just a bit further!"

As the military aircrafts neared striking distance, Sairin yelled from the center of the group, "Spread apart or they'll kill us all!"

The Guild separated from one another and continued sprinting toward the hyperloop entranceway, some seeking cover from what remained of the buildings in Treton. After several minutes, Heron spotted the general area of the hyperloop entranceway. In that moment, the military aircrafts came within firing range. The first bomb was fired from a military aircraft, followed by a grouping of smaller bombs. The first bomb blasted the ground within the latter half ot the rebel army, and the small bombs landed short distances apart from each other throughout the trailing stampede of wrights. Many lives were claimed instantly by the horrific detonations, while many rebels were left with maimed limbs to bleed to their deaths beside the further crumbling components of the Treton infrastructure. Elsan scanned around in terror as his legs seemed to uncontrollably pick up speed.

Heron reached the hyperloop entranceway, but before he could guide his followers into the hyperloop, a bomb exploded at the top of the entranceway. As Heron's life, and the lives of several followers, abruptly came to an end, the entrance to the hyperloop widened, petrified soils launching into the air like fireworks. Wrights started to storm over fragments of metal sheets, poles and walls, some stumbling over chunks of concrete. Bombs continued to drop from the first military aircraft, as the second began striking the crowds of panicked men and women, who wanted nothing more than to find safety as quickly as they could. Ears ringing from the overwhelming blasts of nearby bombs, Elsan reached the gaping entranceway and awaited his mother, Mora, and Sairin as they neared the hyperloop.

Paxtus, Davlin, Macrum, and Karum were able to enter the hyperloop entranceway unharmed, while Garik was left behind in a mass of smoke, misery, and lifeless men and women. Most bomb fragments pierced into the crusted soil, while some penetrated the legs, backs, arms, necks, chests, sides and heads of the rebels. Chests pounding, no one knew if they would be next, where the bombs would land, or where the bomb fragments would strike them. Many died upon impact, while others laid wounded in the legs and sides with no hope to survive the day. In horror, Elsan continued to search for Tera, Mora, and Sairin.

"Just a bit further!" Mora shouted as Tera and Sairin followed closely behind, coming into Elsan's sight for the first time.

Suddenly, Sairin dropped directly flat to the arid ground with bomb fragments piercing his neck and chest, curling his fingers and hunching his back as he rolled over and gasped desparately for air. Mora halted and turned to see her brother's chest, then completely still, bleeding out. Tears filled her eyes as she cried in vexing trauma, though Elsan snatched her off of her feet and carried her toward the tunnel entrance. Mora wailed and flailed her arms and legs as Tera grabbed her arm, forcing her to move forward after Elsan lowered her feet back down to the ground.

"Sairin!" Mora screamed, eyes filling with tears, face red with agony and brown with dirt, as Tera held her still and pulled her closer to the hyperloop entranceway. "Sairin, no!"

After Tera and Mora descended into the hyperloop, Elsan waved more of his counterparts inside. Five rebels were able to enter safely, though another round of bombs were fired from the four military aircrafts. The entranceway was not struck, though the bombs dismantled many more of the trailing wrights as Elsan watched, sickened, from a distance.

Mora bawled profusely, looking back at Elsan with the smoke from the detonations beyond him as she was tugged further toward the hyperloop by Tera. Elsan turned to Tera and Mora to grasp both of their hands so he could descend into the hyperloop before the next barrage of bombs. The expanded entranceway allowed several other wrights to enter alongside Elsan at once, and many more followed.

Bombs again erupted the surrounding soils, killing several more wrights as they attempted to enter the underground. Only a small group of rebels remained on the outside. They raced into the beginning of the entranceway as several small bombs were dropped in their vicinity. Nearly half were slain, while the other half were able to enter the hyperloop without harm, each of them panting heavily, trying to slow their racing hearts to continue forward without fainting.

The air assault claimed the lives of nearly a third of the Guild before the last remaining wrights funneled into the escape tunnel, falling over one another as they skipped over the bent rungs of the broken concrete and the contorted aluminum and steel. Within the hyperloop, disturbed rebels stared at one another in both fear and grief, though some were too busy wrapping cloth tightly around the lacerated arms of agonized rebels. Spattered blood and coatings from clouds of dirt spotted the skin of the living wrights as they processed their devastating losses, though they knew there was little time to mourn their beloved friends and family.

Elsan held Mora firmly within his solacing arms. Tears trickled down his face, while streams spouted from Mora's eyes. For her lamented brother, a devout combatant for the rebel cause, would only be reborn in eternal spirit.

Though the rebel militia was hidden from view, they were aware that the other end of the hyperloop would soon be found, so they ran toward the vanishing point. The rout of rebels sprinted with all of the strength left in their legs. Tears of trauma dried while they trickled down their faces, as there was no time to weep for the lives that were so curtly consumed by the cruelty of war—not while they were still at war themselves. Their tired legs managed to continue moving them forward, instinctually, as they knew that they could not turn back.

At the thud of the two military aircrafts landing above their heads, the wrights scurried more hastily through the hyperloop as the dim, amber lights began to flicker. After several seconds, rebels turned their heads, expecting to see bullets bouncing toward them, ricocheting off of the distant walls. Yet, still not a single guard was in sight.

Suddenly, a detonation was heard in the direction of the entranceway of the tunnel, but a bit closer to the wrights. It was sharp enough to halt the hoards of rebels in their tracks. Wrights turned and watched as the ceiling of the hyperloop and the soil above fell between the Guild and the lifeless bodies of those last killed at the entranceway of the hyperloop, sending a rumble through the floor of the hyperloop passageway. The tunnel lights, the electricity that Riklin spent years masking, turned off, causing the rebel militia to be engulfed by a daunting darkness.

The wrights again sprinted forward. Some held flashlights as steadily as possible, while others reached for the shoulders of those in front. Stumbling over each other's feet, the rebels chaotically proceeded through the deep black of the underground.

*   *   *

Rebel supporters flocked into the ductways, as well as supporters of the Republic. Many confused residents lingered at home with their bloodshot eyes fixated on television projectors, hopelessly awaiting some more comforting words from their Chancellor. That moment never came, and many residents proceeded to the Forum for safety, crying and mumbling hopeful words before the cast stone statue of Medrik Malva, though the Muttin family remained at home.

Without his parents seeing, Ermin left the Muttin home and strayed toward Wrexon's End Ductway to stand alongside residents protesting the leaders of the Republic, who chanted in unison. Daemyn and Moriah Muttin searched throughout their home for Ermin, becoming more and more agitated as they went room to room. With the ghastly semblence of their faces, Daemyn and Moriah knew they would need to find their son and drag him back home.

Dodging residents in the streets, Daemyn and Moriah focused their frightened eyes on anyone who looked like Ermin from a distance, though it became difficult as residents bustled frenetically in all directions.

They became frustrated, overwhelmed by the vast, divergent streets. Setting their sites north, they saw crowds of residents entering the staircase to Wrexon's End Ductway, so they followed.

"Ermin!" Moriah screamed after arising one floor to Wrexon's End Ductway.

"Ermin!" Daemyn shouted desparately as he began drowning between countless residents who walked slowly behind the many others pushing forward in front of them. "Ermin!"

Within the Zanoma Tower, Commander Nap rushed to Chancellor Tibs' office after hearing a report from one of the pilots. Panting, he walked into the office with one hand at his side. His eyes were wide in alarm, his back more hunched than was typical of him.

"Chancellor Tibs," he said, catching his breath. "The rebels are going to pass below the city border. They entered the underground in the path of the hyperloop. Our pilots were able to kill many of them, and they were able to collapse the tunnel west of Zanoma, so they can only move in one direction. We must send our men to the hyperloop entranceway in the Industrial District. We must prepare for the arrival of the rebel army."

"Your orders are approved," Chancellor Tibs said. "You may send the message to our men who are scattered around the city. Tell those in Wrexon's End, Milbon Hill and South Village to shift their focus to the Industrial District and the hyperloop pathway. Tell them to ready their weapons."

Commander Nap nodded, pulled his tablet from his side and spoke into its microphone, "Men in Wrexon's End, Milbon Hill and South Village, report to the Industrial District, near the hyperloop entranceway. The rebel militia may be approaching as we speak. Move swiftly, and be aware that they will likely come through the hyperloop entranceway very soon. More importantly, prepare for combat."

Guards moved toward the Industrial District as Commander Nap ordered them to. Every one of them gripped their guns tightly, keeping a finger on the trigger, knowing that the rebel army could arise from the underground at any moment.

"They'll be waiting in the Industrial District," Paxtus said to Macrum as the Guild approached the vertical conduit of the ventilation shaft on an abandoned industrial lot on the northern side of Milbon Hill. "We should go up here."

"You're right," Macrum said, before raising his voice to speak to the rest of the Guild. "We will rise through the ventilation shaft here. After we remove the grate, we will need to escape the shaft one by one as quickly as possible. We will be spotted, and they will come to get us."

The Guild began climbing up the ventilation shaft, led by Macrum, Paxtus, Davlin, Garik, Karum, and Heron. Macrum detached the grate and ducked out of the ventilation shaft structure to the abandoned lot, immediately raising his weapon and scanning in all directions. Wrights followed one by one and raised their weapons as well.

The front line consisted of Paxtus, Davlin, Macrum, Karum and many of the rebel army's top shooters. They spread along the lot. As they lifted their guns, several guards came into sight, taking aim at the Guild.

"Drop your wea-" one wright started to yell before being interrupted by a bullet to the neck.

At that moment, bullets began flying through the air. Flashes of flickering steel darted past the eyes of some and struck others. Two of the Guild's top shooters fell back onto the asphalt. The front line had been depleted, but the first wave of guards had been killed off. With just a small window of time to spare, the wrights continued to surge from the underground like a boiling geyser.

19

"Lower your weapons!" Davlin yelled, stepping toward another group of guards with his gun raised and his finger on the trigger, but the guards kept their guns held high. "Lower your weapons or we will take you out! Lower your weapons!"

As more and more rebels arose from the underground, the guards gradually retreated further and further. Still, the standoff became more and more overwrought with the arrival of guards from other directions. The retreating guards were growing more fortified by the incoming support as both sides continued to leave their triggers still.

"Lower your weapons!" Davlin yelled again.

The guards instead fired toward the Guild, and the front line of the rebel militia started to fire back at the guards, not only in retaliation, but in knowing that they could not allow all of the guards throughout the city grounds to come and overpower them while they were still out of sight from most residents, who aggregated toward the Industrial District. Other wrights joined, shooting bullets at the front line of guards. Several guards were killed, while others chose to give up their weapons and allow the Guild to move forward toward the entrance of Milbon Hill Ductway.

"Protect the Amaranths!" Davlin commanded. "Move quickly and be ready to fire!"

The rebel militia encircled Tera, Mora, and Elsan while continuing to aim their guns at the guards. As the Guild moved under the ductways, they continued to quash guards who threatened them, while deterring and detaining others, intimidating them into dropping their weapons and laying with their faces to the ground. Within sight was the entrance to the staircase up to Milbon Hill Ductway, where guards were stationed along the walls, monitoring the route to the Central Node. Residents in Milbon Hill Ductway saw the rebel rampage occurring below and ran for the Central Node, regardless of who they supported.

"Run!" Elsan hollered as a small grenade suddenly appeared in the air, soaring in the direction of the Guild.

The Guild took off, sprinting in the direction of the Central Node, attempting to clear the area they anticipated the grenade to land on. The grenade exploded on the back end of the group of wrights, killing several instantly. Some rebels cried at the loss of their friends, while others forced them forward. Fearful of retaliation, the guard who threw the grenade, and those around him, entered the staircase leading up to Milbon Hill Ductway. The Guild slowed its pace and the wrights raised their weapons, gripping them tightly, faces pressed against the sides, as they approached the doorway to the staircase.

The Guild's formation loosened and the back line backpedaled, so as to protect the rebel militia's rear. Some guards chased from behind, though the back line of rebels were able to shoot some down while scaring away the others. At the front, a bullet from a distance struck Davlin's neck, killing him within seconds, while two more bullets took the lives of two others along the back line. Wrights in the front line quickly swung the doorway open.

Backpedaling wrights turned to enter the staircase behind the rest of the Guild, as there was no longer a threat coming from behind. Bullets ricocheted off of the metal exterior of the staircase, killing several more wrights before they could enter the staircase. Guards in Milbon Hill Ductway prepared their weapons. Paxtus, Garik, Macrum, and Karum climbed the staircase with countless wrights ascending behind them. They raised their weapons as well, their fingers trembling over the triggers.

"Move aside!" Paxtus yelled after thrusting open the doorway at the top of the staircase to Milbon Hill Ductway, though the guards inside remained still with their weapons raised. "Move aside or you will be shot dead! Move now!"

The guards ran toward the Central Node in a panic to find greater numbers, allowing the Guild to march untouched toward the Central Node with untiring tenacity. Elsan, Tera, and Mora were pushed through the remaining rebels toward the front while being defended from all angles still. Wrights entered the Central Node and spread to gather residents, some of whom were frightened and frantically ran for cover behind guards, while others were receptive of the Guild's intentions.

"May I have everyone's attention, please?" Tera said, projecting her voice throughout the Central Node and through the nearby ductways, attracting residents to surround the great number of rebels, both between the wrights and the guards and behind the guards, whose numbers were increasing as others filtered in. "This is a very important announcement. What you have been hearing from Chancellor Tibs is not true. The fear that many of you have of the rebel group is because he associates us with the violent ramifications of anarchy. There is an image of who we are engrained within you by Chancellor Tibs, Amon Sarato, and their propaganda machine. The rebel group has never had ill intentions for the people of Zanoma. We have and always will defend the future of the people of Zanoma. We are creating a new world, a world shaped by the lessons of the past, no longer stuck in its ways."

While residents both heckled and cheered Tera, Elsan stepped through the crowd of rebels to stand in front with Tera and said, "To all of you that have followed the words of Chancellor Tibs, today is the day that those words become meaningless. My father, Riklin Amaranth, was killed at the hands of Evarand Nap, as Medrik Malva was, for attempting to expose the Republic's agenda. Chancellor Tibs has made you believe that my father died while attempting to bring lawlessness to Zanoma, but that is nothing more than a mischaracterization of my father's true message. Tibs has made you believe that the rebel group poisoned the food and water of the people we are actually trying to protect. It was Chancellor Tibs and Shylo Cob who commanded the chemical warfare against their own people, who poisoned and murdered the poor as they had done to the rest of the world. They will continue to let the South Village Slums starve, as well as the distant survivors of the world that they've been funneling morsels of food to and essentially governing, without the people of Zanoma knowing, since the Black War. They will continue to put bullets in those who give them even the slightest justifaction. They will continue to hoard resources for themselves and their most loyal followers. They will continue to protect their power and control the world for their own welfare. We must not act out of refusal to doubt our leaders, for conspiracy has plagued our planet before the Black War, during the Black War, and to this day. With your support, we can defeat their regime once and for all!"

All with narrowed eyes and gritted teeth, some residents clamored in support, thrusting their fists into the air, while others screamed, "Anarchists!"

In an attempt to overcome being pilloried by angry residents, Elsan raised his voice louder and continued, "Yes, anarchist is the label Chancellor Tibs has used to demonize us, but that is not who we are, and anarchy is not what we represent. We simply want to bring justice, trust, and long-term sustainability to Zanoma. Chancellor Tibs and his closest followers have lied to you all for too long. These are sick sociopaths who slipped into insanity a decade ago. They aimed to steal wealth and defend that wealth from the rest of the world through the Black War, and they aim to defend what remains of that wealth from our own people now. Other world leaders had the same idea, and this greed is what caused the destruction of the planet. Yet, we stand here today with a chance to create a new world. We will expose Chancellor Tibs and his accomplices. We will will not let them determine our fate!"

Rebel supporters roared as Elsan finished his impassioned speech, though supporters of the Republic continued to scorn Elsan, Tera, the rebel leaders to their sides, and the wrights behind them, distrusting them still. After looking into the eyes of those who opposed him, Elsan noticed that none were subdued. His heart raced, knowing that the unconditional devotion to the order of the Republic, the worship of the legacy of Medrik Malva that they had defined through the words of Chancellor Tibs, would overpower his words. Paxtus and Karum noticed as well, sensing that supporters of the Republic could respond violently against the rebel militia in that moment, so they pulled Elsan back and between them. They raised their weapons, as did Macrum and other front-line shooters. Rebel supporters also merged in front of the Guild, pushing supporters of the Republic back toward the frozen guards on the opposite side of the Central Node.

Chatter spread like wildfire throughout the ductways leading away from the Central Node. More and more people gravitated toward the Central Node as guards rushed through the incoming hoards of residents with the intention of weakening the Guild's position. Elsan looked at his sprightly mother, who nodded at him while residents began arguing amongst each other. The rabbling of the residents within the Central Node, and within the ductways leading away from the Central Node, grew louder by the second.

Elsan peered over the crowd of Zanoma residents in the center of the Central Node and down Wrexon's End Ductway, straight ahead. Behind a clogged coterie of energized men and women was a fleet of guards. The same was true for the other four ductways, and the unyielding tension escalated, as supporters of the Republic were fortified, confident in the forces surrounding them. Ermin suddenly appeared within the crowd, weaving through the dense groupings of unrelenting residents.

"Elsan!" Ermin yelled from beyond several residents scuffling with one another, waving his hand in the air in hopes that Elsan would see his face above the shoulders of the others. "Elsan!"

Elsan's eyes widened at the sight of Ermin, whose head bobbed up and down within the crowd as he moved closer, through the chaos, toward the rebel front. His angry heart suddenly felt warm, as it had for a moment when reuniting with his mother, as it had the last time he had eaten dinner with his father. Memories of their younger years rushed through their minds as they found one another in a situation they had never imagined they would experience together. Yet, through the commotion, with their eyes connected, they knew deep inside that they had the other's support, that their friendship was no weaker through the blur.

"Ermin," Elsan said, pulling his friend through the row of armed rebels and embracing him. "It's great to see you."

"I worried about you, Elsan," Ermin said. "I knew you were innocent deep down, but I didn't understand what was going on. I didn't know what your father was involved with."

"I didn't either," Elsan said. "But it was all for the better. It was to bring the good back to power."

"I see that now. I believe you. I believe everything you said. I wish I understood sooner, so I could have found you and your mother sooner."

"Don't worry. It's hard to know good from bad, watching those puppets on the monitors."

"Tell that to my parents."

"Well, the living tell the tales of our world," Tera said, approaching Ermin to embrace him as well. "We have a battle to win. You should go home, Ermin. It isn't safe here. Go to your parents."

"I'll fight alongside you," Ermin said.

"Ermin, now is not the time," Elsan said. "Go back home. You aren't prepared for this."

"I'm not going to leave you."

Bickering between residents and guards, as well as residents and rebels, escalated to an uproar, saturating the Central Node with its smog. Elsan, Tera, and Ermin peeped over the shoulders of the Guild's front line, hoping to find a way to abate the increasingly chaotic situation. Mora stepped in from behind and wrapped her hand around Elsan's inner arm.

"Let them speak!" a man yelled from the Zanoma Tower Ductway as a fleet of guards approached.

"These are criminals, mass murderers, anarchists!" a guard shouted, projecting his voice over a crowd of rebel supporters as supporters of the Republic stepped behind the fleet of guards for safety. "Now, step aside or we will use our forces to move you aside! Do I make myself clear?"

"Get behind us!" Paxtus shouted over the crowd of rebel supporters as he pushed through the crowd alongside other armed wrights, attempting to get the rebel supporters to safety as well, but they did not listen, and instead pushed closer to the guards. "Step back from the guards. Get behind us and we will protect you! Get back!"

"Scum!" another man screamed at the guards, alongside other rebel supporters who also ignored Paxtus in an attempt to resist the guards themselves. "You'll pay for this!"

The guards in each ductway pulled their black bats from their belts and began swinging them at the rebel supporters, who seemed to doubt the willingness of the guards to attack them with so many spectators surrounding, but the bats struck the residents with severe impact. Several men fell to the ground, holding their legs, sides, and heads. However, just as it appeared that the guards would plow through and scare the rebel supporters into surrendering, so as to open a path to the rebel militia, the rebel supporters collectively stood firm against the front line of guards.

The air fell still, as one guard took aim at a rebel supporter and fired two bullets. The rebel supporter died instantly, falling flat to the surface of the ductway. Wrights and other rebel supporters stood in shock, as did many supporters of the Republic, and even several guards. Some supporters of the Republic continued to bellow and howl like animals behind the group of guards, while the eyes of some in shock became limpid. Rebel supporters lifted their heads after backing away and staring down at their deceased neighbor, their eyes reddening like the ductway floor between them and the guards.

A rush was carried out by the rebel supporters, and they were joined from the other side of the group of guards by previous supporters of the Republic who had suddenly changed their stance. Bats and guns were stolen from each guard, so many of the guards resorted to paralyzing electrical prods, but those were quickly ripped from the guards' hands while residents swung bats at their backs. In Wrexon's End Ductway, the guards were disarmed and left to lay on the floor with their hands curled over their heads, watched over by rebel supporters. The guards in the other ductways fled, as did many of those that still supported the Republic.

The rebel militia and their followers trooped toward the Zanoma Tower. Hundreds and hundreds more residents joined the rebels to push past guards and supporters of the Republic, allowing the rebel army into the Zanoma Tower Ductway.

Countless men, women, and children, however, remained in their homes, fearfully watching their projector screens, awaiting the next announcement from Chancellor Tibs. They would not participate in the civil war, and would instead wait for the war to be won.

Those praying to the heavens within the comfort of their homes needed to be saved, whether it was by the bidding of Chancellor Tibs or by the grace of the Guild. For the inert residents of Zanoma who chose to lock their doors, there would only be the torturous time spent squeezing their families closer than grains of sand. Unaware of the events near the Zanoma Tower, they watched Zanoma's inactive news station, oblivious, sitting in silence.

The sun was setting over the western forests, sitting atop the blackened bark of the forest edge. The lights of the ductways, of the suites atop the Zanoma Tower, and of the tower blocks illuminated. Residents of the City of Zanoma embraced the contained light, for with its reflection off of translucent walls and windows, all would be blinded from the burden of night.

20

On both sides of the battle leading into the second floor of the Zanoma Tower, warriors collapsed like crumbling statues. Several wrights were killed in combat as several guards were as well. Elsan, Tera, Ermin, and Mora were in position toward the back of the rebel militia, hoping for the gunshots to fade so they could move forward in safety.

The Guild continued to force the guards onto their heels. Ermin grabbed a confiscated gun, though he had never shot one before. Although the wrights had inferior weapons, their numbers outweighed the number of guards within the Zanoma Tower. As guards murdered rebels, rebels killed guards in retaliation, but only the guards appeared scared, their hands beginning to shake as they pulled their triggers while the grip of the rebels became firm. Eventually, on all corners of the second floor of the Zanoma Tower, the guards were depleted to so few that they simply began ducking for cover while the rebel militia marched toward the staircases. The Guild sprinted after the remaining guards, rallying with a lust for revenge before disarming them.

Chancellor Tibs, Commander Nap, and Morin Malva watched security footage fretfully from a projector screen within Chancellor Tibs' office. Their men continued to fight for the Republic, but as time passed, they became more and more overpowered by the rebel army. Chancellor Tibs shook his head from side to side, as he saw on the projector screen that some of his men, including some that were stationed in Ornaia, had joined the rebel militia.

"That can't be," Tibs said.

"What?" Nap replied.

"Our men," Tibs continued. "They're with the rebels. They got to them."

Nap looked closer, eyes widening, and murmured, "Traitors."

"Well, you should have kept them at bay!" Tibs shouted at Nap, leaning forward, teeth gritted, face flaring, while Morin kept a stern expression behind them.

Daemyn and Moriah Muttin sat on their couch at their home in Wrexon's End, watching the inactive news station. As they stared, rarely blinking, at the steady television screen, they prayed to the heavens for the safety of their son. They could not connect with him through his tablet, and had no idea of where he was. They worried that their prayers might not have been enough.

Daemyn and Moriah held each other closer and looked at each other with glossy eyes. Meanwhile, within the Zanoma Tower, Ermin stood behind Elsan as they continued to walk toward the staircases. He placed his hand atop Elsan's shoulder and tilted him back a bit before the group split apart.

Several guards suddenly rushed from the staircases, firing their guns aimlessly in all directions, killing many rebels in the process. Elsan ducked and looked up in a panic for Tera, Mora, and Ermin. Tera and Mora were safe, hiding behind heavily armed rebels, though armed themselves. Elsan then spotted Ermin, who was lying along the center of the Zanoma Tower lobby, gushing blood from his split stomach. Hysterically, Elsan sprinted to him and knelt down, his horrified eyes becoming bloodshot. He pulled off his shirt, folded it, and pressed it firmly upon Ermin's stomach, where bullets tore open Ermin's skin.

"E-Ermin," Elsan stammered, tears forming in the corners of his eyes as he stared at Ermin, whose eyes failed to focus as his mind drifted toward the next realm. "Ermin. Talk to me, Ermin. I'm right here. Talk to me. Please, Ermin."

Ermin gasped for air, and with all of his might, he said with a choppy, hushed voice, "Go. Go now."

"No, Ermin," Elsan said, tears falling from the pools of his eyes. "I'm not leaving you like this. You can be saved, Ermin. You don't have to die."

"Elsan, we need to go!" Tera shouted, grabbing Elsan by the arm and pulling him from Ermin as she held back her own detriment with all of her might. "We need to go now! We can't save him!"

"No!" Elsan screamed, ripping his arm from his mother's grasp as images of he and Ermin venturing through Tocano as young boys flashed through his head, images of he and Ermin on their first day at work in the Zanoma Tower.

Another bullet darted by, several feet from Elsan, causing him to roll onto his side, hearing nothing but a ring in his ear. The world encompassed him in slow-moving, staged images, and his vision clouded entirely as he turned his head away from Ermin. His mind surfaced images of he, Ermin, and his family hiking through the Tocano Mountains, with the luminous sunrays leaking through the branches of the hemlock trees.

The ringing started to dissipate along with the taupe smoke. Ermin came back into sight, just feet away, so Elsan began calling his name, though his own voice was muffled. He cried louder.

"Ermin!" he hollered as his hearing started to come back. "Ermin! Wake up!"

"Elsan, we need to go!" Tera yelled once again, joined by Paxtus in grabbing Elsan's arms and pulling him away from Ermin's lifeless body.

"Ermin!" Elsan cried, tears pouring from his traumatized eyes. "Let me go!"

Tera and Paxtus held tightly onto Elsan's arms, dragging his feet along the Zanoma Tower floor. Mora ran in front with her eyes set on Zanoma Tower's staircase entrance. Elsan remained fixated on Ermin, who laid dead in the distance, beyond scattered shrouds of settling debris.

As they approached one of the staircases, Tera held Elsan firmly and said, "We must move on for now, Elsan. We must move on and mourn later."

Tera held Elsan out by the shoulders, and a shirtless Elsan nodded, panting and wheezing with flushed cheeks, and said, "Yes, Mom."

Armed rebels marched up the three staircases from the second floor, scowling at the napes of rebels in front of them. Some wrights stayed within the staircase on the second floor to protect from guards anticipated to be stationed in the Forum. With each step, more and more sweat squeezed from their pores, and the intimidation of the impending bloodshed sunk deeper into their stomachs. Yet, their minds were numb in acceptance of the inevitable acts of violence they would soon commit.

More guards stood on the third floor, on either side of the doors to the staircases, which muted the echo of footsteps. They gripped their guns and turned their backs away from the doors so as to prepare for a standoff. Suddenly, the footsteps stopped.

Within the staircases, wrights braced for the imminent confrontations. At each side of the Zanoma Tower, wrights nodded to the six top shooters aligned along the third step from the top. Those on the right reached out their hands and inched them toward the push plates on the doors. After one final look at their peers, the shooters on the right pushed open the doors.

Guards opened fire, piercing the chests of several wrights. Many guards fell to the ground as well, bleeding from their sides as others rushed toward each doorway. On the western side, where both doorway defenders were killed, rebels spewed through like hornets through a hassled hive. Elsan, alongside Mora and his mother, ran through the western doorway after over twenty of his fellow wrights, his gun held high and his eyes oscillating in alert and anger.

Flocking from the center lobby of the third floor, guards abandoned the elevators they were monitoring. They stationed in the outer ring, where they prepared for the rebel infiltration along the staircases from the Forum to the fifth floor. Unlike their counterparts on the lower levels, guards on the third floor attempted to flee, caught unprepared by the rebel army's confidence to act without stealth.

Supporters of the Guild outnumbered supporters of the Republic, keeping them lingering in the Central Node to question their sentiment toward the Republic with a wall of rebel supporters between them and the Zanoma Tower. Meanwhile, wrights continued up all staircases after containing all guards on the third floor. A flash flood of rebels enterred the fourth floor. On each side of the tower, top shooters in the front were shot, dropping backwards one by one, dodged by those behind them. Some guards who continued to shoot at the wrights were struck and killed, while others placed their weapons on the ground to surrender and were held in place by at least two wrights each. Still, wrights were dropping dead at the hands of guards, but the guards on the north, south, and west sides of the tower were forced to retreat with their backs to the east.

Some rebels were still stuck within the eastern staircase, including Karum, who took a bullet to the heart. Each time a guard was killed by a rebel in the eastern staircase, another stepped into sight, weapon raised, willing to take out as many rebels as it would take to defeat the militia, but guards retreating from other angles backed into their counterparts. Some fired shots in a desparate attempt to weaken the rebel army, though they were quickly killed, causing most guards on the floor to realize their weakened position. Elsan followed behind a front line of wrights with his finger on the trigger of his gun, while Mora and Tera pointed their guns at the heads of guards who had been captured. Several of those in the front line of wrights were shot down by a last round of bullets from the guards, so Elsan stepped into the front line and helped take them down, pausing for a moment after releasing the trigger to take in the atrocity he commited.

All guards on the fourth floor were seemingly detained, but more guards appeared from the openings of the central lobby. Many rebels were abruptly killed, while Paxtus was struck in the leg, causing him to shriek in agony into the thickening air. The other wrights fought back, wiping out several of the guards and containing the others. Elsan turned to see Paxtus, who laid on the ground, blood bursting from his thigh.

"Paxtus!" he screamed, water surfacing in his eyes as he ran to Paxtus' aid.

"Keep going," Paxtus said, panting and pressing his hand over the wound. "I'll be alright. It's just a leg wound. I'll be fine. I promise."

"We can't do this without you!"

"You must. I'll wrap this up. I-I'll be alright. They need you. You can do this without me."

Without another word, Elsan nodded, stood upright, and turned back toward the east, where the remaining guards were starting to place their weapons on the ground. Elsan grabbed the last guard to drop his gun by his vest as another wright picked up the unoccupied weapon. Eyes bloodshot and cheeks crimson red, Elsan shoved the guard into the wall beside the doorway to the staircase on the eastern side of the Zanoma Tower. Wrights still within the eastern staircase stormed onto the fourth floor over lifeless bodies, past detained guards and accompanying wrights. Recent recruits were traumatized by the bodies, which laid in streams of blood, trickling down the staircase toward the third floor. Yet, they stood behind Elsan with their chins held high, breathing heavily, so as to stay composed through the gore of battle, for the fate of the world rested in their hands.

"Where are the rest of your men stationed?" Elsan screamed at the guard, droplets of spit hitting the guard's face. "Tell me everything you know! What floors are the rest stationed on?"

"I-I don't know," the guard said. "I swear; I don't know anything. I was just stationed on this floor. I don't know about the others."

"Of course you know," Elsan said, glaring into the eyes of the guard. "Tell me what you know! Tell me Nap's orders!"

"I don't know!" the frightened guard said in response, raising the volume of his voice. "P-Please give me a chance. I've surrendered. Please, I was just doing what they told me to do. I was just doing what was best for my family."

"Then tell me where the others are stationed," Elsan said with a softer tone. "Tell me and you will be spared. Do you understand?"

"I-I don't know for sure," the guard stuttered, so Elsan thrusted his forearm into his neck. "B-But I know most are either on the fifth floor or near the suites. I don't know exactly."

"Get this man on the ground," Elsan commanded another rebel, who, in turn, waved two armed wrights over to watch over the guard. "Don't take your eyes off of him. Keep him on the ground indefinitely."

The two wrights and two unarmed recruits shoved the guard to the ground. Guns were pointed at his face. Elsan weaved through the rebels toward the central lobby of the fourth floor in order to find Paxtus. He spotted Paxtus lying against the inner wall of the hallway, accompanied by Mora, who was replaced by another wright in watching over a captured guard, instead pressing her hand against Paxtus' leg, slowing the bleeding.

"Paxtus," Elsan said as he approached the great rebel leader, who clenched his fists as Mora started to wrap more cloth around his thigh. "Paxtus, how do you feel?"

"I'm alright, Elsan," Paxtus said with a shrug. "I can't walk, but I'll be alright."

With water again surfacing in his eyes, Elsan stood upright and replied, "You, my mother, and Mora can stay on this floor. We don't have many left. I might not come back."

"I trust you'll finish this," Paxtus said, and Elsan walked back toward the eastern staircase.

Many guards were still held against the ground by multiple rebels each, while many others laid lifelessly along the lobby floors of the Zanoma Tower. Still, a strong army of wrights stood without a challenge in sight. Elsan walked through the idle militia toward a group of four wrights, including Macrum.

"We shouldn't approach by elevator," one said as Elsan entered the circle. "It's too risky."

"I agree," another wright said. "We need to be as stealthy as possible until we get to Tibs' suite. They'll be prepared for us."

"We should continue to rise through the staircases," Elsan said. "And we should capture anyone on the floors beneath them with whoever else we can bring with us."

"Spread evenly to each staircase," Macrum said, changing his tone and backing up in order to give direction to the others. "Spread evenly to each staircase. We have a long climb to begin. Make sure that those that are most capable are with us through the ascent, and that those that are less capable stay with the captured guards. We must move quickly."

Elsan and the wrights aggregated groups of several men, while unarmed residents controlled the ductways, keeping stolen guns pointed at the captured guards and holding off supporters of the Republic. Elsan marched behind one of the top shooters and toward the western staircase, helping to lead the many men that followed through the center.

Mora stood by Paxtus still, near the opening between the central lobby of the fourth floor and the hallway. For a moment, she turned her eyes toward Elsan, who walked by and gave her a subtle nod. Mora nodded back with a sparkle of credence in her eyes and turned her attention back toward Paxtus.

After the group reached the doorway of the western staircase, a rebel turned to Elsan and said, "You stay toward the back. We've come too far to risk your life at this point."

"My life isn't more important than the other men here," Elsan said as another top shooter walked over and joined the group for the ascent. "I'll fight just like they all will. There's no need to spare me."

"Yes there is, Elsan," Macrum said, approaching Elsan to join him. "You are Riklin's son. Even if you're half the man he is, you'll be a better leader than any of us. Your life has a special purpose for the new age. We must protect you, for Riklin and Tera."

Elsan nodded slightly as the fleet of wrights turned toward the western staircase doorway. Rebels forced Elsan toward the back of the militia and began marching upstairs. Other rebel groups also arose through the other staircases.

Without hesitation, rebel leaders ordered the best remaining shooters to the front and charged with them through the fifth-floor doorways. Only a few guards were stationed on the fifth floor, and without a bullet being fired by either side, they were captured within seconds. Three men stayed with each of the captured guards on the fifth floor in order to keep them contained as the rest of the rebels continued up to the sixth floor.

Although no rebel had kept count of the guards' death and detainment toll, they were surprised not to find a single guard stationed on the sixth floor. The seventh floor was the same, eerily empty and void of Zanoma forces. When the rebels came to find not a single guard stationed on the eighth floor, Elsan and the rebel leaders met in the central lobby of the eighth floor, forming a circle.

"Should we go straight to Tibs through the staircases?" Elsan asked.

"I'm not sure we should take the risk of leaving one of them behind," a wright answered.

"Yes," another rebel said. "But we must not let Chancellor Tibs come up with a new plan before we reach him. We must find him as soon as we can."

"I agree," Elsan said. "They could attempt to flee at any moment. They must be watching surveillance. They must be worried."

"That may be," Macrum said. "But he knows he is no safer in Ornaia than he is here. He's more vulnerable in Ornaia."

"Well, we shouldn't waste our time looking on every preceding floor," Elsan said. "We need to find Tibs and Nap now."

"I agree," all of the others said simultaneously.

Elsan and the rebels returned to their groups and reentered the staircases. At the words of their leaders, the remainder of the rebel militia marched step by step up the steep staircases of the Zanoma Tower. To reach the suites, it would take the rebel army hundreds more steps, enough to make them weak and shaky at the knees. They were hungry, hunching over their empty stomachs as they climbed higher and higher, but they craved revenge most of all.

Sweat soaked into their collars after dripping down their necks. Their eyes were bloodshot with both fatigue and a thirst for revenge. As they trooped in unison up the seemingly endless staircases, not a single word was spoken. The only noise came from the increasingly heavy breathing of each wright.

Passing a doorway, Elsan spotted a surveillance camera on the upper corner of the ceiling, but it was of no matter. Although he knew the battle had not yet finished, he no longer feared Chancellor Tibs or any of his faithful followers. It was Tibs who feared the Guild, who continued to follow their rebel leaders, passing by dozens of emptied floors, some reserved for guards to find shelter, some for military offices, and some for surveillance and intelligence personnel.

Soon after, the Guild ascended to a set of five floors, rarely used for special government events. Some were surprised to learn that the staircases ended after the fifth. Elsan peered through the window of the staircase door, only to see an empty room with a wide cylindrical beam in the center. It seemed to be an area for social gatherings of the elitists in that a bench wrapped around the center beam and divots in the beam held bottles of aged liquor. Macrum held Elsan back, pulled the door open, and stepped inside, along with a top shooter from each of the other staircases, looking from side to side, cautiously, so as to identify any form of threat before it became fatal.

Suddenly, the drone of mechanical motion froze Macrum and the rebel leaders' feet to the floor. Each of them tilted their heads up at the top of the cylindrical beam, where sixteen automatic guns were being deployed from behind the walls. Without further hesitation, Elsan and the rebel guards launched their bodies toward the staircase doors.

"Wait!" a voice rang as the automatic guns stopped in dead silence.

It was one of Nap's men, entering through the doorway of a staircase within the center beam of the floor, followed by five other guards. Several floors above, in Tibs' office, Nap and Tibs watched the surveillance screen, astonished by the disruption of the automatic guns and by the lack of combat, or even weapons drawn. Morin stood behind them, holding his chin high with pride, unbeknownst to his leaders. The wrights were confused, holding still with their hands hovering over their guns. After a moment passed, their narrowed eyes relaxed, they pulled their hands away from their weapons, and they turned to face the guards. Macrum gauged the motive in their eyes.

"Come with us," the guard said. "We'll take you to them."

Macrum and the wrights nodded and marched on behind the guards, their vision fading to the peril of the past before musing on the leaders of the Republic pleading for pity. Eyes became bloodshot with barbarity. Within minutes, the rebel militia reached Tibs' floor, where a narrow hallway surrounded Tibs' suite. After a guard placed his pointer finger on the identification pad to Tibs' suite, Elsan stepped in, with a team of guards and wrights around him, intimidating the guards by Chancellor Tibs' side to lower their weapons and be detained by their counterparts on the Guild's side. Tibs and Nap stood side-by-side, staring at the incoming rebels with squirrelly smiles on their faces. Morin paced over to Elsan's side, causing Tibs and Nap to glare at him.

"I see," Tibs said, nodding. "Well done, rebels. You've turned our men against us, apparently. I must say, I am very impressed. I knew there was something special about you all compared to past groups. I must congratulate you, for you and your men have done something truly incredible."

Elsan simply stared at Tibs with narrowed eyes and retorted, "I'm glad you recognize that your reign has come to an end."

"That may be," Tibs replied. "But while a fight for freedom is worthy of applause, it is also worthy of scrutiny, because the future of humanity may no longer rest in my hands, and not yet in yours."

"What are you saying?" Elsan said, appearing unamused.

"While our plans for the future required the sacrifice of those unfit for the system, this rebellion has caused more bloodshed and brutality than we've seen since the Black War."

"It was a worthy sacrifice. That's how you justified your war crimes, right?"

"Perhaps, but if you are to set the rules for the new age based on your father's teachings, some groups of people will still live at a disadvantage. You cannot rid the world of despair, Elsan."

"We would continue to destroy ourselves if we allowed you to continue to deceive the people and control everything. Future generations deserve better."

"That may be, but you must convince the people of Zanoma of that. You will need to convince the people of Zanoma that the lives lost in the process of overthrowing the Republic were worth the world that you all will create."

Elsan's chin began to quiver as images flashed in his mind of the cold, pale bodies lying in the Zanoma Tower, in the streets, in the eastern base, and in Treton. His hands trembled as he questioned whether the ultimate goal of collective prosperity, of freedom and love, was worth this mess. His chest throbbed at the thought of Daemyn and Moriah Muttin's faces when they would find out that Ermin had been killed in fighting for the cause that Riklin created.

"You will need to convince them all that this was a worthy war, Elsan," Tibs continued as Elsan fell down on one knee, wiping tears from his eyes as his neck wilted like a crippling carnation. "Just as I did before the Black War. The people of Zanoma will question you. You see, your father, and you, are not much different than Evarand and I. The people will tear you apart until you doubt your foundations. The people don't want chaos. The people want stability. When they see the leaders of the rebel army in power, when they see the power of the new age in the hands of an Amaranth, they

will come for your head. They will force you to justify
the price of death. The trust has already been lost, Elsan.
Your only option seems to be to flee Zanoma, to flee
Zanoma's borders and never return, for you will never
be accepted. You will be brought to justice if you
remain. The people of Zanoma will lust for your blood."

Chancellor Tibs leaned back into a table behind
him as Elsan knelt still, with his hand wrapped under his
chin and his eyes fixated on the polished concrete floor
beneath him, tears trickling down his cheeks as his chin
continued to quiver. His chest throbbed in pain as he
began to contemplate his actions, the actions of his
parents, and the actions of the Guild. He began to doubt
his foundations, as Tibs said.

He did not know if he and his mother would be
safe from the distraught people of Zanoma, who, for
years, were invested in ideas that contrasted Riklin's, the
ideas that demonized free will as the tolerance of
madness and merciless rage. He wondered whether the
lives of Ermin, Sairin, rebel leaders, new recruits, loyal
rebels, and guards were worth the sacrifice. The room
clung onto Elsan's every breath, until a distant memory
struck him.

*Whatever path we set foot upon is ultimately a route back
home*, Elsan remembered his mother saying,
understanding in this moment, more so than ever
before, what she meant with those words.

Elsan stood upright, his eyes still focused on the
floor beneath his nose, beneath his suddenly stabilizing
chin. Chancellor Tibs and Commander Nap were

eagerly awaiting his words, a devious flare in their eyes. Elsan tilted his head up, stared Tibs in the eyes, and took a deep breath.

"You gave us no choice," he said, pulling his gun from his side.

He pulled the trigger, sending a bullet into the Commander Nap's forehead. After a moment to relish in the gravity, he handed the gun to Morin Malva. Tibs stared at Morin, seemingly cracking his mouth open to speak, but Morin pulled the trigger, sending a bullet into Chancellor Tibs' forehead.

The Guild incarcerated the captured guards in the Zanoma Detention Center. Innocent prisoners were released, while Amon Sarato, Shylo Cob, Fydel Cob, Lealan Wiske, and Powman Pent were contained. Zanoma was relieved of the deceit that afflicted it. The warmth of the moonlight melted down as the blue hour of night faded away.

21

After a day of mourning, the people of Zanoma were reborn. The deaths of Daiton Tibs and Evarand Nap were justified in the minds of most people, while brainwashed doubters kept quiet. Shylo Cob was sentenced to death as well due to his involvement in countless murders. With no supreme ruler guiding their daily movements, no major threat from natural forces besides overexposure, nor an implication of further devastation, the people of Zanoma, of the world, were free to govern themselves.

Residents spent time at all hours of each day in the burial grounds, where those who had passed away, including Ermin, Sairin, rebel leaders, guards, and many more were buried and beholden by the people of Zanoma. Countless lives were lost. Yet, humanity at its core was victorious. The image that the leaders of the

Republic of Zanoma created for the Amaranths and for the Guild was proven wrong, and the world had not spiraled into chaos without a current authority. Morin Malva made sure of that with an announcement over every monitor and tablet in Zanoma, rescinding his support for Chancellor Tibs and his closest followers, and supporting the truth behind his father's death, as well as the truth behind Zanoma's control over the other territories of the world. Data and documents stolen by the Guild were released as proof of corrupt dealings. Zanoma's borders were opened after ten years of confinement, for the protection was no longer necessary. It had not been necessary for some time and would not be necessary so long as the message of the Guild survived. Rebels were released from scrutiny, and they clamored for Tera Amaranth as she stood alongside her son and several others on a small platform on the side of the burial grounds closest to the Zanoma Tower.

"You know," Tera uttered close to Elsan as residents of Zanoma continued to gather in front of them. "My biggest fear throughout the past three years was that you would find out what your father and I were up to and it would threaten your life."

"So, your biggest fear actually came to be?" Elsan said with a smirk.

"Well, yes," Tera said. "But what I didn't realize was that you would become such an important part of the movement, like your father was."

"The Guild did a good job of keeping me alive," Elsan replied.

Elsan and Tera turned as Zanoma residents were clapping and chanting. Mora, Macrum, Paxtus, and many other rebels, who could once again live as typical residents of Zanoma, stood at the sides of the platform with smiles on their faces, waving at their neighbors in the crowd. Paxtus wore a thick layer of bandages around his leg, leaning on a pair of crutches for support. Wrights from other territories of the world stood near the platform with the others, though they still dreamed of a day when they could return to the lands they held dear, and they would. Elsan gazed over the thousands and thousands of exhuberant faces.

Tera gave a slight smile, placed her hand on Elsan's shoulder, and said, "I think the people of Zanoma need to hear from me."

"Good people of Zanoma," Tera began, turning her attention toward the enormous audience of Zanoma residents, who stopped chanting in order to listen. "It took ten long years, and three years of courageous organization by my late partner, Riklin, and countless others. Even our son, Elsan, was unaware of the crimes being commited in the shadows of Zanoma until just recently. Our lives have changed in the blink of an eye, but for the better. Humanity is now free of the greed, cruelty, and apathy that had plagued us before the Black War, throughout the Black War, and throughout the past ten years. Unfortunately, evil forces sometimes need to be defeated by force as well. For the violence that has transpired, we owe this world a relentless pursuit toward peace. We must continue to fight for fairness, and for the prosperity of all. We will live with great health, joy, and most importantly, love. We can soon venture into the world we have forgotten. There have been countless heroes that have made our future possible, heroes that deserve far more praise than me, heroes that lost their lives fighting so we could enjoy this gift of life, a gift granted to us by earlier generations, not by our governments. From this day forward, we will bring upon a new age while holding onto the lessons of the past. Elections will be organized together, and together, we will restructure the Republic of Zanoma as a true republic, with our freedom in mind. Together, we will bring back the food stored in Ornaia. Together, we will free survivors around the world from our control, and we will restore those relationships. The true potential of the people of Zanoma will shine through. Thank you all."

Zanoma residents again cheered for Tera and the Guild as she waved to the crowd. Elsan waved as well, and the mother and son descended from the platform side by side to be embraced by Mora. The people of Zanoma left for their respective homes, knowing that Zanoma needed time to continue mourning the countless men, women, and children lost throughout the decade after the Black War, as well as those lost to the same depravity before and during the Black War.

Elsan, Tera, and Mora returned to the Amaranth home to enjoy each other's company as they too healed from their losses. Although they were grateful for their own lives to continue, they remained silent at the kitchen table, struggling to find words that were warranted on such a day. For lunch, they ate a traditional meal, including cabbage and mung beans, as they had been used to.

"Thank you both for allowing me to stay for a while," Mora said. "You've both been so kind."

"Consider yourself family now, Mora," Tera said. "We would love for you to stick around as long as you need to. Don't you think so, Elsan?"

"Yes," Elsan said, smiling at Mora. "Of course she can stay."

After lunch, the three of them separated to different rooms. Tera left to rest her eyes in her bedroom. Elsan went to his bedroom for a moment to change into comfortable clothes while Mora waited in the living room for him. She sat patiently until there was a knock at the front door. Uncomfortable with answering the door herself, she looked around the room, expecting someone to come out from their bedroom to answer it. After about ten seconds, no one came out from their respective rooms and there was another knock. Rather than answering the door herself, Mora decided to go into Elsan's bedroom to see what he was doing.

"Elsan," she said, creaking open his bedroom door. "There's someone at the do-"

Mora gasped at the sight of Elsan, who was standing with his bare back turned from the door, along the left wall, with a rifle in his tightly gripped hands. His torso moved up and down as he breathed heavily. He remained facing away from Mora.

"Elsan," Mora said again, her hazel eyes alert. "Put down the gun, Elsan. What are you doing? Someone is at the door."

"They're coming for my head," Elsan said, his voice trembling and his back convulsing. "I'm not expecting any visitors. They're here to take me down. Tibs said this would happen."

"Elsan," Mora began. "Your name is clear. No one is coming after you. If you put the gun away, I will get the door myself."

"No!" Elsan shouted, spinning around with his eyes piercing Mora's, the gun in both hands, pointed toward the ceiling.

"Elsan," Mora said, nearing him with a soothing stare and rubbing her hand on his shoulder. "Trust me. No one is out to hurt you. Please, Elsan. Trust me."

After seconds of staring at Mora with frightened eyes, Elsan nodded his head up and down, so as to signal Mora to answer the door. Mora walked out of Elsan's bedroom, through the kitchen and to the front door. She peered through the peephole of the door to see if the visitor was still there and opened the door.

"Hello," she said with a cheerful smile. "My name is Mora Storm. I'm staying with the Amaranth family for some time."

"It's nice to meet you, Mora," Daemyn Muttin replied with Moriah by his side. "We are Daemyn and Moriah Muttin. We came to speak with Elsan and Tera."

"Sure," Mora said. "Let me see what they're doing. Hang on for one minute. You can sit at the kitchen table or in the common room if you'd like."

"Thank you, Mora," Moriah replied as she and Daemyn sat at the kitchen table.

Mora left the room to get Elsan and Tera from their respective bedrooms. This caused a bit of discomfort for Tera, and more extreme trepidation for Elsan. They then left their bedrooms to meet with Ermin's mourning parents. The two of them approached the kitchen table, locking eyes with Daemyn and Moriah, who sat with crooked smiles on their faces. Daemyn was the first to stand up and hug Tera and Elsan, followed by Moriah.

"We thought that we should take some time to talk with both of you about what's happened," Daemyn said as he sat back down next to his partner and across from Tera and Elsan. "I hope this isn't a bad time."

"Not at all," Tera replied. "You're always welcome in our home. You know that."

As Daemyn opened his mouth to speak again, Elsan's eyes watered as he stuttered, "I-I'm sorry."

"Elsan," Moriah began, placing her hand on Elsan's shoulder, but Elsan continued.

"I'm s-so sorry," he stammered again, his chin quivering, tears forming in the corners of his eyes. "I'm so sorry. I didn't me-"

Tears surfaced in Moriah's eyes as well as she consoled Elsan and said, "It's not your fault, Elsan. Ermin chose to risk his life for the movement. Many people did. He and the others were brave to make that sacrifice. We should have listened to him and fought to protect him. You are not to blame."

"I-I could have made him go home," Elsan said. "I could have stopped him."

"Elsan," Daemyn said, glancing at Tera as well. "We came here today to tell you and your mother that we were wrong. We doubted both of you, whether you knew it or not, and we were wrong. We were wrong to dismiss your message. We were wrong to refuse support of what you were doing for the people of Zanoma. We could have supported you and protected Ermin, like you, Tera, and Riklin did for you, Elsan. We're here to confess this, and to seek your forgiveness."

"You should not be sorry," Tera said. "You and everyone else who doubted the rebel movement were justified in your views. Everyone wants to trust their leaders. Everyone wants to feel secure, and everyone wants their family to stay safe. I didn't tell Elsan about the rebel group until he found out for himself. Sometimes, as parents, we need to accept that our children are going to find answers elsewhere. There is no one in this room who should feel sorry, though we all are devastated by your loss, as well as our own."

"Ermin was a great friend," Elsan said. "We will never forget him."

"Thank you," Moriah said as Daemyn nodded with a soft smile.

"I'm glad to hear you're managing this so well," Tera said. "Would you two like to come back and share dinner tonight?"

"Sure," Moriah said, a smile slowing a tear that trickled down her face. "That would be great."

After hugging each of Tera, Elsan, and Mora for a moment, Daemyn and Moriah Muttin left the Amaranth home to return to their own. Meanwhile, Tera went back to her bedroom to rest some more. Mora and Elsan decided to take a walk through Wrexon's End, through Zanoma's open gates, and through the open lands outside the city borders. The warmth of the sun soothed Elsan's pounding heart as he walked alongside Mora. She reached for his hand, wrapping her fingers between his. After a moment with his head tilted down and his eyes fixated on the barren ground, he looked up at Mora with a smile.

"This was all so beautiful before the Black War," Elsan said.

"It still is, and it'll be more beautiful when all of the lands become fertile again," Mora said.

Mora's message would stick with Elsan, for the recent events forced him to be more optimistic than ever before. Elsan's world reached its worst, but the years ahead would bring life back to the surface. Mora looked over at Elsan, and he looked back at her, the sun perched over her shoulder. Mora stepped closer to Elsan and touched her finger to the side of his chin. With warm hearts, they wrapped their arms around each other and kissed as their souls intertwined, aloft from the surfaces of the skin with the open air whirling around them. They were free, truly and helplessly free.

The sun slowly crept behind a layer of thin clouds, the sky settling into a soft blue. From that moment forward, the world would grow with the visions of all of those who inhabited it. The new age would be one of free spirits who quest for life itself, and the good would prosper once again.

www.ingramcontent.com/pod-product-compliance
Lightning Source LLC
Chambersburg PA
CBHW020339180626
46812CB00001B/270